THE
MASK
OF
SANITY

THE
MASK
OF
SANITY

Jacob M.
Appel

THE PERMANENT PRESS
Sag Harbor, NY 11963

For information, address:
  The Permanent Press
  4170 Noyac Road
  Sag Harbor, NY 11963
  www.thepermanentpress.com

Library of Congress Cataloging-in-Publication Data

  Appel, Jacob M., author.
    The mask of sanity / Jacob M. Appe.
    Sag Harbor, NY : The Permanent Press, [2017]
    ISBN 978-1-57962-495-8

  PS3601.P662 M37 2017
  813'.6—dc23   2016053018

Printed in the United States of America

For Rosalie

AUTHOR'S FOREWORD

Sociopaths or psychopaths—the two terms are largely interchangeable—have long been familiar to readers of Western literature. From Shakespeare's Iago to Camus's Meursault, these men and women are not merely villains, but villains lacking any moral compass. Rather than being victims of derangement who cannot tell the difference between right and wrong, they are self-interested and calculating creatures who recognize the difference, but simply do not care. During my career as a psychiatrist in New York City, including time spent working in a state forensic facility, I have come to know a number of individuals who wear what the late Hervey M. Cleckley, once the world's foremost authority on sociopathy, termed "The Mask of Sanity," yet at their cores proved incapable of feeling empathy or compassion for their fellow human beings. What follows is an effort to capture as authentically as possible the mind-set of one such miscreant.

Too often, literature encourages us to imagine these amoral villains as dwelling along the margins of society, clinging to the lowest rungs of the economic ladder like Dostoyevsky's Raskolnikov. Only recently, especially as a result of the exposure of gross misdeeds in the financial services industry and of large-scale Ponzi schemes, has the public become aware that many amoral individuals lurk in the highest echelons of power, be it business, law, and even in medicine. They are all around us, smiling and perpetrating evil.

ACT I

CHAPTER ONE

Killing, Balint discovered, was the easy part. *Not* killing required discipline and restraint. Whether his medical career had inured him to death, or his steady constitution enabled him to suppress his emotions, or merely the sheer depth of his need for his wife and his hatred for Warren Sugarman transcended all moral barriers, he grew to see the slayings as a routine matter, even a mundane nuisance, like his four weekends each year as the on-call cardiologist at the hospital. Never, not even with his hands choking the life from innocent strangers, did he experience any guilt. At worst, he suffered a nagging fear of *future* guilt: the apprehension that he'd one day find himself overcome with remorse and confess for no good reason—like Raskolnikov or Leopold and Loeb. Then even these worries faded, leaving behind only the fact of his crimes. All of this occurred much later, of course: after he'd committed himself irreversibly.

His transformation from conscientious physician to calculating assassin had seemed impossible only nine months earlier, on the rain-swept Saturday afternoon when he'd accidentally run over the brindled dachshund and then watched like a stranger as his own life came untethered from its moorings.

He'd been driving home from Hager Heights, following lunch with his mother and stepfather. Amanda had begged off—as she often did—claiming a toothache. Their girls were away at summer camp. Balint recalled being in particularly bright spirits that day, because his promotion to section chief had been approved only the week before, which made him—at thirty-four—the youngest head of any medical division at Laurendale-Methodist Hospital. And then, out of a forsythia hedge, bolted the hapless dog.

On a clear day, he might have stopped in time. In a steady downpour, the brakes of the Mercedes squealed until the animal bounced off the grille.

He was traveling east on Meadow Drive—taking the short-cut between Chestnut Street and Hamilton Boulevard—with no other vehicles in sight. To his left sprawled the country club, where a flock of Canada geese sheltered itself at the edge of the golf course. To his right, thick hedges protected a row of upscale homes; farther along the road, the shrubbery gave way to a wall of whitewashed brick. Balint sat in the vehicle for several minutes, waiting for the shock of the collision to subside. Surely, if anyone had witnessed the accident, they'd have come to offer help. Nobody did. That meant absolutely nothing prevented him from abandoning the dachshund to its fate and driving off. Escape was the rational response to the situation, he told himself. Instead, he did the right thing.

The dog lay unconscious, but breathing. Blood had colored its left eye crimson and a bone protruded through the fur below its left front knee. The luckless animal's body shivered, either from cold or pain. Balint wrapped the creature inside his sport jacket. Rain matted his shirt to his chest—and it struck him, too late, that the water might cause his hospital pager to malfunction. His initial intention had been to carry the beast back to his car and to drive it to the emergency room. Yet as Balint lifted the heavy, sopping body, he suddenly recalled that Sugarman, the transplant surgeon, lived hardly a block away. In an instant, he made the decision that would lead to so many others, and he carried the bleeding animal around the corner toward Sugarman's house.

Sugarman's son and his own older daughter attended the same grade at Laurendale Prep. Amanda and the boy's mother played tennis together. Over the past several years, a friendship had arisen between Balint and his colleague—not an intimate friendship, but a convivial relationship built around common circumstances and shared worldviews and overlapping social circles. Both men had graduated from Columbia within three years of each other and from its medical school in the same class; both attended the same synagogue on High Holidays. When Balint ran into Sugarman on the ward service, he enjoyed his coworker's easygoing good cheer. In all likelihood, if Balint's daughters married someday, Sugarman would attend the weddings, although the surgeon's recent, bitter divorce threatened to complicate the seating chart. At the same time, if Sugarman vanished suddenly—accepted a job in a different state or even burst an aneurysm—Balint couldn't say that he'd have suffered any genuine sense of loss. What mattered at the moment was that Sugarman lived nearby, and that he might be capable of stabilizing an injured dog.

Later Balint reflected on how many unfortunate contingencies led to what transpired next. After all, had the asphalt been dry, or had he left his mother's place only seconds earlier, he might have avoided the smashup entirely. Or he might not have recollected that Sugarman lived on Meadow Court. Or he might have decided that a transplant surgeon could offer little service to an injured canine. An infinite number of other possibilities *might* have happened; what actually did happen was that he approached Sugarman's driveway, his forearms straining under the weight of his cargo, and he spotted a familiar silver Saab sedan parked beneath the basketball hoop. Again he had an opportunity to avoid calamity—to return to the main road and go in search of help. Instead he stole around the side of the building.

Sugarman's backyard looked almost indistinguishable from his own: a slate patio equipped with a kettle barbecue, a swing set, a vegetable patch ringed with chicken wire. All that differentiated the surgeon's property was the absence of a swimming pool. Despite the pelting rain, Sugarman's sprinklers ran at full tilt—likely on a timer.

Balint climbed the wooden steps onto the deck. He peered into the nearest window and was rewarded with a view of an empty kitchen. The second window belonged to a dimly lit bathroom. Beyond the third window—at the far corner of the patio—stood a spacious den, furnished much like Balint's own family room, with two love seats and a sofa focused upon a large-screen television.

The transplant surgeon relaxed on the sofa. He sipped from a brandy snifter. Amanda's head nestled in Sugarman's lap, her bare feet resting on the far arm of the couch. His fingers toyed with her chestnut hair. While Balint's mind struggled to place an innocent spin on what could not plausibly have been an innocent encounter, his colleague set down the snifter and allowed his free hand—that same hand trained to shear human flesh—to trace Amanda's cheek, her neckline, the curve of her breast. And then, without warning, the surgeon leaned forward and rubbed his nose against hers, a gesture as intimate as it was sensual.

Balint watched, paralyzed, still clutching the injured dachshund to his chest. And then the weight on his forearms felt heavier, almost imperceptibly, but just enough to tell him the poor creature had expired. That was too much for him. He retreated down the patio stairs and dropped the dachshund's remains into the flowerbeds. Not his problem.

On the journey home, his entire body shuddered violently—just like the dog's had done—and as he crossed the highway overpass onto Roosevelt Avenue, an intense urge seized him to veer into the traffic below. Somehow he managed to resist.

———

AMANDA URANSKY hadn't been the prettiest girl Balint ever dated. In fact, they'd slept together for a brief spell in college—and then he'd cast her aside, rather unfairly, to forage in different pastures. Yet she'd taken her rejection in stride, unlike several of the other women he'd mistreated; instead of crying and pleading, she merely gave him a farewell hug and sent him a card on his birthday for each of the next four years. So when chance reunited them in the medical school library, where he was cramming for his anatomy final while she interned at the circulation desk, he found her company a warm refuge from his cold, unforgiving nights of memorizing pharmacological mechanisms and the symptoms of obscure diseases. Soon enough, he didn't even notice the extra flesh on her hips or that her deep-set black eyes, otherwise enthralling, sat slightly too close together. Even as they planned their wedding, Balint knew he'd chosen wisely. His bride possessed all the practical skills he lacked: she could haggle with a caterer, threaten to discharge a florist. When they blew a tire on the way to the rehearsal dinner, she climbed down on her knees beside him and showed him how to install the spare.

That had been nine years earlier. Two daughters ago. Balint tried to remember who he'd been before his marriage, but the Jeremy Balint of his bachelor days was as inaccessible to him as his months inside the womb.

At home, he found a note from Amanda on the letter table in the foyer: "Tooth better. Gone shopping. Back at four."

He did not experience anger, not at first. He didn't feel numb. What swept over him was a sense of helplessness. How would he handle life without Amanda? He had no clue how to prepare his estimated taxes for the accountant, or where the key to their safe-deposit box was hidden, or the telephone number for the pediatrician. He didn't know in which banks they held accounts or even how much money they had. Even if he divorced Amanda and won full custody of the girls—not an impossibility with the right attorney—he had no idea how to raise children on his own. All he knew was cardiology, and that Amanda attended to everything else—and now one of those two pillars of faith appeared in jeopardy of toppling.

He passed the afternoon scouring the bumper of the Mercedes for dachshund blood and scrubbing it from the sleeves of his shirt. The sport jacket proved unsalvageable; he dug a shallow hole behind the woodpile and buried it.

Amanda returned at precisely four o'clock. The backseat of the Saab was loaded with grocery bags and she asked for his help carrying them into the kitchen. Now the sky had cleared; puddles still pocked the front walk.

"They had a special on paper towels," she said. "Eighty-nine cents a roll. So I bought twenty."

"I suppose we can never have too many paper towels," replied Balint. "What made you limit yourself to only twenty?"

What he wanted to ask was: How long has this been going on? How could you betray our daughters in this way? And what does Warren Sugarman have that I don't? And are you going to leave me? But he didn't dare, because he feared the answers.

He deposited the last of the paper grocery bags on the countertop.

"Aren't you glad they didn't have a special on anvils?" asked Amanda.

She sounded so nonchalant. As though she had indeed spent the entire day searching for discounts on paper products.

"How's your mouth?" he asked.

"Better. Not good, but better."

"I'm glad," he said.

Even a simple phrase like "I'm glad" now sounded strange to him. Had his inflection hinted at doubt? Would she think he was mocking her? On an ordinary afternoon, was this something he might have said?

"Are you up for dinner on the town?" his wife asked. "Someplace romantic."

"I really should get paperwork done," he lied.

Amanda approached him from behind and wrapped her arms around his abdomen. This was *not* something she normally did, he thought; she was obviously overcompensating for what had occurred that morning. Balint racked his brain to recall other recent episodes of uncharacteristic behavior.

"Come on, Jer. You can do all the paperwork you want next month when the kids get back from camp." She rested her chin on his shoulder. "How many nights do you get to spend alone with your devoted wife?"

If he were going to hate Amanda, that would have been the moment. But what he actually felt was confusion. An oppressive sense of psychological bedlam. So he accompanied her to the candle-lit bistro overlooking the harbor and then for ice cream cones at the old-fashioned parlor opposite the railroad station. He made conversation—but as he spoke, mostly about the girls, but also about the family vacation to Disney World they had planned for November, he felt like an actor in a play.

In the back of his head, he was planning how to rebuff Amanda if she sought to get frisky that evening. He would refuse—he had to draw a line somewhere. But to his relief, and also disappointment, she didn't try.

———

BALINT'S ENCOUNTER with Warren Sugarman two days later could not reasonably have been termed a coincidence. He was not the service attending that month, and he had only a handful of private patients in the hospital, so he had no reason to be wandering through the wards. Yet he somehow found excuses for multiple forays onto the acute care units. He'd spot a specialist he hadn't seen in some time—and they'd stand at the nursing station, chatting, while the interns and residents typed away on their progress notes. Inevitably he crossed paths with his wife's lover.

Sugarman stepped off the elevator with a pack of house officers in aquamarine scrubs nipping at his heels. The burly surgeon sported a copper-tone business suit over a burgundy shirt and lavender bow tie; a matching handkerchief protruded from his breast pocket. He walked backward like a tour guide, declaiming to his minions as he went. When he spotted Balint, who was in the process of purchasing a soda from a vending machine, he broke off his lecture and dispatched his disciples to their tasks.

"Balint!" he hailed. "How's the new division?"

"I'm still trying to figure that out."

Sugarman strode up to him and actually slapped him on the back. "You medicine people never cease to astound me," he said. "I keep telling myself that I'll relearn physiology someday, but I never get much further than one heart, two kidneys." He glanced at his wristwatch. "I'm far better off sticking to plumbing, I know. Everybody needs a plumber."

"Especially on a weekend afternoon," replied Balint.

"Agreed," said Sugarman—without a hint of discomfort. "Especially on a weekend afternoon."

The doors to the transport elevator opened. They stepped aside, allowing a crew of orderlies to maneuver a lunch-tray rack into the corridor.

"Damnedest thing happened to me," said Sugarman. "Someone killed my neighbor's dog and tossed the carcass into my tea roses. Isn't that the damnedest thing?"

"When did this happen?" inquired Balint.

Was that a reasonable question? Had he displayed too much curiosity?

"Over the weekend," said Sugarman. "I went outside to check on my gladiolas yesterday—I'm trying a new breed this year—and smack in the middle of my rose garden is a god-damn dog carcass. Smelled like hell too." He waved his palm in front of his nose. "Flies everywhere."

"Flies," echoed Balint. "Nothing good about flies."

He had hoped to run into Sugarman all morning, but now that he stood face-to-face with the man, he longed to be rid of him. What could the two of them possibly have to talk about? A certain caliber of husband, Balint recognized, would have challenged the surgeon directly: fisticuffs, pistols at dawn. And he had also heard of so-called "enlightened" spouses who might take the affair in stride, wishing their rivals the best of luck—or even comparing notes. Balint was neither brave nor liberated. He didn't want to fight his colleague, or to tolerate him. No, what he wanted was for Sugarman to stop screwing his wife. Nothing more or less. But that wasn't the kind of request you could make without humiliating yourself.

"Balint? You okay?"

Sugarman had been talking to him—probably more non-sense about the dead dog—but he hadn't been listening. "I'm fine. Just a migraine."

"You've got to take care of yourself, Balint. None of us is getting any younger," Sugarman said, patting his own paunch. "Want to hear my idea for a new novelty item? Of course, you don't—but I'm going to tell you anyway." He punctuated his remark with a chuckle. "*Dementia cookies*, that's my million-dollar gag. Just like fortune cookies, only they all say the same thing inside: 'This is a cookie.' Half of the twenty-five-year-olds in the country would buy a box for their fathers. Now am I right or am I right?"

"It's certainly an idea."

"Anyway, enough of my brilliant schemes. I'd better catch up with that chief resident of mine before she takes my job. But you and Amanda ought to come over to the bachelor pad one night for dinner. Gloria may squeeze every last dime out of me, but I'm not going to let her walk away with my friends. What do you say?"

"We'll see," replied Balint. "It's a busy month . . ."

Sugarman nodded—with no apparent sense that he was being snubbed. "I'll call you. We'll set something up. Now take a triptan before your head explodes."

Balint's rival slapped him on the back a second time and then lumbered down the corridor, leaving him alone in the elevator bay. A moment later, a Code 7000 blared over the public address system—a cardiac arrest—and then the resuscitation team charged past with their crash cart and defibrillator. Balint said a brief prayer for the dying patient, as he always did—more force of habit than faith; and for a moment, he wished it were himself.

———

BALINT WENT through the motions of treating his patients that afternoon: checking blood pressures in both arms, ordering EKGs. What amazed him was how much medical care one could deliver while on autopilot. He managed to interrogate and console and even engage in small talk with the elderly congestive heart failure victims who comprised the bulk of his practice—and he was confident none noticed anything amiss. For six hours straight, he inquired after children, grandchildren, the status of college applications. He praised the talents of his patients' other medical specialists, armies of ophthalmologists and endocrinologists whose names sounded vaguely familiar. He even removed a wood splinter from the thumb of a teenage girl who'd accompanied her great-aunt to an appointment. But if, at the end of the workday, anyone had quizzed Balint about these exchanges, he'd have conceded that he remembered absolutely nothing he'd said—and often not even which patients he had examined.

He longed to speak to someone about his own problems. *Anyone.* To discuss how his life had unraveled so quickly and how he might patch it back together. Alas, he now confronted the second stark discovery of the week: he had nobody to talk to. Not one single human being. He had friends, of course, lots of them. College pals, medical school buddies, a handful of high school baseball teammates he met up with every Memorial Day weekend. If he'd wanted to hit the squash courts, or to go on a fishing trip, or even to shoot a round of pool, he had a Rolodex of colleagues and neighbors to invite. But for an intimate tête-à-tête, he had no place to turn.

There was Steinhoff, the hip young Israeli who'd replaced Rabbi Felder, but he hardly knew the man. He could always make an appointment with a therapist, but his previous bout with psychiatry—after his father's fatal asthma attack, when he was sixteen—had left him angrier and more mixed up than ever. He had no siblings, no close cousins. Other than Amanda and the girls, his mother and stepfather provided his only intimate connections, but his parents' sole coping mechanism was denial. When his Aunt Clara's liver cancer metastasized to her spine, Balint's mother had attributed her sister's pain to rheumatism. When he'd been rejected from Princeton, his first choice for college, she'd wanted him to phone the admissions office to make certain that he hadn't fallen victim to a clerical error. So Balint *could* speak to his parents, but the last thing he wanted was his mother insisting that Sugarman's nose rubbing had a hidden, nonsexual purpose. He already envisioned her asking, "Are you sure it wasn't a medical procedure? Maybe he feared she was choking and he was trying to get a better look . . ." No, at the end of the day, he was utterly and incontrovertibly alone.

After he'd attended to his final patient of the afternoon, Balint found himself in no hurry to return home. For what? So that he and Amanda could continue their game of make-believe until she decided to call it quits. For all he knew, she was already in the process of shifting their property into her own name—of setting herself up for the day when she transferred her address to Meadow Court. That's what he would have done, he told himself, if he stood in her shoes. Of course, he *didn't* stand in her shoes. Because he wasn't the one having an extramarital affair. No matter how many attractive women he'd met since their wedding—nurses, flight attendants, bleached-blonde pharmaceutical sales reps who accompanied him to dinner talks—he'd never considered cheating. Never once. Not that he didn't have desires. Didn't everyone? But he valued the welfare of his daughters—the stability of their home—over any fleeting lust for personal gratification. Although it hadn't actually crossed his mind that Amanda might cheat on him—why would she?—if it ever had, he'd have assumed that she also valued their children's well-being over her sordid passions. So much, he lamented, for playing by the rules.

Balint completed his electronic billing for the month and killed an hour reorganizing his filing cabinet. The sun already had dipped behind the adjoining laboratory building when he shut off the lights and drifted downstairs to the parking garage. Then he drove the streets aimlessly until the last light vanished in the western sky. To torment himself, he cruised past Sugarman's house, but found no sign of the silver Saab. He flipped on the radio and half-listened to news of the latest war.

What have you learned from this, Balint? he asked himself. That was the question he always posed after an unexpected negative outcome at the hospital—a medication error or a catheterization gone awry. It was probably the reason for his administrative successes. Yet now, applying the same question to his personal life, he came up with only one answer: playing by the rules was for losers.

He'd lived his entire adult life as an upstanding citizen: hardworking, honest, faithful. He placed his patients' interests first, honored his mother and stepdad, strove to set a good example for his children. He long ago had accepted that probity didn't guarantee him immunity from the vagaries of misfortune—traffic accidents, stock sell-offs, fatal asthma attacks—but he couldn't help but believe that virtuous living ought to insulate a man from betrayal by his own friends and family. Obviously it did not. Sugarman—glad-handing, oafish, two-faced Sugarman—had flouted the most fundamental of rules, and he'd been rewarded with Amanda.

So what now? Even if he could find a confidante to bounce his ideas off, did he have any ideas genuinely worth sharing? What Balint really yearned to do was to clasp his bare hands around his rival's fat neck and to squeeze until the man's eyeballs turned blue. The image arose before him of Warren Sugarman prying at his knuckles, his lips quivering, his mottled face pleading for another chance. And then he imagined Sugarman's tongue hanging limp from his bloated mouth, and he literally sensed the man's weight as he eased his lifeless body to the ground.

If he'd been able to kill his adversary without facing any consequences, Balint thought, he had no doubt he'd actually do it. Why not? And then a second idea struck him: Why should he get caught? He wasn't your average petty criminal: he'd finished first in his class in medical school—seventy places ahead of his potential victim. If he was smart enough to run a cardiology division at thirty-four, wasn't he also intelligent enough to eliminate his wife's lover with impunity? Of course he was!

That was how, as he drove along Van Buren Turnpike past Laurendale Preparatory Academy, where his innocent daughters would be attending the first and the third grades respectively, toward the house where they lived, Balint decided to murder his former friend and classmate, Warren Sugarman.

CHAPTER TWO

And then a miracle occurred: nothing happened.

Balint had anticipated that his life with Amanda would change drastically after his discovery, but the reality was that their routine continued without any noticeable differences. He kept an eye out for pretexts she might use for contacting Sugarman, but nothing in her conduct struck him as unusual. There were no late-night phone calls from inside the pantry, no efforts to skip out on their social engagements. The only time she ever extricated herself from his company was on Saturday afternoons, every other week, when he drove to Hager Heights to lunch with his parents. He tried to remember the first time she had ducked out of one of these meals—but the alarming reality was that she'd been avoiding his mother for years. Could it be, he wondered, that his wife's affair with Sugarman had really been going on for that long? It was possible the pair also rendezvoused during the workweek, when Amanda was allegedly employed at the library, but Balint telephoned her in the reference room over the ensuing days, on various pretexts, and she always answered immediately.

He considered visiting his parents again the following weekend—just to find out whether she met up with Sugarman in his absence—but he wanted to avoid provoking her suspicions. Instead he waited until the next Saturday. This time, Amanda didn't even offer an excuse for staying home: no toothache, no stomach flu, no emergency staff meeting. She merely smiled at him over breakfast and said, "I don't think I'm up to dealing with your mother today. You're okay going on your own, aren't you?"

"You haven't seen my parents in months."

"I'm sure they don't mind." She poured him a second cup of coffee. "Send them my love. I'll see them when the girls come home from camp."

"And what will you do while I'm gone?"

"I was thinking I might buy a dress for Allison Sucram's wedding."

Balint vaguely remembered the Sucrams, one of the couples who played bridge with Amanda every fourth Tuesday. He assumed Allison was their daughter, but he wasn't positive, and he certainly didn't recall that the woman was getting married. "When *is* the wedding?" he asked.

"October. First weekend. *Please* tell me you put it on your calendar."

"I'm sure it's there," Balint lied.

"It had better be. And one more thing," said Amanda. "Warren Sugarman called. He said you agreed to have dinner with him."

"He *asked*. I didn't exactly agree . . ."

"I didn't want to be rude. On the other hand, I don't want Gloria to think we're betraying her—that we're taking his side. You know how she is . . ."

Balint eyed his wife warily. Was she probing him—trying to see how much he knew? Or was her life so compartmentalized that she could sleep with Sugarman and still worry sincerely about offending the man's ex-wife? "She's *your* friend," said Balint. "If you want to tell Sugarman to go to hell, it's fine by me."

"I thought you liked him."

"Not particularly. He's a butcher in the operating room," said Balint—unable to resist a jab, even an overtly dishonest one. Sugarman actually had the steadiest hands in New Jersey. "The nurses call him Sweeney Todd behind his back."

A flicker of displeasure panned across Amanda's features and then dissolved. "That's too bad," she replied. "But I imagine Gloria will be thrilled to hear it. In any case, I couldn't say no without offending him, so we're on for next month."

"Suit yourself. Just don't have any surgical emergencies during dinner."

He stood up and kissed his wife on the forehead, a part of their morning ritual for nearly a decade, and he assured her that he'd be home by two o'clock. Then he drove the fifteen miles to Hager Heights, where his parents resided in a freestanding duplex on the campus of a planned retirement community. They'd moved there when his stepfather turned seventy. The development, Hager Estates, offered three levels of care: independent, supportive, and skilled. Basically, if you couldn't fend for yourself, they moved you to an assisted-living facility, and ultimately to a nursing home, all three positioned around the same patch of manicured gardens. Balint's stepfather had been a veterinarian and amateur inventor, and he'd once brimmed with intriguing zoological tidbits, but all he talked about these days was which neighbors had been shunted up the supervision ladder.

Balint found his parents encamped on their veranda. The homemade lunch lay under aluminum foil on the wrought iron table. His stepfather set aside the morning newspaper and shook his hand vigorously. "How's the hardworking man?"

"Surviving," answered Balint.

His mother removed the Saran wrap from a bowl of tossed salad and began scooping iceberg lettuce and cherry tomatoes onto plates. "You're alone?"

"Unfortunately. Amanda's still having dental problems."

His mother frowned. "How many teeth does that girl have? You should buy her a pair of dentures so we can have the privilege of her company every once in a while."

"She sends her regards."

"When was the last time we saw her? Three months ago? Four?" His mother set a dish of salad in front of him. "I'm starting to think she's vanished. Or run off. If you get divorced without telling us, Jeremy, that will be the death of me."

"Nobody is getting divorced, Lilly," snapped his stepfather. "Don't even say such things."

"I wasn't serious," replied his mother. "Of course nobody's getting divorced. For God's sake, Henry, why can't you sprout a sense of humor in your old age?" She turned toward Balint. "The important thing is that *you're* here. Now what kind of blintzes would you like? Either cheese or strawberry . . ."

Balint knew that his mother *had* been joking, that he'd probably endured similar remarks about Amanda disappearing on countless other occasions without ever registering them. At the same time, he wondered how his mother might react if he informed her that he was indeed filing for divorce—if he announced his plans that very moment, right there at the lunch table, effectively making it so. She'd be devastated, he feared, even though Amanda was leagues away from being the model daughter-in-law, or even an adequate one, because then she'd have to confront the possibility that her faultless son had somehow made a mistake. But now that he'd decided to kill Sugarman—an idea that he had grown increasingly comfortable with over the previous twelve days—he no longer saw any need for his marriage to end.

Balint forced himself to act normally, although his mind remained focused on whether Amanda's silver Saab would be parked at the foot of Sugarman's driveway. He felt the blood pounding in his temples, but he made certain to stay with his parents until the usual hour, suffering through his mother's display of her latest watercolors. Yet as soon at the clock struck one—the cue for his stepdad's afternoon nap—he raced down the flagstone path and drove at top speed toward the surgeon's address.

En route, he flipped the radio to his favorite Golden Oldies station. The Mercedes filled with lyrics about teenage lovers, and he felt sorry for himself. Also stupid. What a fool he'd been to take Amanda for granted! Why had he failed to appreciate how good he'd had it for so many years? He recalled a moment shortly after they'd first moved to Laurendale, when Amanda had flown to visit her dying grandmother in Florida, and he'd heard on the radio that a New York-bound jet had crashed on the tarmac in Miami—and although he rationally knew that his wife wasn't aboard the doomed plane, that she wasn't due to return until the following day, he'd experienced an overwhelming and paralyzing yearning to hear her voice. Of course even then Amanda might have been screwing Sugarman on the sly.

He turned off Chestnut Street onto Meadow Drive. It was a balmy August afternoon. On the golf course, the Canada geese had yielded their territory to motorized carts and teenage caddies. No trace of the accident marked the spot where he'd collided with the dachshund. This surprised him. He'd feared some vestige of the calamity—maybe a faint bloodstain on the asphalt—although he also understood that his concerns were foolish to the brink of paranoia.

A sinewy, tight-faced woman jogged past on the opposite sidewalk—a friend of his wife's named Bonnie Kluger who

lived on their block and was always voicing contrarian opinions. Either she didn't see Balint at the wheel, or she chose
to ignore him. Behind the whitewashed brick wall rose the
barking of a dog, startling Balint for an instant. He eased the
Mercedes around the corner onto Meadow Court.

As he'd expected—and dreaded—Amanda's silver Saab
basked at the top of the drive. This time, Balint did not
attempt to explore any further. Instead, he pulled over to the
side of the road and sobbed.

———

THE GIRLS returned from sleepaway camp the following Friday.
In the ensuing hugging and tickling and reading of bedtime
stories, Balint sensed some of his warmth for Amanda returning. They even made love on the night of the girls' arrival—
for the first time in a month—and he somehow managed
to lose himself in the experience. But he wasn't doing it for
pleasure, he realized. Certainly not out of affection. He was
having sex with Amanda in order to lull her into a false sense
of security, to ensure that nobody suspected him of a motive
for murdering her lover. It was a definitive moment for Balint:
his entire existence, from that point forward, was aimed at
one specific goal.

The irony was that the more he thought about killing
Sugarman—the more he trained all of his anger and disappointment upon this one objective—the more tolerable all of
life's smaller indignities seemed. When he was on weekend
call over Labor Day, and Amanda deposited the girls with a
neighbor for "a quick trip to the hairdresser," which he recognized as code for a dash to Meadow Court, Balint relaxed in
the physicians' lounge at the hospital, calm as ever, reassured
in the knowledge that he would ultimately savor his revenge.
As the weeks passed, the more he thought about Sugarman,

the more abstract the notion of murdering the man became. The reason he intended to kill his rival transcended the affair and the betrayal and even Sugarman's very existence. It boiled down to something so much simpler: the real reason that he was going to eliminate Amanda's lover was simply that he had decided he was going to do so—nothing more, nothing less. Because, like graduating first in his medical school class, he wanted to prove to himself that he could. Even on the occasions that he ran into Sugarman at the hospital, or consulted with him about a heart-transplant case, he found the encounters surprisingly tolerable—because, in the end, he knew that he'd have the last laugh. No matter what task occupied him at any given moment—raking leaves, delivering lectures to the medical students, taking the girls cranberry picking—in the back of his mind lurked the conviction that comforted him through all his daily troubles.

He no longer felt any urgency. If he was going to commit a murder, he was going to bide his time and avoid any mistakes. So whenever he had moments to spare, he found himself pondering various methods of execution. He considered staging a robbery, cutting the brake lines in the surgeon's BMW, slipping incremental doses of arsenic into Sugarman's food. During quiet afternoons at the office, he sneaked over to the branch library in the adjacent township and read accounts of unsolved crimes from the Black Dahlia murder to the Tylenol scare of 1982. He was careful never to check out any books, to browse when no other patrons stood nearby, donning leather gloves to conceal his fingerprints. One could never take too many precautions. By mid-September, he knew every detail of the Zodiac killings, Diane Suzuki's disappearance, the paraquat spree in Japan. He'd read Dreiser's *An American Tragedy* and Capote's *In Cold Blood* as "how *not* to" books. What he realized, after his month of research, was that most "perfect crimes" stemmed at least partially from luck. Many victims found themselves in the wrong place at the wrong time; perpetrators often escaped identification through shoddy police work. Had he been conducting a controlled experiment, in which he was afforded multiple chances, Balint might have risked relying on a combination of skill and good fortune. But he had only one opportunity, only one life, so he refused to leave even the most trivial detail to circumstance. He thought of the horrors of prison, and about his own daughters, and he knew he had to get it right.

A third alternate Saturday arrived and he again visited his parents in Hager Heights. More truck-ripened tomatoes. More watercolors. More doting praise from his mother and crisp admiration from his stepdad.

Balint still did not have a plan. Yet he had made considerable progress: in only six weeks, he already had identified dozens of ways in which he would *not* kill Warren Sugarman.

———

ANOTHER ODD thing occurred: he accompanied his girls to a farm in Marston Moor to purchase pumpkins for Halloween, on a Sunday when Amanda actually did have to cover the reference desk at the library, and he ran into Gloria Sugarman and her son. He'd encountered his wife's friend many times in his own living room, and at dinners with their spouses, but he couldn't recall the last time he'd crossed paths with her at random—certainly not forty-five minutes away from home. She'd aged a decade since he'd last seen her: crow's-feet limned her eyes and her skin had acquired a sallow tone. The child, Davey, was a pale, pudgy creature; he reminded Balint of the cartoon piglet on Phoebe's favorite television show. The notion crossed his mind that the boy was divine retribution, also that he didn't particularly look like Sugarman. His own daughters, he reassured himself, both boasted the distinctive Balint family chin.

Gloria spotted him in the pies and preserves aisle.

"Jeremy," she cried. "Jeremy Balint!"

"What a surprise . . ."

He dispatched Jessie and Phoebe to explore a stand of enormous pumpkins.

"It's *so* good to see you," said Gloria. "Truly."

They stood facing each other in the fertile air. A hay cart entered the parking lot, discharging a swarm of raucous adolescents. Grackles and starlings scavenged on the gravel in front of the apple-weighing station. Balint had nothing to say.

"Have you seen Warren?" she asked.

"Here and there. In the hospital. Not socially."

He didn't mention the upcoming dinner they had planned—which he vaguely recalled was still on his calendar.

"It's okay, if you do," said Gloria. "I fully understand. But he's an asshole. Just so you know."

I *do* know, thought Balint. Yet he held his tongue. He found himself thinking: *You may hate him, Gloria, but I'm going to kill him.* The certainty of this vow brought a genuine smile to his lips.

"A real asshole," she emphasized. "Not to be trusted."

Balint glanced around to make sure that his kids were out of earshot; he didn't need them repeating Gloria's remarks to Amanda. In one of the true crime digests at the Pontefract Library, he'd read about a scarlet macaw that had unwittingly divulged his owner's career as a cat burglar.

"I do hope you've landed on your feet," said Balint. "You're looking well."

"Nonsense. I look like shit," answered Gloria. "I'm using my maiden name now, incidentally. Gloria Picardo. I always despised Sugarman . . . It sounds like a gingerbread cookie, doesn't it?"

"Gloria Picardo," said Balint. "I'll let Amanda know."

He turned toward the pumpkin grove—pretending that he'd heard one of his daughters summoning him. "So good to see you," he said, already inching along the aisle. "I'm sure we'll cross paths again soon."

He did not mention the encounter to Amanda.

———

THE DINNER at Sugarman's was actually scheduled for that Thursday. Amanda had arranged for a babysitter—a mousy girl who had previously worked for a cousin of a woman with whom his wife had once taken a pottery class. Or something like that. He couldn't keep Amanda's hobbies straight and he couldn't keep her friends straight. If she in fact had been learning sculpting, after all, and not screwing some dashing art instructor. Yet deep down, Balint suspected that there were no other Sugarmans in her life. Her lover might be playing around with scores of women, but that wasn't Amanda's nature. One affair, maybe. But not two. Or, at least, that's what he told himself. If his rival really had seduced his wife away from a life of fidelity, that justified the man's murder all the more.

Balint felt no desire to spend an evening in Sugarman's company. On the other hand, he might postpone the dinner, but he couldn't avoid it forever. Eventually, if he sent enough regrets, his rival was bound to grow suspicious. So far better to get the engagement over with as quickly as possible. Like lancing a boil. It might be torture. Yet even torture proved bearable when one knew that it wouldn't last forever.

They drove to dinner in the Saab. Amanda didn't park under the basketball hoop, however, but at the curbside. Balint brought along a bottle of Cabernet Sauvignon. He took pride in the knowledge that he hadn't tampered with the wine— that he was not the sort of dimwitted killer who'd let emotion cloud his judgment.

Sugarman greeted him with a handshake, then had the nerve to clasp him around the shoulders. He didn't attempt any physical contact with Amanda.

"So here are the options," declared their host. "We can order in Italian. Or we can order in Indian. Or we can order in sushi." He handed Balint a stack of paper delivery menus. "Alternatively, we can show up at Gloria's condominium, and demand that she cook us dinner, but she's likely to sprinkle mine with cyanide. So what will it be?"

"I vote cyanide," said Balint. "I hear it tastes like almonds."

The surgeon led them into the den—the very room where the traitor's nose had rubbed on Amanda's. "*Smells* like almonds," he said. "They claim it tastes bitter, but it probably anesthetizes the tongue on contact, so it's hard to say . . ."

"You know a lot about poisons," mused Balint.

"Just enough. You can't be too careful. Definitely not with Gloria on the loose."

Balint watched his rival closely, on guard for any subtle exchanges between him and Amanda. He saw none. Sugarman blathered about his transplant cases, which he described using medical terminology, addressing Balint as though his wife weren't even in the room. He sat on one of the love seats, leaving the sofa to his guests. Over cognac, they decided upon Indian, and Sugarman phoned in their order. Then his eyes gleamed, as though lit with a photographer's flash, and he said, "I almost forgot. I've been meaning to give you follow-up on that dead dog business."

Balint's ears perked up.

"Turns out it was some troubled kid from Hager Park. They caught him stabbing a woman's German shepherd last week—and he's already confessed to at least two other animal killings. So far, he's denying responsibility for my neighbor's dog, but it seems rather implausible that he's behind every *other* dog murder except this one. Strange, isn't it, how criminals will confess to almost all of their crimes and then hold back and insist they're innocent of only one or two."

"Maybe they really are innocent," offered Amanda.

"Could be. But I think a far more likely explanation is that people want to feel that they've been victimized. Even a serial killer can take pleasure in indignation. If he can say, I've done *almost* all you've accused me of—except not *that*—it lets him focus on the way he's been wronged by the authorities, rather than on the wrongs that he's done to others. It's a coping mechanism."

Balint savored his good fortune; now even the dead dachshund wouldn't be traced back to him. "Interesting theory, Warren. You sure you're not thinking of transitioning into psychiatry?"

"Only as a patient. And hopefully no time soon," quipped Sugarman with a broad grin. "Seriously, headshrinking's not for me. Do you know what the problem with psychiatry is?"

Balint waited for his rival to answer his own question.

"The problem with psychiatry is that you can't sleep with your patients." Sugarman beamed. "Or I suppose you can. But only until someone catches you."

He poured himself a second cognac and topped off Balint's glass.

"That was a joke, for the record," he added. "In case you're thinking of reporting me to the medical board. Anyway, what have you two been up to?"

"The usual," said Amanda. "Carpool. Violin. Ballet. I love my girls—don't get me wrong—but I'm starting to understand the appeal of Swiss boarding school."

"Davey is with Gloria full-time now," said Sugarman. "Probably for the best. We were never good at dividing responsibilities. You two, on the other hand . . . I admire how you work so well together." He took a sip of cognac and nodded—but Balint couldn't discern if he approved of the brandy or of his guests' parenting. "You know, Jeremy, I should be angry with you. Gloria was always holding you up as an example in order to shame me. Practically every time you drove your kids to a birthday party or a music lesson. You're lucky I didn't name you as a corespondent in my divorce."

"I'm the luckiest guy on earth," said Balint.

He pictured his fingers choking off the air to his host's lungs.

"I do have an interesting case to tell you about," continued Sugarman—apropos of absolutely nothing. "I'm actually going to be an expert witness in criminal court."

"Very impressive," said Amanda.

"It's a manslaughter trial. You may have heard about it. Surgery resident up in Somerset County accidentally requested the wrong medication for a patient a few years back. He was supposed to order intravenous metoclopramide for nausea—and instead he ordered meperidine. Demerol. Sent the patient into a hypertensive crisis. Nearly killed him."

"Sounds like gross negligence, at a minimum," said Balint.

"That's just the tip of the iceberg. So this kid—he's only two years out of med school, after all—insists that he *did* order metoclopramide. That the nurse must have filled the syringe wrong. They were still using paper charts at this hospital at the time, mind you, so there's no electronic record . . . and when the auditors searched for the carbon copy of the order slip, they found it had been torn from the logbook."

"Clever. His word against the nurse's."

"But here's the insane part, Balint. This resident gets it into his sociopathic head that they might not believe him. That he might *still* get fired. So for the next two months, every time that particular nurse is on duty—it's a male nurse, a relatively new hire—the resident sneaks into the medication room and fills a metoclopramide bottle with Demerol, hoping to frame the guy. The nurse unwittingly injects four *other* patients before the hospital gets wind that something's terribly wrong and suspends him. Two of those patients died."

"That's awful," cried Amanda.

"You've got to wonder who let this nutcase into med school," said Sugarman. "Nurse nearly ended up going on trial for murder too. You know what saved him?"

"The resident had a guilty conscience?" suggested Balint.

"Appendicitis. The lucky bastard comes down with appendicitis and has to skip his nursing shift at the last minute. So a different nurse is on duty for the fifth injection." Sugarman leaned toward them, his face flushed. "The best part is that the resident was actually part of the team that scrubbed in on the appendectomy. That fellow must have been shitting bricks when he realized who was on the table. Talk about irony."

The doorbell rang. Sugarman set his drink on a coaster.

"Every time one of my own residents makes a mistake," he observed as he strode toward the door, "I'm just thankful he's not that kid."

"At least the guy was smart," said Amanda.

"Not so smart," objected Sugarman. "He got caught."

Yes, thought Balint. He got caught. But I won't. And his plan for murder suddenly came into focus.

CHAPTER THREE

Most of Balint's patients were hopeless cases. These men and women had already failed fluid restriction, digoxin, aldosterone antagonists. They'd visited cardiologists up and down the East Coast, paid out-of-pocket for third and fourth opinions. Unfortunately, what they needed were new hearts, substitute organs to replace their own failing tissue, but new hearts were in critically short supply. So they waited. And they suffered, sleeping on stacks of pillows to help them breathe. And a lucky few survived long enough for Warren Sugarman or Chester Pastarnack to slice open their chests and to rejuvenate them with a blood pump salvaged from a motorcycle fatality or a gunshot victim. For that's all the human heart really is: a relentless blood pump. Several times a month, Balint had the unpleasant duty of phoning the family members of one of his patients and informing them that, in the case of their loved one, the original pump had stopped working too soon.

Norman Navare was such a hopeless case. He'd been referred to Laurendale from a community hospital in Elizabeth Lakes on the remote chance that Balint might be able to slip him onto the transplant list. One look at his chart was all it took to recognize that the odds were grim. Navare was

sixty-four—at the cusp of too old. He had diabetes, another
strike. But his largest problem was that his heart's ejection
fraction had been measured at 14 percent. Anything below 15
percent was dire, a number below 10 percent usually incom-
patible with life. Even if he were eligible for an organ, he had
little prospect of surviving until one became available. But
Balint had agreed to see him—cultivating good relationships
with Laurendale's satellite hospitals was a crucial aspect of
what made an effective division chief—and in late September,
the man had arrived for his first appointment in the company
of his adult daughter. Navare, despite his bleak health, displayed the confidence and flair of a man who had once been
exceedingly handsome. He sported a guayabera and a Panama
hat that gave him the look of a playboy from prerevolution
Havana. But Balint hardly noticed the man's rugged features,
because he was immediately captivated by the black-eyed brunette at his patient's side: Navare's daughter was the most
beautiful woman that Balint had ever laid eyes upon.

"We're so grateful to you for seeing us," she said. She
appeared to be about twenty-five. "We tried to get an appointment at Cornell, but they wanted us to wait six weeks. The
Brigham in Boston wouldn't see us at all."

Balint noted the girl wasn't wearing a wedding ring. He
hoped that she hadn't spotted his own. As the diseased man
settled himself into a chair, Balint concealed his hands beneath
the desk and clandestinely slid the gold band off his finger.
What authority did Amanda have to complain? If she spent
her Saturdays on the sofa in Sugarman's den, he had every
right to flirt with anyone he damn pleased.

"Well, that's their loss," said Balint. "Some of these fancy
hospitals take only the easy cases. They're more concerned
about padding numbers than with saving lives. It's sad. But I
promise you we'll do the best for your father."

"So you think you can get him a heart?"

Usually, this was the moment where Balint warned patients and families that he couldn't make any promises. Instead, he said, "I'm certainly going to try like hell. If my own father needed a heart, I wouldn't try any harder."

The girl's eyes glowed. "Did you hear that, Papa? That's not something you hear every day from a doctor."

Her father nodded. "We'll see what happens."

Navare sounded short of breath. Balint listened to his heart and lungs with a stethoscope. He held his own shoulders out and sucked in his stomach while conducting the physical, striving to appear dashing—or, at least, professional.

"I'm Delilah, by the way," said the girl. "Like the woman in the Bible who gives Samson that nasty haircut. But I'm a nurse, not a hairdresser. A nursing *student*, really—for another nine months." Her voice was tender and intensely feminine, a striking contrast to Amanda's no-nonsense manner of speaking. "Forgive me for saying this, Dr. Balint, but I want you to know that we've seen God-knows-how-many cardiologists over the past few years, and you're the first one who didn't treat Papa like a number. Most of them look at his ejection fraction and more or less bury him alive."

"There's a lesson in that. Don't die on one doctor's opinion," said Balint. Then he took a risk and added, "But please, call me Jeremy. In Hebrew, it's Jeremiah. Like the guy in the Bible who complains a lot."

To his surprise, Delilah Navare laughed. A high-pitched, almost musical laugh. Even her father cracked a thin smile.

"I'd like to see you every three weeks, Mr. Navare," said Balint—which was twice as often as he usually booked his heart failure patients. "We'll set up some evaluations for you and get you on as many transplant lists as possible . . . and then we'll have to keep you alive until you reach the top. There's no choice in the matter. How does that sound?"

"Sounds reasonable," answered Navare. "If it happens, then it will sound good."

"Fair enough." Balint liked the man's style, the sort of stoic reserve that comes from a lifetime of disappointment. "I'm going to give my cell phone number to your daughter. You have any concerns or questions—*any at all*—you call me. Night or day. I mean it. If I find out you have an emergency and you *don't* call me, I'm going to be mad as hell." He wrote his private number on the flip side of a business card. "I'm also going to include my pager number. It's always on—so no excuses."

Balint passed the card to Delilah and she thanked him. Then he took the liberty of escorting the patient and his daughter out to the elevators. He found himself wondering whether this girl was truly the most beautiful woman he'd ever seen, or whether there had been others whom he hadn't noticed because he'd been fully committed to Amanda. He couldn't be certain. What he did know was that Delilah Navare was stunningly attractive—and he had every intention of seeing her outside his office.

———

DELILAH INTRIGUED him; she didn't distract him from his mission. Once he'd mapped out the general contours of his scheme, Balint set about methodically laying the groundwork. Most murderers killed in haste, desperation trumping their common sense. But Balint promised himself that he wouldn't act prematurely. Whether it took him two years to bump off Sugarman, or ten, was entirely beside the point. Hadn't it taken Oppenheimer half a decade to build an atomic bomb? Every step from acquiring the materials to selecting his victims—he'd decided that his plan required multiple victims—deserved the same painstaking care as a heart transplant. So while he'd charted his strategy in his head, Balint held off an entire month before launching his first preparations. *If a month goes by and I still don't uncover any glitches*, he assured himself, *that will be my cue to act.*

In early October, he finally felt comfortable enough with his plan to begin assembling his equipment. Even before he purchased any supplies, he required a safe place to store them. Balint didn't dare conceal them inside his home, where one of the girls might stumble upon the evidence at the bottom of a drawer or behind the boiler. For a few days, he contemplated stashing his materials in his office—possibly in the locked cabinet where he kept an emergency supply of tranquilizers and analgesics—but he knew that he'd never sleep easy while the cleaning crew had access to the suite at night. It was true that he possessed the only key to the cabinet; he could even have installed a second strongbox beyond its steel doors. Yet he couldn't risk one of the maintenance workers jimmying the lock in search of pharmaceuticals or cash. Eventually he decided that the safest hiding place was his stepfather's fishing cabin on Lake Shearwater, an hour west of Laurendale in the Onaswego Hills.

The two-room cedar cabin had been in Henry Serspinsky's family for multiple generations. Shortly after he'd married Balint's mother—her second marriage, his third—the veterinarian invited his new stepson out for a weekend of hooking trout. Balint had been in college at the time. They'd repeated the pilgrimage annually, for another eight years, until Balint acquired children of his own and the retired vet declared himself "too old" to survive without creature comforts. On the final few excursions, the old man had needed to return to shore frequently to self-catheterize. Every year,

Balint promised himself he'd make the trip on his own—or at least help Serspinsky rent out the cabin for a profit—but all he ever managed to do was drive to the site for a couple of hours to check on the upkeep and make sure squatters hadn't burned down the place. It was a secluded structure at the end of a shaded dirt lane, and since the state's Fish and Game Bureau had stopped stocking Lake Shearwater with trout several years earlier, even the neighboring lodges went largely unvisited. In short, the cabin offered the perfect spot to salt away his supplies.

Balint drove out one day after work. Nothing strange about that, he assured himself. Early autumn was usually the season he inspected the property. Yet even as he steered up the poorly maintained roadway, his adrenaline surged. After weeks of planning, he was finally taking action.

The cabin was almost exactly as he'd left it twelve months earlier: same squeaking front step, same burned-out light bulb in the bedroom, same aroma of wood chips. None of the dust on the floorboards appeared disturbed. Along the far wall, Serspinsky's shelf of "inventor's tools" gathered dust. Someone or something had shattered one of the cabin's windowpanes, but the lock on the sash below didn't bear any indications of tampering. Balint slipped into a pair of gloves. No reason to risk leaving stray fingerprints in whatever nook he selected as a hiding place—on the extremely remote chance that the authorities ever did search the cabin. But where to conceal his gear? His first instinct had been among the box springs beneath the bed; then it crossed his mind that a potential squatter might shift the mattress if he found himself unable to sleep. Instead Balint located a steamer trunk inside one of the closets that contained an assortment of tablecloths and draperies and vintage women's undergarments. A few strands of ribbon and a pair of scissors, tucked into the bottom of such a chest, would hardly draw notice.

On his way out, Balint dusted the entire cabin and fractured a second, larger windowpane, creating the illusion that a squatter had been trespassing on the premises. Even if the police ever found his supplies, he could deny knowing how they'd gotten there.

His next step was to acquire the ribbon itself. He had to obtain a sufficient length to last him through his spree—but not so much that buying it attracted notice. Obviously he did not want to have to purchase additional ribbon after the initial murder. Here, he congratulated himself on making his first wise choice. Although he had a hypertension conference in Las Vegas on his calendar for the second weekend of the month, where he could easily have bought the ribbon at a local stationery shop—far from New Jersey, in case anybody ever tracked the materials to their point-of-sale—he realized that he'd draw suspicion if he wore gloves into a store in the Nevada desert during October. *Not* wearing gloves, however, ran the risk of leaving fingerprints on the ribbon. So he held off. Two weeks later, at the American Cardiology Association meetings in Minneapolis, he drove out to a suburban shopping plaza and purchased his supplies. (He avoided the city itself, because he'd read that some urban centers—New York, Washington—now had police cameras mounted along every block. He hadn't been able to find any evidence of Big Brother in Minneapolis, but why take chances?) It was a windy, bracing afternoon and his leather gloves, if not essential, didn't stand out.

Balint chose green ribbon. His inspiration was the Red Ribbon Strangler, who'd terrorized Creve Coeur, Rhode Island, in the 1960s, but he feared—irrationally—that someone might associate red with blood, and from blood it was a short leap to cardiology. He also considered yellow, but too many families used yellow ribbon for a military tribute, and he didn't want the authorities thinking the choice of yellow ribbon was incidental, that he'd found the trimming at the crime scene and made use of it. No, he needed them to think the killings were carefully planned. Black posed similar problems. Lots of people already owned black ribbons—employed them to transform hats and dresses into funeral attire. So green. He bought enough ribbon to produce thirty-two identical two-foot-long strands, far more than he anticipated using. He also purchased three packages of wrapping paper, an assortment of children's toys, a pin-the-tail-on-the-donkey set, and sufficient party favors to entertain every six-year-old child in Minnesota.

"What birthday is this for your kid?" asked the sales clerk.

"My niece," he replied, correcting the girl in an effort to make his deception sound authentic. "Six—going on sixteen."

Balint found himself glancing at the girl's cleavage, something he would never have done in his previous existence. She was cute. Not stunning like Delilah, but pretty enough. Under different circumstances—had he not been accruing supplies for his killing spree—he might have flirted, or even invited her out for a cup of coffee. Instead he thanked her politely and asked her to double bag his purchases. Then he traveled across the city to a different suburban shopping plaza and deposited all of the merchandise, except for the ribbon and scissors, into a Salvation Army dumpster. The following Tuesday morning, he detoured to Lake Shearwater on his way home from the airport and secured his equipment inside the steamer trunk.

———

WHILE BALINT led a second life, amassing the accoutrements for his vengeance, his first life continued in all its regular chaos. He attended Allison Sucram's wedding, to a red-haired woman in a wheelchair, and spent the reception discussing with the tax attorney seated to his right whether it was grammatically preferable to refer to the couple as two brides, or as spouse and spouse. He remembered only one other event from the evening: an aunt of the bride—the bride whose parents played bridge with Amanda—approached him in the cloakroom of the Waldorf Astoria Hotel, where the reception had taken place, to ask whether her diuretic could be responsible for her rash. At the end of the evening, he still wasn't sure whether he'd ever met the Sucrams before.

Later that month, he also attended a bar mitzvah in Philadelphia for the son of Amanda's childhood piano teacher and a funeral for the father of a woman from her former "babies group." He strove to appear extra attentive to his wife and to avoid arguments. He deferred to her on matters over which they might previously have bickered—like whether Jessie was too young to trick-or-treat without a chaperone. To outsiders, they must have appeared the perfect couple. To Balint, it felt as though they talked much less than they had previously— or, at least, less intimately—but he couldn't actually pinpoint any specific examples. Maybe, it crossed his mind, they'd *never* spoken to each other with much intimacy.

In mid-October, Balint's mother tripped in the produce aisle at the Shop 'n Save and fractured her hip and her collarbone. She required a two-day stay in the hospital, six weeks of casting, and then another three months of rehab. She also required twenty-four-hour attention—a level of care that her husband couldn't manage alone. During her first few weeks at home, Balint spent nearly every night in Hager Heights. Even Amanda had no excuse to justify staying away. He derived particular pleasure in insisting that his wife join him and the girls for lunch at the retirement village the following Saturday, claiming that he couldn't look after both his mother and his daughters at the same time, all the while knowing this would disrupt Amanda's date with Sugarman. She offered no objection. For a woman conducting an affair, she had a frustrating knack for prioritizing her own family—and this made it difficult for Balint to stay angry with her.

Work also kept Balint busy. Chester Pastarnack, the senior heart-transplant surgeon at Laurendale-Methodist, announced his retirement—effective the first of November. Shortly afterward, Warren Sugarman, at thirty-five, was appointed acting head of thoracic surgery. That meant he joined the Wednesday morning leadership meetings that Balint attended each week, forcing him to endure his rival's banter over croissants and coffee. It also meant that if he murdered Sugarman before Laurendale recruited a second heart-transplant surgeon, his crime would effectively shut down the hospital's entire program for the time being. Unless, of course, Pastarnack agreed to come out of retirement during the crisis. Balint crossed paths with Sugarman at the synagogue on the second day of Rosh Hashanah and congratulated his rival on his promotion. "More like a punishment," observed Sugarman. "I work harder . . . and Gloria gets more alimony." But he sensed the smug bastard was pleased as punch.

Balint found himself acutely aware of how peculiar it felt to be preparing for another man's assassination—attending to the gruesome business in a detached, practical manner, as though arranging a medical symposium—but he refused to let these feelings trouble him. Occasionally, he even saw the matter-of-fact nature of his preparations as humorous. For instance, one day Jessie repeated a John Lennon quotation she'd picked up at school: "Life is what happens while you're busy making other plans." How very true. At the same time,

Balint thought to himself with amusement, he highly doubted that *his* variety of plans were what the singer had meant.

———

DELILAH NAVARE telephoned after nine o'clock on a Sunday evening. Balint had finished reading *The Remarkable Story of Chicken Little* to the girls, and was sitting in his study, his legs propped atop his ink blotter, proofreading a review article on valvular diseases. Amanda lay in bed upstairs, watching a documentary about female aviators. Or perhaps she'd already drifted off to sleep. He answered the call with irritation, assuming the hospital's page operator had phoned the wrong service attending by mistake.

"Dr. Balint?" asked the delicate voice. "I'm so sorry to call you this late. I hope I didn't wake you."

He recognized her immediately. "Delilah?"

"You said we should call anytime—or I never would have interrupted your weekend. Is now an okay moment?"

"It's fine. Just fine. What's going on?"

"Papa's getting worse," she explained. "I'm scared."

She had phoned from the emergency room at Laurendale. As soon as he hung up the receiver, Balint tracked down the night resident in the ER and learned that the team planned to admit Norman Navare for management of fluid overload. Thirty-five minutes later—after kissing his daughters and urging Amanda not to remain awake—he strode across the ambulance bay in his crisp, knee-length white coat.

"Dr. Balint. Chief of cardiology," he introduced himself to the dumbstruck emergency resident. "You can admit Mr. Navare under my name. VIP. If we have any private rooms that we can comp for him, make it happen."

"Sure thing," agreed the junior clinician. "I didn't realize . . ."

"Of course, you didn't. If Jesus Christ showed up at this hospital, you'd tag him as a homeless dude wearing a loincloth and keep him waiting for hours. Now please do your best to keep Mr. Navare comfortable."

He poked his head around several curtains before he found the out-of-the-way alcove to which they'd consigned Delilah's father. The patient sat propped at a right angle to the bed, on cannular oxygen, yet he still appeared desperate for air. Some idiot hadn't properly removed the EKG electrodes from his chest, leaving the poor man's hirsute body dappled with adhesives. His daughter stood beneath the cardiac monitor, dabbing his forehead with a damp towel. "Dr. Balint," she exclaimed in surprise. "I figured you'd stop by in the morning. I didn't dream you'd show up tonight."

"Jeremy," he corrected her. "Please."

Something in his tone penetrated her reserve—and registered his intentions. This was her opportunity to draw a line in the sand, if she so desired, to remind him ever so subtly that he was her father's cardiologist, not her friend. Balint actually felt as nervous as a teenager for a moment—as on edge as he'd been sixteen years earlier when he'd invited Molly what's-her-name to the senior class prom. Certainly far more tense than he had felt while stockpiling materials for his murder plot. But to his relief, Delilah smiled—a gentle, unmistakably inviting smile—and she said, "Jeremy." Just his name. Nothing more. But in those three syllables, she'd communicated everything Balint needed to know.

Once the overnight nursing administrator learned to her surprise that Norman Navare, a Venezuelan-born disabled housepainter, was a VIP patient, and that the chief of cardiology had come to see him in person on a Sunday evening, she managed to find the man a complimentary private room in under an hour. Navare's lab values came back better than

Balint had anticipated. His oxygen saturation improved. With the appropriate pills and fluid regulation, he'd do fine—at least in the short run. Over the long haul, of course, he'd end up in the emergency room again sooner rather than later.

"I do believe we have everything under control," Balint assured both father and daughter, once the patient was safely ensconced in his room on the hospital's luxurious top floor. Outside, the lights of the mansions along Laurendale Beach twinkled down to the coast. "You'll be back on your feet in a couple of days—tops. Maybe tomorrow."

"From your mouth to God's ears," said Navare.

"I'm sorry I dragged you out of bed," said Delilah, but now she sounded affectionate and not particularly apologetic. "I didn't know where else to turn. It's just been the two of us since my mother passed away . . ."

"I'm *glad* you dragged me out of bed. I'll stop by in the morning, but I'll have my phone on all night."

Suddenly, Delilah clasped his hand and squeezed it. "Thank you, *Jeremy*," she said. "I trust you."

———

This LATE-NIGHT exchange with Delilah reminded Balint of the key advantage he had in comparison with history's other murderers. People trusted doctors. People also harbored strong prejudices regarding serial killers. The men who shot strangers or blew up public fountains were assumed to be loners, delinquents, enemies of civilization. Poor, hungry bastards who thought too much. Theodore Kaczynski. Not leading cardiologists at tertiary medical centers, certainly not the husbands of tennis-playing librarians or the fathers of adorable, well-adjusted princesses. Never Alpha Omega Alpha graduates of Ivy League medical schools and fellows of the American College of Physicians and founding members of the Hager

Park Racquetball Association. In short, beyond all of his painstaking preparations, he benefited from the simple reality that he didn't remotely fit the bill of what people expected from a sociopath. Whether he actually was a sociopath, Balint decided, was not worth thinking about. All that he knew for certain was that life had dealt him an unjust hand and he was evening out the score.

If he'd harbored any doubts—which he didn't—his confrontation with Sugarman the next morning would easily have banished them. The disagreement erupted at the monthly heart-transplant summit, a seven A.M. session during which senior clinicians from various disciplines reviewed which patients should be eligible for organs. When Balint arrived, exhausted after only four hours of sleep, he found his colleague already seated in the conference room. Sugarman raised his Styrofoam coffee cup to acknowledge his arrival. "How are you, Balint?"

"Almost awake."

He retrieved an agenda from the stack at the door. In twos and threes, the representatives of the various departments and services dallied in: anesthesia, nursing, psychiatry. Balint waited for Chester Pastarnack to arrive—but then, to his surprise, Sugarman called the meeting to order. The baton, it appeared, already had been passed. No longer would Pastarnack's bald crown with its enormous brow make final determinations of life and death. They had entered the Sugarman era. Balint's nemesis was now to play God, at least for the short time on earth still allotted to him.

"I saw your patient Navare this morning, Balint," began Sugarman. "You can't seriously want to list him?"

"But I do. Why not? He's under sixty-five. He's got strong family support."

Sugarman shook his head. "Pardon my French, Jeremy, but he's a fucking nightmare. The guy's a poorly controlled diabetic on the brink of renal failure. He could be Dick-goddamn-Cheney and I wouldn't cut open his chest."

An awkward silence settled over the conference room. These transplant summits were usually harmonious affairs, a collaborative effort. Chester Pastarnack rarely spoke until every participant had received an opportunity to offer his ten cents—and he certainly never used profanity. On occasion, Pastarnack had even been known to solicit an opinion from one of the medical students or nursing trainees who observed the meeting from the folding chairs along the rear wall.

"Am I crazy, people?" asked Sugarman. "Or am I missing something?"

Balint's eyes wandered from face to face. He could have kissed the consult-liaison psychiatrist—a dour German woman old enough to be his grandmother—when she offered a tepid word of support. "That man possesses a will to live," she said. "I met with him for two hours last week. Psychologically, he's an excellent candidate."

"Anybody else?" asked Sugarman.

"The daughter is a nursing student," observed one of the nursing coordinators. "I'm just throwing that out there."

Sugarman raised his eyebrows. "Okay, she's a nursing student. Good for her. But what am I supposed to do with that information?"

"She'll be able to look after him," ventured the psychiatrist.

Sugarman grinned—an ugly grin. "If I have to play the bad guy, then I have to play the bad guy. Say we give your friend a heart, Balint, he's got a one-in-three chance of dying on the table. Even money, he's dead in a month. And do you really want to tell the parents of some twenty-year-old athlete with cardiomyopathy who *doesn't* get that heart that we had to kill their kid—which is, in essence, what we'd be doing—so the chief of cardiology could try to buck the odds?"

That was the final verdict. They passed over Delilah's father and moved on to the next candidate. Balint didn't absorb another word that was said all morning. When the meeting ended, he hardly noticed. Only after Sugarman approached him and placed his hand on Balint's shoulder did he register that it was time to leave.

"It's not personal, Jeremy. He's a lousy candidate. If we had more organs, it would be different. You know how it is . . ."

"Of course, it's personal," snapped Balint. "Maybe not for you. But for Norman Navare and his daughter, you bet your ass it's damn personal. Where do you get off playing God all of a sudden, Sugarman? Are you even an organ donor?"

"Whoa, cowboy. What's gotten into you?"

Balint realized he was on the brink of ruining everything. If word got around that bad blood had brewed between him and Sugarman before the murder, it would only be a matter of time before the authorities discovered Amanda's affair—and then all would be lost. His only option was to swallow his pride and apologize.

"I'm sorry, Warren. I shouldn't have said that. I was way out of line," he said.

"Don't think twice. We all have our moments." He flashed Balint a benevolent smile. "No harm, no foul."

Balint placed his hand atop of the surgeon's. It was the only way. "Navare is a family friend . . ."

"I had no idea. I'm sorry," said Sugarman. Balint hated the man now more than ever—despised him for his sympathy above all else. "If I thought he had a remote chance, you understand, I'd bend over backward . . ."

Balint stood up and Sugarman gave him a hug—the sort of macho half embrace exchanged by clergymen and mobsters. Perfect. At least a dozen witnesses had seen them make up. But to Balint, his rival's embrace was more than hypocrisy. The arms locked around his torso were already the icy limbs of a cadaver.

CHAPTER FOUR

He had decided upon the *how*. His next step was to determine the *where*.

Balint bought himself a Rand McNally *Road Atlas* at a service station. He might have searched for promising locations on the Internet, but he did not want to leave behind an electronic trail. Circumstantial evidence had sent nearly as many men to prison as eyewitness accounts. A similar calculus shaped his choice to center the spree in New York City, using Manhattan as his hub and the Tri-State suburbs for spokes. The distances were longer than he would have preferred—it was a two-and-a-half-hour drive from Laurendale to Westchester and Long Island, nearly three to Fairfield County in Connecticut—but they were tolerable. Suburban Philadelphia had been his other option, but he'd grown up in nearby Bucks County, and he sought to avoid even the remotest ties to the crime scenes. Of course, choosing the suburbs of either New York or Philadelphia put him way ahead of the average killer. A less-intelligent perpetrator would have concentrated the crimes around Laurendale itself, murdering once in North Jersey and then in the Trenton area and on another day down by Atlantic City—until the police required only a protractor and a piece of string to home in upon their suspect. Balint's research confirmed what he'd already suspected: most criminals were indeed not very bright. If you marked the sites of a serial killer's crimes on a map, nine times out of ten you could then predict the murderer's address within half a mile.

The first rule Balint settled upon, in regard to choosing his targets, was not to be governed by sentiment. He resolved against shying away from potential victims because they cared for young children or elderly parents. If he were to succeed, he had to be willing to strangle nuns and kindergarten teachers and firefighters, disabled veterans and elderly widows, even pregnant women and adolescents, all with equal voracity. He planned to avoid younger children, but for a practical reason: he feared strangling elementary school kids might impact the psychological profile of the killer that the police inevitably would generate. He hoped to have the authorities searching for a disaffected dropout or derelict—often the perpetrators of serial killings. In contrast, he'd read, methodical child butchers lurked in all segments of society. Balint's first priority had to be to murder Sugarman without getting caught. Inevitably, avoiding detection meant selecting additional targets. Vulnerable targets. The alternative was to assume greater risks, and while he might have been willing to take such chances where only his own welfare was concerned, he refused to play Russian roulette with the futures of his daughters.

After several days of reflection, he concluded that New York's Westchester County offered as good a place to start as any. But where in Westchester? He proceeded by process of elimination—avoiding large municipalities, which might already possess street cameras, such as Yonkers, and those like Mount Vernon, where a violent crime would not draw much attention. At the opposite end of the spectrum, he feared homes in the tiny suburbs of Scarsdale and Chappaqua could confound him with high-tech security systems. Above all else, he avoided towns to which he could claim even the remotest connection: he had a second cousin in Ardsley and a former girlfriend in Mamaroneck, so he scratched these communities from his list. Ultimately he settled upon the village of Cobb's Crossing, because it contained both a small college and a planned retirement community, each of which might afford easy targets, and because, in a pinch, its position at the intersection of four major highways promised access to numerous escape routes.

Balint circled the hamlet on the Westchester County map in his atlas. Then he thought the better of leaving behind any vestige of his planning, so he tore the page from the Rand McNally and ignited it on the gas range. As he watched the flame burning toward his fingers, his spirits surged on a wave of power, a glorious wave that carried him aloft like a phoenix rising from ash.

———

Norman Navare returned home from the hospital three days later, as Balint had anticipated, and he scheduled a follow-up appointment for early the next week. This time, he booked a full-hour block with his priority patient. All weekend long, he found himself looking forward to the encounter, and when the time finally arrived, he actually suffered a mild case of the jitters. Adding to his anxiety, Navare ran late—Delilah later explained that she'd accidentally locked her keys inside her car—and Balint was on the brink of giving up hope when the old man and his daughter stepped through the office door. Navare's complexion had assumed the blue-gray tinge of an ice floe.

"I'm so sorry," apologized Delilah. "But I come bearing gifts."

She handed Balint a colorfully striped paper bag.

"A little something to say thank you . . ."

Her offering was more than a *little* something. She'd baked him cookies, literally hundreds of cookies, shaped like hearts with red and blue sprinkles. These weren't valentine-style hearts; they actually looked like human organs. Upon closer inspection, Balint realized the red and blue sprinkles had not been randomly distributed: the red patches marked the oxygenated blood of arteries, while the blue area indicated the relatively deoxygenated blood of veins.

"Anatomically correct," observed Balint. "Very impressive."

"You've been so kind to us," she replied. "To me . . ."

Usually Balint replied to this sort of remark with the observation that he was merely doing his job. To Delilah, he answered, "Don't be foolish. It's the least I could do for my favorite patient." Of course, what he actually meant was that *she* was his favorite patient, so to speak, and they both knew it. Her father was merely some debilitated housepainter with heart disease—not a person Balint had any reason to favor over countless other critically ill men and women.

Balint examined Navare and ordered several diagnostic tests. "Your father could use another echocardiogram," he explained. "To make sure that his ejection fraction is holding steady."

"Any news on the heart?" asked Delilah.

He hadn't yet told her about Sugarman's decision.

"I'm still working on getting him listed. We've hit a minor snag regarding your father's eligibility, but nothing we shouldn't be able to overcome . . ."

"Are you sure?"

"I thought you trusted me. I *am* going to get your father a heart, even if it means poisoning all the other candidates on the list."

Navare shook his head. "Don't worry too much about me, doc. You should give your hearts to the most deserving people . . ."

Delilah patted his knee. "You're as deserving as anyone, Papa . . ."

"I am an old man," said Navare. "If it comes down to me or someone younger . . . a father of small children . . ."

Balint closed the man's chart. "I understand your concerns, Mr. Navare. But we *do* give the hearts to the most deserving candidates. In this case, I'm optimistic that there will be enough to go around . . ."

He completed Navare's physical exam and asked him to step into the lavatory to provide a urine sample. Urinalysis was entirely unnecessary, but it afforded Balint a moment alone with Delilah. The nursing student looked radiant with her onyx hair braided into cornrows and her breasts snug under a cotton halter. He guessed that she'd done herself up for the appointment.

"I hope I'm not out of line," Balint said, trying to mask his own confidence, "but I was wondering—I swear to you I've never asked this of a patient's family member before, and I could probably get in big trouble for doing it—but I was wondering if you might want to have dinner with me sometime?"

"Do you mean *go on a date*?"

He looked away. "I shouldn't have asked."

From the next room, they heard the rhythm of Norman Navare's urine hitting a specimen cup.

"*Now* who's being foolish?" asked Delilah. "And yes, Jeremy, I would be very happy to have dinner with you."

At that moment, the bathroom door opened and Navare shuffled back into the examination suite. He was still tucking his undershirt into his trousers with one hand and he held the cup of urine in the other. His fly wasn't zipped. Balint took the specimen from him to label it, while his daughter assisted with his clothes.

"I should see you in another three weeks, Mr. Navare. After the echo results come back. But I'll obviously call you sooner if we uncover anything alarming."

He opened the door for the old man and his daughter.

In a softer voice, he asked, "And I'll see you . . . ?"

"Name your day."

"Tomorrow?"

She smiled. "Sure. Tomorrow."

"My last patient is scheduled for five thirty. Do you want to meet downstairs in the lobby at six fifteen tomorrow night?"

She agreed.

Balint watched the beauty as she helped her father past the receptionist's desk and across the packed waiting room. He regretted for a moment that he hadn't thanked her one final time for the cookies. Then he returned to his desk, opened Navare's electronic chart, and recorded that he'd discussed the man's present ineligibility for cardiac transplantation with both the patient and his daughter.

———

BALINT AWOKE so giddy the next morning that he considered canceling all of his patients and taking the day off to relax. He might have done so—except that his alibi with Amanda depended upon a long day at the office. As far as his wife was concerned, he'd be delivering a dinner lecture on anti-cholesterol medications for a drug company that evening, a lucrative gig of the sort that fell into his lap on occasion; this time, Balint told her that he'd be filling in at the last minute for a colleague whose child had become seriously ill. Unfortunately Amanda managed their finances, so he ran the risk that she might eventually notice that he'd never been reimbursed for this nonexistent presentation, but he was hoping that as months passed, the matter would slide through the cracks. Of course, if he didn't go to work at all, she'd notice something amiss.

Skipping out on the hospital *without* staying home wasn't an option either, as it might have been most days, when he could have split his time between the gym and the library. But this was also the afternoon Balint was slated to speak with Rabbi Steinhoff. Amanda had arranged the meeting—and if he postponed, she was bound to go through the roof. After all, his wife served on the synagogue committee that had hired the handsome young Israeli, a decorated veteran of his nation's air force.

The incongruity was not lost on Balint that the very same day he planned to cheat on his wife for the first time, after nine years of marriage, he was also consulting with a clergyman about charitable work. If this were a film, he imagined, Steinhoff would gain his confidence, ultimately causing his conscience to get the better of him, and he'd end up revealing the murder scheme to the rabbi. But this was *not* a movie and he had no intention of divulging anything.

Balint met Steinhoff on the elevator as he was returning from lunch; the pair shared an awkward ride in the crowded car. They exchanged handshakes in the corridor, then strolled in silence until they reached Balint's office. The rabbi stood a head taller than he did, but was far too thin for his frame, and Balint found himself reminded of the line from Shakespeare's *Julius Caesar* about Cassius boasting a "lean and hungry" look. He'd seen the play with Amanda one summer in the Berkshires—and this was among the few passages that had lodged inside his nonpoetic skull. Since this wasn't a medical visit, Balint seated himself opposite the rabbi in one of the

upholstered patient chairs, rather than behind his own imposing mahogany desk.

"Thank you for your time, Dr. Balint." The rabbi spoke
rapidly—with no trace of a Hebrew accent. "I realize you're
busy. *I'm* busy. Everyone is busy these days. My wife likes to
say that she's too busy to be busy . . ." Obviously Steinhoff
thought this remark rather witty, so Balint resisted the urge
to insinuate that the man's wife might be busy sampling merchandise elsewhere. "So I am grateful that you've made the
time for me, and I will try to be as brief as possible . . ."

"No rush," said Balint. "It's a quiet afternoon."

Steinhoff raised his eyebrows in surprise, as though the
notion of a quiet afternoon was a first perilous step toward
adultery and murder. Balint missed the late Rabbi Felder,
an irreverent, hearing-impaired clergyman who had probably
never been busy for a single day of his life.

"I've come to propose a joint venture," pitched Steinhoff.
"Are you familiar with Project Cain?"

"Amanda told me something about it. You try to keep
Jewish kids from committing crimes."

"Not only Jewish kids. Kids of all backgrounds." Steinhoff
leaned forward, dropping his voice nearly to a whisper—even
though they sat alone in the office with the door shut. "We
operate in Newark. Mostly in the black community. My guess
is that none of the children we assist are actually Jewish."

"Maybe you can convert them," proposed Balint.

The rabbi winced. "That's not our objective, Dr. Balint."
He then explained the nature of the initiative in painstaking
detail: a coalition of local synagogues dispatched suburban
housewives into inner-city neighborhoods to serve as "supplemental mothers" to children ages eight to eleven. The goal
was violence prevention—to use maternal affection to steer
the children away from crime. If Eve had been more devoted

to Cain, their reasoning went, he'd have thought twice before slaying Abel—hence the project's idiosyncratic name.

"Several good studies show that lack of quality time with their mothers is directly correlated with school-age children's risk for arrest as adolescents," expounded Steinhoff. "But the solution is harder to implement than you might think. These mothers *want* to spend time with their sons and daughters, but they're often single, and they're too busy earning their livings at Walmart or some fast-food joint. So that's where our volunteers come in. While the biological mothers are on the job, our supplemental mothers run workshops for the kids . . ."

Balint couldn't imagine Emmanuel Felder hatching such a harebrained scheme; he doubted Felder had ever stepped foot in Newark. "Why not just have the volunteers work at Walmart?" he asked.

"Excuse me?"

"You could ask your enthusiastic housewives to do the menial work at Walmart or McDonald's or wherever, freeing up the biological mothers to spend time with their kids. And then your volunteers could donate their earnings directly to the bio moms . . ."

Steinhoff didn't appear to realize that he was being mocked. "I imagine that might work too, Dr. Balint. But the organizers prefer this approach. They believe the supplemental mothers will provide good role models." He removed a handkerchief from his pocket and blew his nose, then tucked the cloth back into his jacket. "It's a *great* program. Trust me on that. The only problem we have is convincing these inner-city families to participate."

"Too much competition from other charities?" asked Balint.

"We're not sure what the hurdle is. We've even tried offering free pediatric checkups to participating children . . . But it didn't work. Most of these kids are already eligible for free care via CHIP or Medicaid . . ."

"Maybe you could pay them cash," suggested Balint. He was beginning to relish poking fun at the oblivious rabbi. "If you shelled out fifty dollars a session, I bet you'd increase your participation rate rather quickly . . . Or I have an even better idea: Why not just figure out the average salary at Walmart and offer a dollar more per hour? You'd have a packed house every afternoon . . ."

Balint kept a straight face. Steinhoff appeared flummoxed. "We need your help, Dr. Balint," he said. "What we're hoping to do is to establish a free medical clinic *for the parents.* As an incentive for them to bring their kids to our program . . ."

"And let me guess. You'd like me to set it up for you."

"It would be a great mitzvah, Dr. Balint."

"Not just a little mitzvah?"

The rabbi smiled. "I think you were joking," he said. "But that's my fault. I should simply have said a mitzvah. Not great or small. One should not measure good deeds against each other . . . So can we count on you?"

Needless to say, the decision had been reached long before Steinhoff ever stepped foot inside Balint's office. Amanda had practically ordered him to tender his services and to recruit his colleagues to work at the site one afternoon each month. On the other hand, he relished keeping his visitor on coals.

"Let me ask you something, rabbi. Do you really believe a program like this will make a difference?"

"I can send you the studies."

"No need. I'm sure the data says what you're telling me. But I'm more interested in the psychological aspects. The philosophical dimensions, if you will. Isn't it possible that some of these children are just bad apples?"

"What do you mean?"

"Have you read Dreiser's *An American Tragedy*? Or seen the film?"

The rabbi had not.

"Well, I'd take a look. I think Dreiser was onto something." Balint had pointedly avoided mentioning a book about serial or spree killers—although he might as easily have cited *The Stranger Beside Me* or even *The Strange Case of Dr. Jekyll and Mr. Hyde*. "I've always been curious myself about individuals with antisocial personality disorder. What you might call sociopaths. And it seems to me that they're naturally evil—*born* rotten to the core—and no after-school program with a herd of swanky housewives is going to fix that. You might steer these kids into more upscale versions of sociopathy, so they end up like Bernie Madoff or the folks who ran Enron, but you can't alter their inherent natures."

The rabbi rubbed his eyes. "If I truly believed that, Dr. Balint, I don't think I'd be able to put on my tefillin in the morning."

Balint wondered if he believed that himself. He knew he was capable of murder—but why? Because he'd suffered? Because of his father's death and the sudden financial hardship that followed? Or because of something deep inside him that made him different from other human beings? He honestly didn't know. What he did know was that if life had treated him more kindly—if *Amanda* had treated him more kindly— he'd have had no reason to kill. So maybe Steinhoff had a point: when society gave people what they wanted—what they needed—they had no cause to test its rules.

"Maybe I'm too much of a cynic," he said. "In any case, my wife is a great admirer of your program—and I'm a big fan of my wife. So my personal misgivings and instinctive pessimism aside, I'll be glad to help you."

"You'll serve as medical director?"

"If you'd like," agreed Balint. "I suppose I'll win extra points with Saint Peter."

"In a manner of speaking."

"That's right. We don't do Saint Peter. But whoever the Jewish version of Saint Peter is, I'm banking on his being impressed."

Steinhoff opened his mouth as though he intended to educate Balint regarding Talmudic approaches toward admission to heaven. Then he seemed to think the better of it and merely thanked him for his support.

———

BALINT'S FINAL patient of the afternoon proved to be a complicated case. She was an elderly blind woman who lived alone—and she'd apparently been concealing an increasingly severe state of cognitive decline. She was, as his rival might have said, a good candidate for dementia cookies. As a result, she'd been ingesting her heart failure medications haphazardly. On a different day, Balint might have gone "above and beyond" to coordinate a home-care nurse for Mrs. April, but that inevitably required numerous phone calls and several hours of paperwork. Instead he arranged for her to be admitted to the hospital's medical service. Let the social worker on the ward find her a nurse, he decided. But even the process of arranging for transport to the cardiac-care unit took far too much time. He waited with the confused woman, his own heart sinking as the minute hand on his watch advanced relentlessly toward six fifteen—and beyond. At twenty past the hour, the orderlies finally wheeled Mrs. April away on a gurney.

Balint's nerves were just starting to slacken when, in the elevator, he bumped into Warren Sugarman. His rival carried a dozen vermillion roses wrapped in paper. He was whistling

"Alexander's Ragtime Band," perfectly on key, but broke off when Balint entered. They had the car entirely to themselves.

"Hot date, Sugarman?" asked Balint.

The words were already out of his mouth when he registered that the "hot date" must have been with his own wife—that while he was supposedly lecturing on cholesterol, Amanda had arranged a tryst with his foe. Sugarman paused before answering, confirming Balint's suspicions.

"I'm meeting up with an old flame," said Sugarman. "A woman I knew long before I met Gloria."

"Someone from college or med school?" inquired Balint. Sugarman had obviously forgotten, for an instant, that they'd been at school together—twice. He toyed with his wedding ring inside the pocket of his slacks and decided to press his advantage. "Does this hot date of yours have a name?"

"Not one you'd recognize." Sugarman looked up at the elevator console, where the green light illuminated the numbers of the passing floors as they descended. "No need to mention this to your wife, Balint . . . She's bound to tell you-know-who, and the less Gloria finds out about my private life, the better."

"Your secret is safe with me," promised Balint. Yet he found himself seething at his rival's audacity, so he added, "Of course Amanda may find out on her own. It wouldn't surprise me if she already knew. That woman practically has eyes in the back of her skull when it comes to these sorts of affairs."

Balint prided himself on choosing the word *affairs*.

"I'm sure she does." The elevator doors opened and Sugarman stepped out. "Good night, Balint," he said—and strode briskly toward the exit.

Any rage Balint felt melted as soon as he spotted Delilah.

If the nursing student looked gorgeous in casual attire, then decked out for dinner—in a floral-print skirt and ruffled yellow blouse—she was dazzling enough to induce an arrhythmia. Possibly a fatal one. Balint had dated his share of attractive women in his day, but even he found himself awed that Delilah Navare had agreed to join him on a date. It was hard to believe she was single. She greeted him with an adorable wave, flickering her fingertips. He glanced around the lobby, kicking himself for not choosing a less public meeting place. Fortunately, other than the security guard, he didn't see any familiar faces.

"I'm sorry I'm late. We had an emergency upstairs."

She flashed a mock frown. "You've got to stop apologizing for yourself, Jeremy. I'm sure whatever you were doing was far more important than meeting me . . ."

"Far from it."

He steered her rapidly through the revolving doors and onto the pedestrian mall. At least he'd had the good sense to park on the street—to avoid the hospital lot, where he'd have been forced to chat with coworkers while waiting in line to pay. Outside, dusk had settled over the granite plaza and its marble statues of medical pioneers. A crisp chill hung in the air. Balint opened the passenger door of the Mercedes for his date, then whisked the two of them off to a seafood restaurant in Hager Park. It wasn't his favorite eatery—far from it— but it was an establishment that Amanda despised, because she found the waitstaff oppressively attentive. He'd originally intended to take Delilah to the romantic bistro overlooking the harbor—he'd even booked a reservation—but he suddenly feared that he'd run into Amanda and Sugarman.

"So tell me about your work," Delilah said, after they'd been installed at a snug table beyond the lobster tank. "Can I ask what your emergency was—or are you not allowed to tell me?"

"I'll tell you anything," said Balint. "Just please don't shout it from the rooftops. Or post it on the Internet."

"I won't even tell Papa."

Balint felt the girl's warmth radiating toward him and he longed to impress her. "The big news of the day is that we're setting up a free medical clinic for the parents of inner-city youth," he said. "I met with one of our local rabbis today. The goal will be to give the parents an incentive to bring their kids to crime-reduction workshops."

He filled in the details on Project Cain, embellishing and fabricating as necessary. Delilah was left with the impression that the program had been entirely his brainchild, although he never claimed as much overtly. He also neglected to mention that he'd met Steinhoff through his wife—or that he even had a wife—which necessitated further half-truths to paper over inconsistencies. He didn't even reveal that he was Jewish, and gave the distinct impression that he wasn't, as he'd discovered that his potential mistress was a practicing Catholic, albeit a lax one, and he wanted to minimize their differences.

As he shared his life story, or at least the version that didn't include a wife and two daughters, and as he listened to Delilah's own innocent tales of girlhood visits to cousins in Caracas and of deciding between a career in nursing and social work, he was struck by how easily he might embrace a new life with this exquisite creature—how he could simply abandon Amanda, cast off all thought of harming Sugarman, and enjoy fifty years alongside the earth's most beautiful specimen of femininity. He was confident that, if he admitted to Delilah that he was married, but was in the process of getting divorced, she would forgive him. Alas, that wasn't what he wanted. If he didn't yet know his endgame with this attractive woman, he had no intention of disrupting his daughters' lives for his own personal pleasure. Balint also acknowledged another, more troublesome reality: he was genuinely looking forward to wrapping his hands around Warren Sugarman's neck.

Together they polished off a carafe of wine. The notion entered Balint's mind that he might be over the legal limit, but he felt in control enough to drive.

"Shall I take you home?" he asked.

"You don't have to."

So they kissed. Tentatively at first, then less so. And soon Balint found himself checking in to the Hager Heights Motor Inn.

THE FINAL logistical decision was the *when*.

Selecting a date for a first attack was as important in serial killings as it was in military onslaughts. Balint would be choosing his D-Day, his H-Hour. Now that he had supplies and a location to target, he had no excuse to hold off.

Amanda inadvertently decided the matter for him. He'd arrived home from his date with Delilah to find his wife watching television in bed. It was approaching midnight. "The girls are having a sleepover at Ellen Arcaya's. They begged," she announced. "I hope you don't mind."

"Why would I mind?"

He removed his tie and draped it over the back of a chair.

"On a less pleasant note," continued Amanda, "do you remember Herb Pickering?"

"Should I?"

"Dentist with bad teeth. His daughter is in Jessie's ballet class."

Balint didn't recall any dentists with bad teeth. He *did* know an ophthalmologist with a glass eye—but that seemed less than topical.

"Are we having dinner with him?" asked Balint.

"I hope not. Herb's dead. Ruptured his aorta yesterday morning."

"And why are you telling me this?"

"Because we have to make a condolence call. Tomorrow night. *Both* of us." Amanda looked at him directly for the first time. "Don't drop dead on me," she said.

"I'm not planning to."

But the thought took hold of him that he *could* drop dead—that thirty-four-year-old men did keel over from ruptured aortas and massive MIs and rare parasitic infections. During the three hours he endured in Alyssa Pickering's parlor the next evening, he kept thinking: that sobbing little girl could be my Phoebe. *This could be me.* The logical corollary to these morbid thoughts was that he required additional life insurance, particularly if he planned on turning to a career of violent crime. In a pinch, he promised himself, he could always choose suicide—which was far preferable to a life of confinement. Assured that his daughters were financially protected and well-cared for, he'd easily choose death over prison. Balint had learned to his amazement, after a patient's intentional overdose several years before, that some life insurance policies actually covered suicide, as long as six months had elapsed between signing up and kicking off.

He intended to buy more insurance—much more. At the same time, he didn't want to raise Amanda's suspicions that anything was amiss, nor did he wish to leave yet another obvious clue for potential investigators. Fortunately their impending trip to Disney World offered an excellent excuse for maximizing his coverage: in case their plane crashed—and by some trick of fate, he was killed, while his wife and the girls survived. It was a preposterous concern, but also a theoretically plausible one; Amanda was easily convinced of his sincerity, even if she thought him paranoid. So that answered the *when*. He'd purchase insurance, enjoy his family time in Florida, and then return to target his first victim before Thanksgiving.

CHAPTER FIVE

Every inch of the vacation bore the stamp of Amanda's meticulous preparations. While he'd been occupied researching the nature of evil and hiding ribbons, his wife had planned twelve days of nearly continuous activity for the entire family. And yet all of her arrangements almost fell through when Balint was suddenly scheduled for a deposition on the morning of their departure, a crucial piece of his lawsuit against the firm that had installed a defective filtering system in their swimming pool. The contractors, a father and son from Portugal, had also damaged the concrete pavers, leaving a gap where rabbits and woodchucks could climb under the gate. Every few months, Balint had to fish a dead mammal from the water. His attorney assured him the case would ultimately settle in his favor—but opposition counsel appeared determined to make his life hell in the interim. "You can postpone the deposition," the lawyer warned him, "but then they'll ask the judge for a continuance, and we won't get on the docket for another year." Ultimately they decided that Amanda would fly to Orlando with the girls as planned, and that he'd meet up with them the following morning.

The deposition itself was a humdrum affair; it took place in a rented conference room at a local real estate office and lasted less than an hour. Afterward Balint drove Delilah into New York City for dinner at a five-star French restaurant and a night of passion at an equally opulent hotel. She did most of the talking, which was fine by him, as he couldn't discuss either his testimony or his plan to purchase life insurance without revealing his marriage. He paid cash. No need to leave a paper trail on his credit card. As far as Delilah knew, he'd be traveling to Orlando for a meeting of the American College of Physicians. The next morning, Balint boarded a flight to Florida—armed with an additional $800,000 of term life insurance that he'd purchased from an unctuous agent at the airport.

He had visited Disney World twice previously—once at the age of nine, when his father had still been alive, and a second time, seventeen years later, while Amanda was pregnant with Jessie. The second trip had been principally business, a brief stint of rest and relaxation after attending a weeklong cardiology conference in nearby Kissimmee. During that stay, they'd spent very little time in the theme park, and exerted most of their energies on the king-sized bed inside their hotel room. In contrast, on this holiday, Amanda was determined that the girls sample every ride in the Magic Kingdom, and taste every exotic culinary delicacy at the Epcot Center, and have themselves photographed on the lap of every animated character along Main Street, USA, who proved capable of sitting down. They played miniature golf atop the deck of a replica pirate ship, watched a one-armed Seminole "warrior" wrestle an alligator, kayaked along the banks of Lake Toho-pekaliga. During these coordinated excursions, which often involved bathroom breaks and temper tantrums, Balint found himself agreeing with Sugarman: he and Amanda *did* parent phenomenally well together. They were an excellent team—although if this was teamwork, his wife did far more than her share of the work.

Balint also arrived at another realization. He woke up before dawn one morning, while Amanda was still sleeping, and watched her breathing for nearly an hour. She looked so helpless as she slept, so much more vulnerable than the no-nonsense voice of authority who, when awake, delivered commands about which toys to pack as though she were ordering a bayonet charge. While she was unconscious, a lunatic might sneak through the window and strangle her, he thought, and the notion—as remote and irrational as he knew it to be—left him feeling empty and unsettled. His second realization, in short, was that he loved his wife immensely.

One of Balint's favorite hobbies had always been people watching. He enjoyed relaxing inconspicuously in a public place and speculating to himself about what was transpiring in the opaque minds and hidden hearts of passersby: which of his fellow human beings was contemplating suicide, or suffering from auditory hallucinations, or plotting to embezzle funds from the till at his firm. Yet as he waited opposite the Hall of Presidents, nibbling fried dough with his daughters while Amanda arranged tickets for a paddleboat excursion, he found his suspicions much darker than usual. If a potential serial killer lurked inside him, what atrocities were these other innocent-appearing strangers capable of perpetrating? Might that grandfather in the fishing cap be a future child molester, grooming that little boy for a dungeon cell? Were those obese sisters stockpiling explosives in their attic? Of course not. Among all of these cheerful, corn-fed heartland families, he was likely the only one with murder on his mind. To Balint's own surprise, that realization didn't alarm him. Instead, the

distinction actually made him feel good about himself—proud
of his ability to think outside the box.

On their final night in Orlando, they attended the
monthly fireworks show above Liberty Square. The evening
proved chilly and Amanda insisted upon bundling the girls
in matching windbreakers. Phoebe hid behind her mother's
knees, afraid one of the ersatz Continental musketeers might
shoot her; Jessie darted around the pavilion wishing strangers
a "Happy Fourth of July." Amanda tucked her hand under
Balint's elbow, something she hadn't done in ages.

"It reminds me of Cape May," she said.

He instantly knew exactly what she was referring to: an
Independence Day display they'd attended the summer before
their wedding. That had seemed a perfect evening, just the
two of them together, possibly the high-water mark of their
romance.

"That was a long time ago," he answered.

They stood in silence for several minutes, the pyrotech-
nics bursting overhead, and then Amanda asked him the most
unexpected question—the sort of question that he'd never
imagined she might carry inside her: "Do you think I'm a
good wife?"

The wind rustled the holly topiaries. A baby wailed in the
crowd.

"How can you even ask that?" he asked.

"I don't know. I was just wondering."

He rubbed her neck affectionately. "Of course you're a
good wife." He meant this too, in spite of her affair with Sugarman. "And a fantastic mother."

———

On the flight home, Balint had already shifted gears from
devoted father to aspiring killer. He'd taken pains to establish

an alibi for the following Saturday, informing Amanda he planned to attend a daylong continuing medical education symposium at the hospital. It was one of those events where you could sign in at eight A.M. and then vanish for the remainder of the day—which is precisely what Balint intended to do. Since the course was also open to nurses and physician's assistants, he imagined Sewell Auditorium would be filled to capacity, and that nobody would notice his absence. He could easily drive to Cobb's Crossing, complete his mission, then return to the hospital in time to pick up his certificate of completion. Or, should he get delayed, they'd mail it to him. If Amanda knew about his plans in advance, he guessed that she'd schedule a tryst with Sugarman for the same afternoon, eliminating any chance that she might phone him during his absence.

Only one barrier stood between Balint and his objective: a nagging fear that he might panic at the last moment. What if he chose a target, secured his fingers around the victim's neck—and then lacked the fortitude to seal the deal? Didn't one-third of soldiers fail to discharge their weapons in combat? The first deed would truly be the most risky, because there was no way of gauging for certain, in advance, whether some inner moral demon wouldn't still his hand at the final second. And yet, deep down, Balint didn't think of himself as the sort of man to freeze under pressure. As a teenager, he'd once rescued a beachgoer from a rip current—diving fully clothed into the surf at Cormorant Beach while on spring break to pluck the woman from the tide—so he had a promising track record. Of course, that effort had involved *saving* a life, not *ending* one, but the difference was really just a matter of perspective. In addition, he claimed six deer and a full-sized bull moose to his credit, as well as countless quail and grouse, all amassed during hunting trips to Wyoming with his college roommate, and not once had he shied away from pulling the trigger. One could never be certain about anything until it happened, but Balint felt the odds favored his nerves.

On Thursday, he rescheduled his afternoon patients for the following week, then drove out to the cabin at Lake Shearwater. He hadn't been to the site that late in the season ever before, and to his dismay, he discovered that several distant fishing lodges were now visible through the barren oak forest. Dead leaves covered the stone path. The cabin itself displayed no signs of recent human exploration. Balint was hit with the insight that when it snowed—which was an inevitability in the Onaswego Hills—anyone visiting the structure would leave tracks on their approach. That left him two options: Either work around the elements, maybe take home enough ribbon to last for several crimes; or buy a pair of larger shoes, possibly with a distinctive soleprint, and discard them afterward. He'd figure all that out later, he decided. He likely had another few weeks, at least, before any chance of a lasting snowfall.

Balint retrieved the spool of green ribbon from the steamer trunk and clipped off a piece roughly twenty-four inches long. Then he slipped the trim into a small ziplock bag and secured it inside his wallet. During the entire process, he wore latex gloves over his own leather pair—precisely as he intended to do when committing the murders. Before he departed, he filled the used outer gloves with pebbles and tossed them into the lake. Balint felt a tad like a surgeon himself as he completed these tasks, but also as though he had embarked upon an adventure. In an alternate universe, he told himself, he'd have written detective novels.

When he arrived home—the ribbon safely stashed inside his slacks pocket—he discovered the front door stood partially ajar. It was past six o'clock. In the living room, Amanda sat comforting an unfamiliar woman. The stranger looked to be about their age, or maybe a few years younger, with a mane of frosted hair and high cheekbones. She was sniffling into a tissue. Balint's arrival seemed to startle her.

"The front door was open," he said—mostly to fill the silence.

"Sorry. It's been a crazy afternoon," answered Amanda. "This is Sally Goldhammer, our new neighbor."

Sally offered him a thin smile.

"Sally has had something of a fright. Her adorable daughter managed to run off, and she's been playing upstairs with Phoebe and Jessie since three o'clock, while Sally had the police out searching for her."

"Abby's only three," added Sally Goldhammer.

Amanda hugged her arm around Sally's shoulder while the neighbor sipped hot chocolate from a mug. "The girls were playing mommy and child. It was actually the sweetest thing you've ever seen. They have no idea how much stress they've put everybody through."

"Tim is going to kill me," said Sally. "He's always on my case about keeping a better eye on her, but I'm just scatterbrained. I really do *try*. You have to believe me . . . Maybe I'm not cut out for this, after all."

"It happens to the best of us," said Balint.

Sally Goldhammer's parenting skills were the last thing he wanted to worry about at the moment. He listened politely while Amanda proposed strategies for revealing the episode to the woman's husband, an international banker away in Europe on a business trip. "Or you could *not* tell him," suggested Amanda. "Sometimes ignorance is bliss."

"I couldn't do that."

"It might be for the best," continued Amanda. "It's your decision, obviously. But if I had told Jeremy about every time our girls did something dangerous, he'd have had a nervous breakdown ages ago. He doesn't have any clue how many near misses we've experienced over the years."

"Let's keep them near misses," interjected Balint.

Their neighbor sniffled again. "I wouldn't be able to live with myself. Tim and I don't have any secrets between us."

As far as you know, thought Balint.

He excused himself and poked his head into Phoebe's bedroom, where both his princesses greeted him with hugs. Abby Goldhammer wrapped her arms around his right leg, as though it were a tree trunk, and refused to let go—a gesture he feared might not be appropriate age-level play. She was an undersized, sickly looking tyke with a small face and enormous eyes, of the sort that, in adolescence, might either prove beautiful or syndromic. Either way, the girl's genetic health would have no bearing on his own existence. To Balint, Phoebe and Jessie mattered above all else: his ultimate legacy, the guardians of his image after his death. Other people's kids were just so much window dressing and clutter. He retreated to the kitchen for a glass of Merlot.

Later, after coaxing Sally Goldhammer and her daughter out the door and narrating a bedtime story about mermaids, he followed Amanda down to the laundry room, and asked, "Have you really had near misses that you haven't told me about?"

Amanda laughed. "You're worse than she is."

"Well, have you?"

His wife continued transferring brights from the washing machine into the dryer. "Do you really think I ever let the girls wander off without noticing? No, I have *not* had any near misses, thank you very much. Oh, except we used to have a third daughter—I forgot to mention her to you—but she was carried off by an escaped baboon." Amanda added fabric softener to the dryer. Her tone turned serious. "I feel genuinely bad for that woman. She *isn't* cut out for this."

"A lot of people aren't, I suppose."

Amanda shut the lid of the dryer. "At least we are. Both of us. Whatever else happens, we'll always have that."

———

D-DAY ARRIVED.

Balint awoke at six A.M., showered, shaved, changed into his tie and sport jacket, and left the house shortly after seven thirty. His daughters were still asleep; he kissed each on the nose and the forehead. Amanda had come downstairs briefly to join him for a cup of coffee, or more accurately, to watch him drink a cup of coffee, but she claimed that she intended to return to bed until ten. He had little doubt that by noon the girls would be under the supervision of Ellen Arcaya or Betsy Sucram—or even, God help them, Sally Goldhammer— and that Amanda would be on her back in Warren Sugarman's bachelor pad. *Get all your goddamn philandering in while you can, Sugarman*, he thought, *because your days are numbered.*

It was the weekend before Thanksgiving and the turnpike teemed with early Christmas shoppers headed into Manhattan. A few cumulus clouds drifted harmlessly across the western sky, but the day loomed otherwise clear and mild. A perfect day for a killing, reflected Balint—its arrival, on that particular morning, a testament to a truly wrathful and beneficent God. He crossed the George Washington Bridge before nine o'clock and took the Cobb's Crossing exit off the interstate at precisely 9:47. A few moments later, he pulled into the parking lot of a small shopping center—a pharmacy, a pet store, a restaurant called Maia's Dinette—and removed his necktie and jacket. Next, he slipped the ribbon from his wallet, holding the ziplock bag loose inside his pocket. Finally, he tore open a packet of latex gloves, appropriated from a hospital he'd lectured at in California, so the package couldn't be traced back to Laurendale-Methodist, and he slid the gloves over the leather pair he already wore. The blood quivered in his arteries; malarial throbs of heat cascaded through his temples. All that remained was to select a target—and to act.

Balint cruised toward the college, past a bustling plant nursery and a sign for the municipal dump, then veered onto a tranquil street of two-story, wood-frame Victorians. The sidewalks were nearly empty; on one of the front porches, two athletic young men smoked cigars. Along the next block, there wasn't a human being in sight. Balint didn't know exactly what he was looking for. He followed the curve of the road, driving slowly, the Mercedes weaving farther from the avenue. He had forgotten how quiet suburbia could be during daylight hours—even on weekends: jack-o'-lanterns rotted on veranda railings; a wheelbarrow waited for attention in a flowerbed. His concern had been encountering too many people, an excess of pedestrian traffic; how ironic it would be if his plan failed for lack of a victim.

At the end of a long driveway, he caught sight of a lanky coed fumbling with her keys outside a basement apartment. She'd propped her bicycle against a nearby drainpipe, and as Balint watched, she carried a potted cactus from the bicycle basket into the flat. The girl had left the door open behind her. He noted a stand of gardening implements—hoes and shovels—leaning against the nearby siding.

Balint pulled the Mercedes to the curbside. He scanned the street: all remained still. As he'd suspected, the girl returned a moment later to chain up the bike. She wore sweatpants and a form-fitting top that exposed her bare midriff. Balint had taken advantage of her momentary absence to conceal himself behind a dumpster at the tail end of the driveway.

His initial plan had been to follow her into the basement apartment—if necessary, to clobber her from behind with one of the gardening implements that rested only feet from the door. Yet as he was about to attack the girl from the rear, he noticed, out of the corner of his eye, that the back door to the house itself also stood open. On closer inspection, he noted other promising signs: A teacup sat on the patio table. So did a pair of spectacles, resting atop a folded newspaper. In an instantaneous decision, for reasons that Balint never fully understood himself, he spared the coed. Instead he waited for the lucky girl to enter her apartment again, and then he climbed the back stairs into the house above.

The vestibule opened onto a tidy kitchen of thirty-year-old appliances. Photographs of young children, obviously related, had been affixed to the refrigerator with magnets. One of the magnets read: "Have you taken your blood pressure pill today?" Another photograph depicted an attractive couple in wedding regalia. Balint warned himself not to be sentimental. He had a job to do. Nothing more. The sound of running water emerged from behind a nearby door, followed by the distinctive whoosh of a toilet flushing. He positioned himself against the adjacent wall—the side nearest to the hinges. That would enable him to see the occupant before the victim had an opportunity to adjust to his presence.

When the door opened, a gray head of hair appeared at the level of Balint's chest—and, in less than a second, he had his fingers locked around the owner's throat. He squeezed with all of his power. The elderly woman emitted a sharp, gurgling noise, before losing consciousness. He released his grip, startled. The woman toppled forward, hitting her face against the linoleum.

Balint stooped to his knees and squeezed the woman's neck for another two minutes—timing the act on his wristwatch.

Then he checked his victim's carotid pulse: to his chagrin, he found that her heart continued to beat. It took another five minutes before the old lady finally arrested. By then, Balint's hands ached from the pressure. But the deed was done. That was what mattered most.

He quickly explored the rest of the ground floor. One spacious room, some sort of conservatory furnished with a piano and a harp, also contained a damask sofa that seemed suitable for displaying a corpse, so he dragged the woman's body across the kitchen and through the foyer, up onto the cushions in the music room. Here too, photographs of small children cluttered both end tables. When Balint flipped over the woman's body to elevate her head on the armrest, two listless brown eyes stared up at him. They struck Balint as more dopey than accusing. Her forehead bore several sizeable abrasions—probably the result of being towed across the carpet; the fall to the linoleum had partially crushed her nose. Other than that, there was nothing remarkable about the pasty, slack-jawed cadaver that had, only moments before, been living flesh and blood. With painstaking care, he unwrapped the green ribbon and wound it around her neck. Done. His nerves had held.

But when he turned to depart, another pair of eyes greeted him. An equally ancient man stood in the doorway, aghast—shocked into paralysis. Only visual contact with Balint released him from his trance. He turned to escape. Miraculously, he did not scream—did not open his mouth at all. The old man had hardly retreated five yards when Balint pounced upon him and literally drove his skull into the hardwood floor of the foyer. A grisly crack reverberated through the house. Balint held his hands away from his own body as he choked the last wind from the man's throat. Then he dragged the second corpse into the conservatory, laying it out on the floor beside the sofa.

Balint surveyed the chamber one final time, admiring his handiwork. He only hoped the second killing hadn't squandered the first, because he didn't have an additional green ribbon to plant as a calling card—and there was always the possibility the police might conclude the woman had simply worn a green ribbon as a choker. In hindsight, he cursed himself for failing to bring along an extra length of ribbon.

The broken skull had left a trail of blood; on his escape, Balint was careful to avoid stepping in it. He pulled the door closed behind him, but did not remove the teacup or newspaper from the patio. He wanted these bodies to be discovered soon—wanted the police to start hunting for a killer. This old couple had nothing to do with him, after all. Or almost nothing. Two more victims, he reassured himself as he drove off, and then the Green Ribbon Strangler could murder Warren Sugarman.

ACT II

CHAPTER SIX

He was the same person.

Balint's fear that the murder would transform him—that he might leave Cobb's Crossing fundamentally altered—did not come to pass. Even before he'd ever contemplated homicide, he had always found the sudden guilt of killers somewhat inexplicable. In college, where he'd suffered through a required English seminar for premeds, Lady Macbeth's remorse had utterly befuddled him. Now that he had proven his own mettle and joined the criminal ranks, the notion of second guessing his deed seemed more alien than ever. On the drive home from Westchester, he had braced himself to feel anxious and unsettled. In reality he experienced a sense of calm that he hadn't enjoyed in months. His future course of action had been determined irrevocably; there was no turning back. When he paused at a rest stop on the interstate and flushed the latex gloves down the toilet, Balint felt only satisfaction. To his delight, despite heavy traffic from the college football games letting out at the arena, he was still able to return to the hospital in time to retrieve his certificate of completion.

Over the next several days, Balint's initial calm gave way to restless energy. Although he'd pledged to himself to wait at least two weeks before attempting a second strike, he now fought against an urge to kill again quickly. It wasn't that he took any pleasure in the slayings—far from it. If anything, the brutality of the offense had repulsed him. But now that he'd started down the path toward exterminating his rival, he longed to finish the job, to put the enterprise behind him. Another motivating factor was Delilah's father: once Sugarman had been eliminated, Balint hoped to persuade the surgeon's replacement—either Chester Pastarnack or a newcomer—to list Norman Navare for an organ. Of course, premature action came with its own drawbacks: if he'd committed any errors during the first killings, he hoped the press would report on his sloppiness, so he could adjust his methods before further attacks. That was the sensible plan. Ultimately he compromised with his own desires and opted to play it by ear.

At first, the media didn't report the double homicide at all. Balint fidgeted in his study while listening to the radio all day Sunday, tuned to a New York City-based news station, awaiting a breaking crime alert. Nothing. He didn't dare search the Internet for information—not even at the public library—for fear the authorities might ultimately track his digital fingerprints. Finally, during his commute to work that Monday morning, the story broke. Balint learned that his victims were Albert and Wilma Rockingham, both in their early eighties. The pair were retired musicology professors from Saint Anselm College. Their bodies had been discovered by their granddaughter, Ruth, who lived in the basement apartment below their home. Balint realized he was the only living human being who could appreciate this irony: the girl he'd spared hadn't been so lucky after all.

What Balint heard next enraged him so greatly that he nearly drove the Mercedes into a tree. Local law enforcement suspected murder-suicide—especially as Albert Rockingham had been suffering from dementia. The radio reporter interviewed a longtime neighbor who described the couple as "inseparable" and "devoted," and a police captain who promised to "explore all angles." Nobody mentioned any green ribbon. Balint was dumbfounded: Hadn't the investigators seen the marks on his victims' necks? Or the abrasions on Wilma's forehead? Her nose was practically crushed, for heaven's sake! How could a frail octogenarian strangle herself with her own bare hands? He resisted a burning impulse to telephone the Keystone Cops in Cobb's Crossing and to inform the chief that his officers were a pack of bungling idiots.

Over the Thanksgiving holiday, the matter disappeared from the news entirely. Balint felt himself growing sullen and despondent. He had promised to take the girls to view the Macy's parade along Fifth Avenue, but at the last minute, he feigned severe back pain and sent Amanda and his daughters to New York on their own. Who cared anymore if his actions appeared suspicious? His problem now was that there was no longer any unsolved crime to be suspected of. Yet puttering around the lifeless house that morning, another idea struck Balint: What if the authorities *weren't* knuckleheads? Could they already suspect a potential serial killer—maybe tipped off by the ribbon—and all that nonsense about "murder-suicide" was merely a ruse? An effort to bait the culprit or lull him into false confidence? The more he considered this scenario, the more plausible it seemed. Over the holiday dinner at his parents' place that evening, listening to Phoebe describe each of the parade floats in painstaking detail, Balint's mood buoyed on the belief that his plan might yet have succeeded. That the police could already be hunting clandestinely for the Green Ribbon Strangler. His head swam with excitement. Four glasses of red wine did nothing to dampen his relief.

Balint took a risk the next morning, visiting the Pontefract Library to skim the Westchester newspapers. While this wasn't an unpardonable error—like searching for "double homicide" or "Rockingham" on his home computer—the possibility always existed that he might be seen. But he felt that he needed to know the state of the investigation. To his dismay, he learned nothing. Apparently, at least for the moment, the press no longer deemed the couple's deaths newsworthy.

And then, on Sunday afternoon, a seemingly minor incident disconcerted him. He was installing a reflective address number on his mailbox—to conform with a new local ordinance that already had led to several warning letters from the town—when his wife's strange friend, Bonnie Kluger, called out to him. She wore a pith helmet; a pair of binoculars hung around her wiry neck.

"I saw you yesterday," she announced—without any introduction.

"Could be," said Balint. "I've been around."

"Not here," said Bonnie. "At the library. In Pontefract."

The smart response—the common sense response—would have been merely to acknowledge the possibility; visiting a suburban library was far from a capital crime. But, on impulse, Balint said, "Not yesterday. I haven't been to Pontefract in ages."

"It was you." Kluger wagged her index finger at him. "And it was yesterday."

Balint regretted his denial immediately. He shrugged. What did it matter, he reminded himself, if Bonnie Kluger thought him dishonest.

"It was you. I know what I know," Bonnie repeated again—and then she trundled away as quickly as she'd appeared. Balint watched her retreat across the street, shouting instructions to her countless outdoor cats before she disappeared into her house.

Although he knew he didn't have anything to fear from Bonnie Kluger—she was nutty, but harmless—the lesson to be drawn was clear: even reading about the slayings in the library was potentially dangerous, as it might lead to other incriminating behaviors like this pointless lie to his peculiar neighbor.

So he waited for developments. At first, each day that passed without additional news left him increasingly frustrated. By the end of the week, he was on the brink of giving up hope—of writing off the Rockingham killings and starting his murder spree from scratch. And then, a few days later, as he unwound in the physicians' lounge after a long morning in the clinic, he caught sight of an article in the Metropolitan Section of the *Times*: "Cobb's Crossing Slayings Reclassified." A coroner's verdict had ruled out murder-suicide and the local authorities now sought a perpetrator. Again, no mention of any green ribbon. The closest the media came to reporting on the ribbon was a cryptic statement that authorities were withholding "a peculiar detail" related to the crime. Good enough. After nearly two weeks of torment, Balint sensed that at last he had the upper hand.

———

THEY HAD just settled down to dinner that evening when the doorbell rang. Balint looked to his wife for an explanation—but she appeared equally puzzled. "I hope it's not Sally again," she said. "Did I tell you she lost that kid a second time? On Thanksgiving Day! The police found the girl sleeping inside the Rothschilds' doghouse."

"You didn't tell me."

"Well, I'm telling you now."

The bell rang twice more.

"I believe someone is at the door," said Jessie—mimicking the English maid on one of her television programs. "I shall answer it."

Jessie raced from the table into the foyer. Balint shrugged at Amanda and then chased after his daughter.

On the porch stood Gloria Picardo, who had once been Gloria Sugarman, and now looked as though she were one straw away from self-destruction. The surgeon's ex-wife didn't carry an umbrella; she made no effort to shield herself from a steady barrage of sleet. Flakes of frost coated her shoulders and peppered her stringy, unkempt hair. Bags of flesh swelled under her bloodshot eyes. "Jeremy! Thank God you're home," she cried, practically falling into the vestibule. "Please tell me Amanda's here."

"She's in the kitchen. Did something happen?"

Balint feared for an instant that Sugarman's ex-wife had killed him herself—which would have achieved his own goals, yet somehow leave him cheated. Gloria didn't answer. She staggered past him into the kitchen and slumped into a chair. *Balint's chair.* Seconds later, the woman was sobbing, her face cupped in her palms.

"Is she hurt?" Jessie asked him.

"I don't think so," answered Balint. "Your mother is a magnet for weeping women. The moment they sense a tear coming on, they're drawn to our doorstep."

Jessie frowned at him, puzzled. "I don't understand."

"That makes two of us." He picked up his daughter's plate. "Why don't you and your sister take your suppers into the living room and watch TV? We'll make it a special night."

"Will you come with us?"

"In a few minutes, princess," he agreed.

He'd dispatched the girls in the nick of time. They'd hardly been out of the room thirty seconds when Gloria started lacing the air with profanity.

"Let it all out," coached Amanda. "You're among friends."

That was rich. One of these "friends" was sleeping with the woman's ex-husband and the other was planning to kill him. Balint drew his plate away from their visitor and devoured his halibut while Gloria filled the kitchen with invective.

"Goddamn, goddamn bastard! Cocksucking bastard!"

"Please," warned Balint. "The children will hear you."

Gloria cut short her cursing and tried to compose herself.

"What happened?" asked Amanda. "Tell us from the beginning."

Their guest dried her face with a napkin.

"He was cheating on me. For years," said Gloria. "I broke into his e-mail account. The bastard's goddamn password was *heart*."

Balint's adrenal glands surged into overdrive. In the next room, Jessie and Phoebe argued over which channel to watch.

"Do you know *who* he was having an affair with?" asked Amanda. "Did he mention a name?"

"Why does it matter?" interjected Balint—with unprovoked cruelty. "Are you friends with Warren's mistress?"

Amanda flashed him a ferocious look.

"I was just curious. And who knows? It's a small, overlapping world."

Gloria glanced from him to Amanda and back. "That's the awful part. There were so many of them. Patti and Sandra and M.W. and someone named C and someone named A . . ."

Amanda's face turned white as gauze. "Well, that's a surprise, isn't it?"

"He's still meeting A on Saturdays and C on Sundays."

"What happened to B?" asked Balint.

Gloria either didn't hear his question or didn't absorb it. The woman removed her pocket mirror from her purse and examined her face. "Heavens, I look terrible," she said. "I'm sorry I barged in on you like this. I didn't know where else to turn . . ."

"You did the right thing," replied Amanda.

Gloria thanked her through another burst of tears. "But what should I do now? What should I *do*?"

"You don't need to do anything, dear," soothed Amanda. "You're done with him. He's A's and C's and Lord-knows-who-else's problem now."

Sugarman's ex-wife clutched her purse to her chest, shell-shocked.

"I think it's time for someone new," said Amanda. It amazed Balint how well his wife kept her emotions in check. "The best revenge is to lead a good life. Maybe Jeremy can fix you up with one of his colleagues . . ."

Like that was going to happen, thought Balint. Even if Gloria Picardo hadn't looked like she'd hired the Ghost of Christmas Past for an image consultant, the pickings were slim among eligible bachelors at the hospital. Some of his older colleagues might not care about her appearance, but her anger—*that* was unsellable. Yet Amanda had a knack for assigning him tasks on behalf of her countless acquaintances—*please recommend a podiatrist, kindly write a letter to an insurance company*—not realizing that these favors mounted up to a hell of a lot of extra work.

"I swear I'd kill him if I could get away with it," Gloria threatened. "I really would kill the bastard."

But you *couldn't* get away with it, mused Balint. They'd catch you in a day.

He cleared the fish bones off his plate and set the dish in the sink. Then he retreated into the living room and watched a double episode of *Dancing Barnacles* with his daughters.

Another two hours elapsed before Amanda managed to ease their visitor out the door. That meant a delayed bedtime for Jessie and Phoebe.

Amanda stepped into the living room as soon as Gloria had departed. "May I have a word with you, Dr. Balint?"

He followed his wife to the cusp of the dining room. The moment they were out of earshot of the girls, she demanded, "What on earth is wrong with you?"

"What's that supposed to mean?"

"*What happened to B? Are you friends with Warren's mistress?*" mimicked Amanda—echoing his earlier questions. "Anyone could see that woman was suffering. Did you really feel the need to make fun of her?"

"She didn't even notice."

"But *I* noticed."

"And I wasn't making fun of her," insisted Balint. "Not really."

"Like hell you weren't." His wife had her tiny hands balled into fists. "Gloria's *so* right. You *are* all a bunch of bastards."

———

He'd learned one clear lesson from those first slayings: his next murder would take place at night. The advantage of the daytime was that it afforded him more time, and more flexibility with his alibi; in the end, Balint decided this wasn't worth the additional risk of being witnessed. If he'd been leading only a double life—dividing his days between his roles as family man and marauding strangler—he'd have had little difficulty finding enough opportunity for both roles. But he was actually leading a triple life—as family man, serial killer, and philanderer—and balancing this triad of obligations proved far more of a challenge. He grudgingly gave Sugarman credit for being able to manage multiple lovers, as even one mistress proved a scheduling nightmare for him. Of course, the surgeon hadn't been married to Amanda—a woman who made a point of knowing *everything* about *everyone*. Balint assured himself that, had he been married to Gloria Sugarman/Picardo—perish the thought—he could have slept with the entire New York Jets cheerleading squad without her noticing.

The best evening alibi that Balint could devise was through his work at Steinhoff's inner-city clinic, which had gotten off the ground with surprising speed. The rabbi had arranged a fully equipped office suite for Monday and Wednesday evenings, renting from a solo practitioner who served the city's Brazilian community. All of the signage was in Portuguese, but the equipment proved first-rate. Balint had persuaded the medicine department chairman, Dr. Sanditz, to assign three senior house officers to the clinic, which he'd convinced his boss to be a good public relations move, while Balint himself had strong-armed the younger members of his division into supervising. He'd even agreed to supervise in his own right two nights each month. But he was flexible, not stupid: it was more than likely, he recognized, that one of Amanda's goals in having him administer the clinic was to keep him away from home in order to facilitate her trysts with Sugarman. His suspicions were confirmed when he returned after his first evening of supervision to find the girls away at yet another sleepover with the Arcaya sisters. If Amanda had agreed to a sleepover on a weekday night, she was obviously up to no good.

His initial plan had been to arrange coverage at the clinic for one evening and then to drive into suburbia in search of his next victim. The only risk was that Amanda might surprise him at the clinic—and find him absent. She'd been threatening to visit her pet project for weeks. His wife's actual aim, Balint understood, was to generate her own alibi, so he wouldn't suspect her of infidelity, but her efforts to conceal her double life promised to crash directly into his own. Rather than waiting for her to surprise him, he decided to preempt her: he phoned Etan Steinhoff and organized a tour.

Amanda was obviously displeased at the sudden change to her schedule, but when Balint told her that Steinhoff would be visiting the clinic the following Monday, she had little choice but to join them. Another official from the synagogue accompanied the group—a statuesque, sheep-faced woman who looked far more Scandinavian than Jewish—as did the squat, acerbic wife of Chairman Sanditz. After exploring the clinic on a Monday night, the cardiologist assured himself, his wife would have little reason to drop by again on a Wednesday.

The clinic was operational, but far from successful. It turned out that another free clinic already operated in the neighborhood—one affiliated with a local African American church. On some nights, Project Cain boasted as many physicians as patients. As a result, much of Balint's VIP tour consisted of showing off unoccupied office space. Without patients, the clinic looked remarkably like any other physician's suite.

"When do you open?" asked Mrs. Sanditz.

"We *are* open," answered Balint.

He steered his entourage across the waiting area into an examination room. One of the house officers relaxed at a computer, playing solitaire. "This is examination room number one," said Balint—as though flaunting the Crown Jewels of England. "This is our supply cabinet. This is our refrigerator. This is Dr. Desai, one of our senior residents."

Dr. Desai smiled awkwardly and shook several hands.

"I'm confused," said the sheep-faced woman. "Why aren't there more patients?"

"Maybe we've cured them all," said Balint. He continued the tour. "And this is the cabinet where we keep the spare gowns. And this is the unisex bathroom. Would any of you like to try out the unisex bathroom?"

Rabbi Steinhoff exchanged a few inaudible words with Amanda. Then he adopted his pulpit voice and said, "I think it's crucial to remember that we've only been open for a month. The community is just beginning to hear about us."

"One wonders," quipped Mrs. Sanditz, "precisely what they're hearing."

"And this is the janitor's closet," said Balint. "And, lo and behold, this is Mr. Paderewsky, the janitor. Would any of you like to say hello to Mr. Paderewsky?"

Amanda didn't utter a word to him all evening. He imagined she was thinking: I can't believe I gave up my night of passion *for this*. But it hadn't been his idea to offer healthcare that nobody actually wanted. His fear now was that Steinhoff might pull the plug on the whole enterprise before he'd had an opportunity to do any killing. Fortunately the rabbi wasn't the plug-pulling type. Balint could already envision the fool doubling down on his clinic—maybe establishing a chain of unwanted healthcare centers—because men like Steinhoff possessed far more hope than life's evidence ever merited.

———

IN AN ideal world, he'd have committed his next murder on Long Island. After studying his atlas, Balint concluded that Nassau County was the preferred location—but also, that the distance would be too far for him to travel on a weekday night. Instead he decided that he'd kill in northern New Jersey this time, then find a weekend night when he would have more time for the next murder. If his fifth victim were Sugarman, that would still leave a wide-enough spread to focus investigators on New York City.

He worked as rapidly as possible. His first task was to arrange coverage at the clinic, which proved more difficult than he'd anticipated. Wednesday evening, it turned out, was the surgery department's Christmas party, and many of the junior medicine attendings planned to crash the shindig for the free booze. After nearly a dozen calls, Balint finally found a visiting pulmonologist from Taiwan whom he was able to cajole with promises of exposure to "unique patient populations."

On Tuesday, he skipped grand rounds and drove out to the fishing cabin. Fortunately the snow on the stone path had melted—although the undergrowth alongside the trail lay buried under several inches. In preparation for the winter, he cut off six yards of ribbon and secured it inside his wallet. What choice did he have? Then he returned to Laurendale-Methodist during his receptionist's lunch break. By the time she was back at her desk, he'd already registered the next patient on his own. Nobody, he was confident, had noted his four-hour absence.

Wednesday dawned clear and cold. Balint spent an hour on the telephone that morning with Delilah, assisting her with the complex dosing problems on her nursing school homework. Ever since he'd informed her that he'd managed to place her father on the transplant list—which wasn't true, *yet*, but might well be soon—the girl had been frolicking at the top of cloud nine. When they met, at least one afternoon each week, she appeared prettier than ever. Fortunately she'd been assigned to an overnight shift for the next three months, at a hospital two counties away—a clinical requirement for graduation—so she rarely placed any additional demands upon his time. He enjoyed helping her with her homework. It made him feel as

though she was also deriving a benefit from their relationship—
as though he wasn't simply using her for his own ends. After
he'd taught her tricks for converting doses of short-acting benzodiazepines into long-acting benzodiazepines, he spent the
remainder of the day auscultating chests and palpating abdo-
mens. His last patient canceled. At four o'clock, he pulled the
Mercedes onto Veterans Boulevard.

This time, he hadn't chosen a particular town in advance.
Instead he cruised up the parkway for an hour and then
took the first exit that appeared vaguely suburban. The village he found himself in was Upper Chadwick, a middle-class
bedroom community of widely spaced, split-level homes. As
though looking ahead to Balint's spree, the town planners had
lined the hamlet's streets with evergreen shrubs—boxwoods,
and laurels, and privet. Most of the sidewalks, especially on
the back streets, were largely shielded from the nearby homes.
Balint didn't have a particular plan for selecting his prey, so
he circled down various lanes and culs-de-sac, hunting for a
promising victim. For a while, he trailed a pair of teenage
girls, hoping they might separate, but they ultimately ducked
up the same front path. He passed a young man leaning over
an open automobile hood, in a particularly quiet stretch of
road opposite a vacant park, but the motorist looked strong
enough to put up a fight. How much easier, reflected Balint,
if he'd been shooting instead of strangling. But guns generated
noise and were more difficult to conceal. And, to be candid,
he had no idea how to purchase a firearm illegally.

The clock on the dashboard had passed six o'clock. He
was feeling desperate, yet he knew not to let his emotions
influence him. If he couldn't find a suitable target, he'd have
to defer until another evening. Slipshod work led to the gas
chamber, at least metaphorically speaking, although there
were no gas chambers left in New Jersey. Yet he had crossed

state lines for the Rockingham murder, he knew, so he could indeed face the death penalty in federal court—all the more reason not to be apprehended.

He allotted himself half an hour more. A few minutes later, he passed a local middle school—and, on a whim, he looped into the parking lot. One glimpse was all he needed to confirm his target.

The kid looked to be thirteen or fourteen. Old enough. He was an overweight creature, not obese, but his limbs were stubby; if this weren't sufficient punishment, genetics had cursed him with a soft chin and a sloping forehead. He sat on a swing set, trailing his feet in the sand below. An enormous backpack rested on the concrete nearby. Not another human being was in sight. The panoramic lights from the middle school roof, affixed at the top of every drainpipe, afforded Balint a complete view of the parking lot, the playground, and the baseball fields beyond. He could not have asked for a more promising victim.

He pulled the Mercedes to the side of the lot. The adolescent looked up for a moment, then returned to his moping. Balint had known boys like this kid before—in high school, fewer in college. They faced miserable futures: What woman wanted to wake up each morning next to a specimen like that? What employer asked a youth like that to sign a contract? The more Balint thought about the boy, the worse he felt for him—and the more convinced he became that, in strangling him, he'd actually be doing the hideous child a favor. Sure, his parents would miss him. Maybe his siblings too. But in the long run, they'd be spared the indignity of watching their homely, hopeless offspring struggle through an adulthood of wretched gloom. He'd spare beautiful women—like Phoebe and Jessie would someday become—from the creature's pestering advances; he'd save public health dollars squandered on the loser's future psychotherapy bills. Killing the Rockinghams could be chalked up as a necessary evil; putting this youth out of his misery might actually qualify as a good deed, even if the authorities didn't see matters that way.

Balint slid on his gloves. He unwrapped the ribbon and stuffed it into his pocket. Even though he'd only done this once before, his actions already seemed like a well-worn routine.

He exited the vehicle and set out across the asphalt. It was a crisp evening. Overhead, in the darkening sky, a solitary planet gleamed. The distance between him and his target was roughly thirty yards. The boy still hadn't looked up.

At twenty yards, the teen noticed his approach. He eyed Balint curiously. At ten yards, he looked as though he might speak. Balint was literally five feet from the swing set when the kid said, "Hi." His was a tentative voice, but deeper and more resonant than Balint had expected.

"Hi," said Balint. "Mind if I join you?"

The teen appeared baffled. He obviously wasn't accustomed to having his isolation interrupted. But what choice did he have? "Okay," said the boy.

Balint stepped alongside him, as though he might mount the adjoining swing. Instead he reached out suddenly and wrapped his hands around the teen's neck. Maybe it was the shock—or maybe the kid felt resigned to what was coming—but he offered surprisingly little resistance. He pried at his assailant's fingers for a few seconds; then his entire body went limp and heavy like a waterlogged blanket.

Balint dragged the corpse to a nearby hedge. With the dexterity of a trained assassin, he removed the boy's winter coat to gain better access to his neck, and using a nearby rock, sliced free twenty-four inches of ribbon. He coiled the ribbon around the flabby neck and tied a bow. Then a better idea struck him—and he cut loose another two strands of trim.

He wrapped the additional green strands around the boy's throat. Three ribbons for victim number three. That would give them a distinctive pattern. Not even the most incompetent of investigators could avoid taking notice.

CHAPTER SEVEN

They *did* take notice.

By midnight that evening, listening to the radio in his study, Balint learned that the state had put out an amber alert for the missing teen; when he drove to work the following morning, a bird-watcher had already discovered the body. He soon found out that his victim hadn't been any ordinary adolescent. Not hardly. From among all the awkward teenagers in the state of New Jersey, he'd managed to stumble upon sixteen-year-old Kenny McCord, the oldest son of State Senate Majority Leader Veronica Sanchez-McCord. So if the killing of the Rockinghams had been fodder for the crime blotter, Balint's third murder blanketed the front pages of newspapers across the state. Local civic groups tripped over each other offering reward money for information leading to an arrest. Soon the bounty topped $100,000. "Justice will be served," warned the Upper Chadwick chief of police, an avuncular officer who perpetually looked as though he'd just been roused from an afternoon nap. "It is hard to imagine anyone wanting to harm an intelligent, well-liked young man like Kenny McCord. But whoever is behind this outrage, rest assured we will find them." Chief Putnam informed a press conference that the last murder in his jurisdiction had occurred in 1958. He did not mention any green ribbon.

So saturating was the media coverage of the killing that even Balint's patients brought it up during their appointments. One elderly woman confessed that she worried about her granddaughters away at college; another blamed the incident on "television and drugs and dancing."

While Balint waited at the fax machine, he heard his receptionist speculating about the case with the man who'd come to fill the watercooler. "Mark my words," said his receptionist. "It will all be about a girl."

"They're saying that kid was some kind of genius," said the watercooler man. "IQ over 200. What a waste."

"No girl is worth dying for."

Balint had heard similar speculation about other crimes, but now that he knew the truth, these musings sounded downright silly. The kid had indeed been murdered over a girl, in a way, although not remotely as his receptionist imagined.

Even Delilah brought up the murder the next afternoon. They'd met at the motor inn for a brief tryst before she drove out to Somerset County for her overnight shift.

"I've always wanted to have children," she said. "But then I hear about something like *that* . . . and I don't really know anymore."

Balint lay beside her, holding her bare, delicate frame to his. "It's a fluke. A one-in-a-million," he reassured her. "The vast majority of children grow up without anything like this ever happening to them . . ."

"But what about those who don't?"

He wanted to change the subject—but feared it might appear odd.

"I know it's not a popular thing to say, but my sense is that most of these tragedies are highly preventable. As a parent, you have to be careful. You can't protect your kids from everything, obviously, but you can make a major difference."

"I guess," said Delilah. She gazed at him thoughtfully. "Do you think you'll have children someday?"

"When I'm ready," replied Balint—but he hated himself for the deception. Denying the existence of his own daughters upset him viscerally, in a way that lying about his marriage or career never did. "And if I do," he added, "I'm going to make absolutely sure nothing like that ever happens to them."

He meant it too.

———

ANOTHER FOUR days passed before the authorities tied the McCord killing to the Rockingham murders—or at least until the media reported on the connection. During those four days, Balint devoted his every free minute either to following developments in the case on the radio or to reading the New York City papers. Now that the story had become national news, he no longer worried about concealing his interest. If he *hadn't* appeared curious—at least mildly so—that might have raised suspicions. Chief Putnam updated the media twice daily, at ten A.M. and six P.M., doing his utmost to debunk conjecture about ransom notes, copycat offenses, even claims of a link to the Lucchese crime family and international terrorism. It was at one of these ten o'clock press conferences that the "Drowsy Detective"—as the chief had been dubbed by the pundits—revealed a potential relationship between the crimes. He stood in front of a seal of the State of New Jersey, flanked by the United States attorney and the FBI's regional bureau chief. Balint watched the spectacle unfold on one of the monitors in the hospital cafeteria.

"We have been in close contact with investigators in West-chester County," declared the soft-spoken chief. "We now have reason to believe that the same perpetrator or perpetrators behind the killing of Kenny McCord were also responsible for the murder of an elderly couple in Cobb's Crossing, New York, on November 24."

Chief Putnam did not use the term serial killer. The television analysts did.

Expert consultants on the news networks generated precisely the profile of the killer that Balint had anticipated: an angry, disaffected white male between ages twenty and forty, probably a loner without stable employment. To be frank, in spite of his extensive reading on the subject, Balint still had no clue how these experts were able to produce such a specific profile from such limited data—but he wasn't complaining. All that mattered to him was that none of these profiles predicted the killer to be a married cardiologist with two daughters and a thriving medical career.

Who first disclosed word of the green ribbon to the media remained an unsettled question long after the murder investigation itself had concluded, and successive inquiries by multiple task forces were never able to establish the source of the leak. Yet within a week of the McCord killing, the detail became public knowledge. Soon the police themselves were making reference to the "Emerald Choker"—which, Balint conceded, had a more romantic flair than the "Green Ribbon Strangler." As a result of the leak, Balint learned of his first decisive victory over the authorities: they had traced the ribbon fibers to a wholesaler who supplied retailers in Minnesota and Wisconsin. He took considerable pride in his foresight. Had he purchased his materials locally, the police might already have been on his trail.

Only once did Balint experience any emotional reaction to the ongoing—and increasingly distorted—accounts of his crimes. Following a week of seclusion, State Senator Sanchez-McCord conducted an exclusive interview with Isabel Crosby of "Trenton Tomorrow." In addition to questions about her son, Crosby asked the young widow about her firefighter husband's recent death in the line of duty. Only halfway through the encounter, *both* women were crying. "This isn't only about Kenny," said Sanchez-McCord after she'd composed herself. "This is about all of our children. My son might easily have been *your* son or *your* daughter." Balint shut off the radio. He didn't experience sympathy for the grieving mother, but raging anger: How dare she connect her stunted loser of a son to his darling princesses?

———

AT MOMENTS, engrossed by the media storm surrounding the "Emerald Choker," Balint almost felt that he'd already accomplished his goal. But then a flesh-and-blood encounter with Warren Sugarman would jolt him back to reality. The first of these occurred on the same evening that the authorities traced the origins of the ribbon to the Midwest, while he was hurrying into the parking lot en route to his daughter's ballet recital. Sugarman called out to him from across the plaza.

"Hold up there, Balint!"

He considered pretending not to hear—but didn't dare. The surgeon shuffled up to him, red-faced and winded.

"Glad I caught you."

"I'm in a rush," answered Balint. "Jessie's performing."

"I'll walk you to your car."

Balint accepted the offer—what choice did he have?—and started toward the far corner of the lot at a rapid clip.

Sugarman kept pace with obvious effort. His rumpled beige raincoat gave him the look of a fleeing flasher.

"I hear you had dinner with Gloria," he said. "That she broke into my e-mail account and got some wild ideas into her head."

Balint stopped short. He suddenly feared that his rival might have followed him to the parking lot to gun him down in cold blood—that he wasn't the only one with lethal intentions on his mind. He kept Sugarman's hands in his line of sight. "Did Amanda tell you that?" he demanded.

"No. When would I see Amanda?"

"Then how . . . ?"

"Gloria told me herself," said Sugarman. "Or wrote to me, to be more accurate. In the nastiest e-mail message you've ever read."

Balint didn't respond. He waited for his rival to say more.

"I just didn't want you to have the wrong impression," Sugarman continued. "Gloria has a knack for putting a sordid spin on everything. She got it into her head that every woman I've ever corresponded with was some sort of mistress."

"That's none of my business," replied Balint.

"Probably not. Nevertheless, I wanted to set the record straight. Don't get me wrong. I'm not claiming to be a vestal virgin. Who is? But I'm also not the sex-craved Don Juan she makes me out to be . . ."

Balint resumed walking toward his car.

"I wouldn't want any rumors to spread, especially around the hospital," said Sugarman. "Even if I did cheat on Gloria here and there, what husband doesn't supplement his income, so to speak, when the opportunity arises?"

"I don't," snapped Balint. "This is entirely between you and Gloria."

Sugarman chuckled. "You're too much, Balint. Half the hospital knows about you and that brunette . . ."

"I have no idea what you're talking about."

He clicked open the lock on the Mercedes.

"If you'll excuse me," said Balint—in a cold, steady voice. "I believe our conversation has ended."

"Jesus, Balint. No need to get worked up."

Balint shut the car door and pulled away. His colleague gazed after him, looking genuinely bewildered by his reaction.

JESSIE WAS the star of her recital—at least in Balint's eyes. She pirouetted and pliéed with the verve of a professional. Her performance proved the ideal antidote to Sugarman's accusations. Afterward they brought the girls out to his daughters' favorite restaurant, Animal Palace, where the waiters dressed like exotic fauna, and he and Amanda shared the afterglow of the family victory. He wondered if Sugarman had told her about Delilah—maybe to deflect her anger over his own double-dealing—but his gut told him that his wife still knew nothing.

The following morning, Saturday, Balint didn't even bother to ask Amanda her plans for the day. Instead he took it for granted that she had no intention of joining him for lunch with his parents. When he told her that he'd be back before five o'clock, she asked him to send her best wishes to his mother and stepfather—without offering any pretext or excuse for not joining them. This was the new normal, it seemed. Surprisingly the arrangement felt far easier than his pretending to believe her excuses. The only downside was that his parents would be unhappy that they weren't going to see their granddaughters that weekend, but he couldn't bring them, as he intended to retrieve more ribbon from the fishing cabin on the way home. As far as Amanda was concerned, he'd be dropping by the hospital to check up on a patient, a delay which dovetailed perfectly with her own plans.

His parents were waiting for him in their cluttered living room. Over decades of travel, the Serspinskys had acquired useless trinkets from six continents, an army of figurines and glass baubles and miniature portraits that filled countless display cases. Every inch of tabletop housed some exotic geode or intricate piece of scrimshaw. In the midst of this "gallery of junk," as Balint thought of it, Henry Serspinsky relaxed, eyes closed, arms folded over his chest, listening to a recording of Tommy Dorsey's orchestra. Balint's mother stood in the kitchenette, attending to the final details of their lunch. Balint let himself in with his own key.

"You're alone?" asked his mother—obviously disappointed.

"It's not Amanda's fault," he explained. "I have to stop at the hospital on the way home. An urgent case."

"She could have taken a second car. What's the point of owning two cars, Jeremy, if you don't *use* them?"

"Next time, Mom. How's your hip feeling?"

"My *hip* is fine. But my mood is terrible. Doesn't a seventy-two-year-old woman have a right to see her grandchildren every once in a blue moon?"

Balint's stepdad blinked open his eyes. "Lay off the boy, Lilly. He's doing the best he can."

Henry Serspinsky rose to his feet and offered Balint a handshake. "It's been a rough week here, Jeremy. The man next door—name was Fontanelle—died in his tub. And another couple we've become friendly with relocated across the quad to a higher level of care. So it has been somewhat stressful."

Balint's mother set the lunch tray on the coffee table. Bagels and blintzes. The word "variety" had long ago been erased from her vocabulary. "A very stressful week," she emphasized.

"We're also worried about the Choker." Balint must have appeared puzzled, because his mother added, "Please don't tell me you haven't heard about the lunatic who has been killing children and old people!"

"I've heard," said Balint.

"It's truly dreadful." His mother served him a blintz. "But we're not taking this sitting down. We've formed a neighborhood watch."

"Don't you think that's a bit extreme? There have only been three murders—and all of them far away from here."

"That's easy enough for you to say. If you were in the madman's target age range, you might feel differently."

"He has a target range? I didn't even know it was a he."

Balint's mother shut off the record player and seated herself beside her husband on the divan. "Show him your invention, Henry."

The retired veterinarian reached beneath the coffee table and removed an eight-inch-wide band of leather with Velcro tabs. As Balint watched, his stepfather fastened the device around his own neck. "It's a security collar," he explained. "Leather mesh with wire and razor blades concealed inside. If the Choker tries to strangle you, he'll cut his fingers to shreds."

"Why can't he just remove it?"

"That will take time. You'll have a chance to fight back."

"But what if he hits you over the head from behind and knocks you out cold? Then he'll have plenty of time to remove your collar . . ."

"Anything is possible," conceded Henry. "But it's better than nothing. This is only the prototype. I'm going to ask the board of managers to provide emergency funding for 200 of them . . ."

Serspinsky's earlier inventions had included a foldaway birdbath and a machine for prechopping multiple strands of dental floss simultaneously. Balint recognized that there was no point in explaining the shortcomings of the "Iron Neck," so he praised his stepfather's ingenuity. "That being said," he added, "I don't think you have to worry about being strangled by a serial killer. You have a far greater chance of being struck by lightning—or kidnapped by pirates."

"And since when are you such an expert?" demanded his mother.

"He's a doctor, Lilly," answered Balint's stepdad as he removed the shield from around his throat, "so he thinks he knows everything."

———

BALINT LEFT his parents shortly after one o'clock and arrived at the fishing cabin before two. A thin veneer of snow already coated the path. Instead of purchasing a distinctive pair of boots, he had decided to wrap his own shoes in cloth, leaving behind a mysterious trail of broad, shapeless prints. Even if the police found these tracks, they could never trace them back to him.

He retrieved enough ribbon for at least two more killings. He dared not take more, as the coil already made his wallet bulge. But that was enough: by the time he next returned to the cabin, Sugarman would be dead. On the drive home, he found himself wondering if his rival were prepared for the end: Had he written a will? Did he own a burial plot? Would his dopey son receive any insurance payout? When Balint's own father had died—without warning, at age forty-one—he'd left his widow and child utterly unprepared for the calamity. Before she'd met Henry Serspinsky, Balint's mother had been bartending at a roadside pub to supplement her teacher's salary. Even then, they'd barely made ends meet. So Balint didn't feel particularly bad for Davey Sugarman, or for Gloria, whose alimony would likely cease. Life was unfair. If you had a lout for a father or an ex-husband, those were the breaks.

Balint saw the glow of the flashing lights before the police cars themselves came into view. There were six of them—lined up along the roadside opposite his house like enormous children's toys. On the lawn, a detective in a white shirt spoke with a pair of plainclothes investigators. Balint's pulse quickened. Had he screwed up? Could they possibly have connected the murders to him already? But there was also a fire truck parked in front of the Rothschilds' house. And then he spotted an ambulance in his own driveway, the doors shutting, a siren suddenly piercing the suburban afternoon. This wasn't a murder investigation, but something far worse.

He stopped the Mercedes abruptly—nearly blowing out the automatic transmission—and charged up to the trio of police officers. "I'm Dr. Jeremy Balint," he announced. "Where are my daughters?"

The detective held up a hand to keep the two plainclothes officers from intervening. "The homeowner," he warned them. Then he turned to Balint and said, "I'm afraid there's been an incident, doctor."

"What's happened? I want to see my daughters!"

The detective was in his early fifties, a lean officer with a thick mustache. "Let's step inside your house for a moment, Dr. Balint, if that's all right."

"Not until you tell me what's going on. Where are my children?" Balint was seconds from grabbing the officer by the throat and strangling him. Meanwhile, the ambulance backed out of the driveway and disappeared up the street. Its sirens faded rapidly, leaving behind a tense and chilling hush.

"I'm their father," shouted Balint. "I have a right to know."

"Your daughters are fine, Dr. Balint," said the detective.

He didn't believe the man. Fortunately, at that moment, Amanda stepped onto the porch with Phoebe clasped against her shoulder. "They're okay," said his wife. "I sent Jessie across the street with Bonnie Kluger."

"Thank God!" exclaimed Balint.

He hugged both his wife and younger daughter in his arms. Then he followed the mustached detective into the house. Half a dozen cops of various ranks milled about his living room. Several carried clipboards and measuring tapes. The officers formed a two-way parade across Balint's kitchen and into his backyard.

The detective steered him into the living room. In one corner of the room sat Matilda Rothschild, the sixtyish matron from down the block, attempting to comfort the seemingly catatonic Sally Goldhammer. His new neighbor mouthed inaudible pleas, rocking back and forth like a mad-woman. As soon as Balint saw her, he understood what must have happened.

"Dead?" he asked the detective.

The man nodded. "In the pool. She'd probably been under for half an hour when we found her."

Balint instantly understood that his position was tenuous. "I've been in litigation with the contractors," he explained to the cop. "They damaged the pavings, but refused to repair them—and I couldn't get anyone else to tackle the job while the matter remained unresolved."

The last part wasn't exactly true: other contractors would have done the work, but only if he'd compensated them upfront—while he'd decided to hold off on additional repairs until his lawsuit had settled. It was just his bad luck that the gap in the damaged pavers, frequented by rabbits and wood-chucks, also was large enough for a toddler.

"So you were aware of the danger?"

"Obviously, I didn't imagine anything like this could happen," Balint objected quickly. "We do have a perimeter fence around the entire yard. I don't understand how anyone managed to get around it."

"She came through the front door," said Amanda. "Jessie let her in while I was giving Phoebe her bath . . . and then she somehow opened the kitchen door on her own . . ."

"You've been home all afternoon?" asked Balint.

"Where did you think I'd be?"

"I don't know," he stammered. She'd caught him off guard. Was it possible that she'd terminated her affair with Sugarman? Or was this merely a strategic ploy, an effort to mislead him? "Out, I guess."

"We were having a quiet day—just the three of us . . ."

Amanda shifted Phoebe to her other shoulder. Two officers walked past them carrying the disembodied wire gate to the swimming pool. Later, when Balint inspected the yard, he'd find the entire opening patched shut with yellow police tape.

"This was an accident," Balint found himself insisting to the detective. "We have a perimeter fence. That's all the law requires." And we have homeowners insurance, he thought— although he didn't know the amount of coverage offhand; that was the sort of detail he left entirely to Amanda. "You don't really plan to pin this on us, do you? She has a responsibility to keep her daughter from wandering off, doesn't she? And you can't hold us to blame for the negligence of an eight-year-old child."

The detective offered a reedy smile and gave nothing away.

"I'm not holding anybody to blame for anything, Dr. Balint," he replied. "That's not my job. I'm just gathering facts."

THAT NIGHT Balint entered into his first serious conversation with his daughters about death. They'd had a more superficial discussion the previous year, when the gourami that Phoebe won at her school's carnival expired after only three days, but at the time Balint had been careful to limit their talk to the fate of invertebrates. When Amanda's father had died, the girls had been too young for any discussion at all. In contrast, the drowning of Abby Goldhammer required a family conclave. What struck Balint immediately was that both of his daughters looked petrified.

"The most important thing to remember is that what happened today wasn't anybody's fault," he reassured them. "Sometimes, God is just ready for somebody to join Him in heaven and there's nothing we can do about it." Balint didn't actually believe in God—he'd given up any faith in a higher being long before he'd first contemplated his killing spree—but he found the supernatural a useful fiction when explaining these matters to his daughters. And then an idea struck him—a premise he remembered vaguely from a European film. "Do you know what chess is?" he asked.

Amanda looked at him quizzically over the girls' heads.

"That's like checkers," said Phoebe. "But harder."

"Exactly. Well, life is like a game of chess that people play with God. And as long as you're winning, God lets you stay down here on earth. But when God wins, that's when He takes you up to heaven."

"And God beat Abby?" asked Jessie.

"That's a good way to think about it," answered Balint. "God beat Abby at chess. So now she lives up in heaven with Him."

A silence fell across the room as the girls digested this strange new information.

"Can you teach me how to play chess?" asked Phoebe.

"It's a very difficult game," said Balint. "Maybe when you're older."

"But what if God wins before I learn how to play?"

Amanda shook her head at him. "We're not going to let that happen, darling. I *promise* that daddy and I won't let that happen. Because as much as God loves you and wants to be with you, we love you even more."

———

NORMAN NAVARE returned to the hospital that weekend for another tune-up; his ejection fraction had fallen to 12 percent. This reminded Balint that, while in an ideal world he should have waited several months for the media clamor to die down before striking again, he could not afford to wait that long if he hoped to save Delilah's father's life. Another bizarre thought also crossed his mind: he didn't want to get caught before he bumped off Warren Sugarman. Should that happen, his entire effort would have been an utter waste. The reason this notion struck him as bizarre was that he had absolutely no intention of getting caught *at all*, so the goal of avoiding getting caught *before* murdering Sugarman had no rightful place in his thinking.

He recognized that his next killing had to take place on Long Island. That would create a triangle around New York City, so that when he strangled Sugarman, it wouldn't draw any particular focus to coastal New Jersey. The problem was that Nassau County was two hours away, which meant he needed to set aside four hours of travel time in addition to whatever was required for the killing itself. There was simply no way he could find that amount of time after dark. Even on a weekend afternoon, four hours was a long interval to desert his wife and daughters. It didn't help matters that he'd already used up all of his good excuses—fake conferences and training sessions and drug company meetings—orchestrating trysts with Delilah. And then good fortune struck: Amanda announced that, the weekend before Christmas, she'd be attending an overnight bridge tournament in Maryland. He suspected that this was an outright lie, that she'd actually be meeting up with Sugarman at a hotel, and that her presence at home the previous Saturday had indeed been part of a maneuver to deceive him. But the last laugh, of course, would be his.

Balint asked few questions about the imaginary tournament, merely wishing his wife good luck when she departed on Friday morning, and then he dropped the girls off with his parents for a full day of grandparent-granddaughter bonding. By midday, he'd crossed the Verrazano Bridge and was cruising the backstreets of Hempstead and Wantagh. He'd listened to the radio news on the two-hour drive and learned—to his amusement—that the FBI believed the case might be linked to a similar strangling in Duluth several years earlier.

Balint pulled into the parking lot of the South Coast Nature Center. Only one other vehicle sat in the lot—a dilapidated pickup. Patches of snow dappled the nearby woods, but much of the dirt trail was dry. The contours of the land, and the waist-high stone walls, limited visibility. This patch of urban parkland appeared to be the ideal location to wait for his next victim.

A fifty-something woman emerged at the head of one of the paths. She walked a Saint Bernard who wore a bright orange parka. After watching the pair for several seconds, Balint registered that the woman was blind. Although it crossed his mind that the service animal might put up a fight, he also entertained the notion of strangling both human and canine—of wrapping a ribbon around the neck of each. That would certainly confound the FBI investigators.

He stepped from the vehicle, leaving the door ajar so that his victim wouldn't hear the sound of it closing. Step by step, he cut the distance between them. Thirty yards. Twenty. The woman looked up: "Is someone there?" Balint said nothing. The dog barked, but its owner appeared to relax. "What's gotten into you today, Excelsior? We can't have you getting all excited over every last rabbit and chipmunk." He advanced another few feet. But at that precise moment, a young couple hiked over the ridge. The owners of the pickup! They'd spotted him—so even after their departure, he couldn't risk murdering this blind woman. Instead, he greeted her and asked for permission to pet her dog.

Balint's stop at the nature center had cost him more than an hour. And now that he'd been seen, he didn't dare commit his crime anywhere near the south shore of Long Island, so he drove all the way across the county to Brockton. The homes there were more upscale than in Upper Chadwick or Cobb's Crossing, but not so exclusive as to require private security. Unfortunately the gloomy weather had driven nearly everyone off the streets. His best bet, Balint realized, was to enter a home through an open back or side door, as he'd done in Westchester, but he struggled to find a suitable target. It was nearly four o'clock, and darkness was already falling, when he caught sight of a man smoking a cigarette on the concrete walkway alongside a Catholic Church. As the Mercedes approached, Balint recognized that the man was a priest.

The cardiologist rounded the corner and parked the Mercedes on a residential block. He pulled his sweatshirt hood over his head and strode quickly toward the church. As he approached the building, the clergyman stubbed out his cigarette and disappeared through a large red door. If that entrance were unlocked, Balint realized, he'd have a perfect opportunity to follow the priest into the building. His heart rate had nearly doubled by the time he reached the red door. He looked around—nobody. Then he gripped the door handle with his gloved hand and pulled. It refused to open. He tugged for several seconds—and then accepted the reality of the situation and let go. Only when he turned around again in disappointment did he notice the security camera tucked into the evergreen hedge.

That ended his day's efforts. He'd nearly blown it. When he reached Hager Heights to pick up his girls two hours later, he'd perspired through his shirt.

CHAPTER EIGHT

The encounter with the hidden security camera convinced Balint that he had to be far more cautious in selecting future targets; it also left him in a disagreeable mood. When Amanda returned home from her "bridge tournament," he peppered her with questions about the event: How had her partner played? How many "master points" did she earn? Had she run into anybody they knew from Laurendale? Initially, his wife had been in bright spirits, but eventually she soaked up his irritability and snapped, "I don't see why you care so much about *my* life all of a sudden." So he withdrew to his den and spent the evening on the phone with Delilah. Amanda could have listened at the door, he realized, but he doubted that she cared enough to bother. When at breakfast the next day, his wife announced that she'd be attending another overnight tournament—on the weekend between Christmas and New Year's—he was neither particularly surprised nor particularly upset. Let her have one final hurrah with Sugarman.

Another matter, however, caused him considerable consternation. Although his attorneys assured him that he was highly unlikely to face charges in the death of Abby Goldhammer, and Amanda had confirmed that any civil claim up to $2 million would be covered by their homeowners' policy, the local press had laid the blame for the episode squarely on his shoulders. An Op-Ed in the *Laurendale Leader* branded him "Dr. Negligent" and the editorial page of the *Hager Heights Beacon* demanded criminal prosecution. It would have been a fitting reflection upon the state of the nation's justice system, he reflected, if he went to prison for an accidental drowning while escaping punishment for a series of calculated killings. But that didn't mean he had to accept this disparagement without a fight. Balint ordered his lawyers to threaten both newspapers with defamation lawsuits, even though the attorneys assured him that he had no chance of winning.

The community's anger over Abby's death took an even more personal turn. While Balint didn't lose any of his current patients, approximately one-third of his new consultations canceled over the following several weeks. This figure was far higher than his usual drop-off rate: a man who was reckless in fixing the stones around his pool might be equally negligent when it came to matters of the human heart. Not that he actually needed the additional business. At a practical level, he was grateful for the extra free time. Yet the cancellations bruised his ego. During the first days after the *Beacon* editorial, he'd also received a handful of angry, anonymous phone calls at home, but these evaporated by the end of the week. Amanda's coterie of friends rapidly circled their wagons around her—only Bonnie Kluger sided with Sally, and Bonnie had always been an odd duck—so the negative social fallout from the incident was also limited. In fact, rumors circulated that the Goldhammers felt so isolated in Laurendale that they planned to move back to Brooklyn. Nonetheless, the entire episode left a bad taste in Balint's mouth.

He had warned his receptionist to keep an eye out for process servers, as it was almost inevitable that Timothy

Goldhammer would eventually subpoena him—and he didn't feel the need to make a civil suit any easier for the banker. So he was already on his guard, when on Christmas Eve, an unfamiliar man in a business suit approached him as he sipped a cup of coffee in the hospital atrium. Another prospective patient had "no-showed," leaving him forty-five free minutes before his noon conference.

The stranger appeared to be in his forties, but with gray-tinged sideburns and a deep groove between his eyes. He carried himself with his chest out—like a man who'd inhaled a balloon full of anger. "Are you Dr. Jeremy Balint?"

"Can I help you?" Balint asked noncommittally.

"I'm looking for Jeremy Balint."

"And what's your business with Dr. Balint?"

The stranger responded by socking him in the jaw. Balint toppled backward and his head slammed into the tile floor. He could actually hear what sounded like the snapping of bone, but he remained conscious. Above him, his attacker had lifted a chair and was about to bring it down upon his face—Balint raised his hands in an effort to deflect the blow—when someone tackled his assailant from behind. Through the haze of struggle, he heard a voice shouting, "That monster killed my daughter. That monster killed my baby girl." And then he blacked out.

—

BALINT AWOKE six hours later on the VIP unit—in a room adjacent to the one where he'd treated Norman Navare. His head throbbed, but a quick check of his limbs revealed full mobility down to his fingertips and toes. At the foot of the bed, a physician sporting a bow tie perused his vital signs on a clipboard. It took Balint a moment to recognize Myron Salt, the director of clinical neurology. "Sure took you long enough," said Salt, when he finally noticed that Balint was awake.

"How bad do I look?"

"No worse than before." Salt set down the clipboard. "Nothing broken either, as hard as that may be to believe. But we did give you some steroids to prevent swelling."

"Aren't they going to make me loopy?"

"Better loopy than dead. It'll teach you not to fight outside your weight class. The guy who slugged you was apparently a boxing champion in college."

His altercation with Tim Goldhammer slowly came back into focus. "What happened to him?" asked Balint.

"No idea. But Andy Price in hematology recognized him from their time together at Princeton. Says the guy was the state middleweight champion three years running. You owe Andy, by the way. If not for him, we'd be prying chair legs out of your eye sockets."

"You neurologists always phrase things so eloquently."

"Nothing more eloquent than the truth. Now try to get a good night's sleep and we'll see about discharging you in the morning."

"You can't seriously plan on keeping me overnight."

"Dead serious. Which is a hell of a lot better than dead."

That was when Balint registered that he'd been changed from his street clothes into a hospital gown—that his wallet was no longer in his possession. And his wallet contained more than seven yards of green ribbon! If they'd inventoried his belongings, he was a goner. "Where's my stuff?" he demanded. "Where's my wallet?"

"That's a question for a nurse," replied Salt.

He patted Balint on the arm and departed. Balint rang the call button.

After a wait of several minutes—during which he pressed the button again multiple times—a portly Filipino matron entered the room. She was not one of the nurses whom he knew well, but he did recognize her from his days as an electrophysiology fellow. "Sorry for the delay, doc," she said. "I was on break."

"Where are my things?" demanded Balint.

At first, the nurse appeared puzzled.

"My wallet," he prompted her. "My keys. My clothing."

The nurse smiled. "Oh, I believe your wife took those home with her. She said that if you woke up, to tell you she'd be back in the morning . . . Now do you think you're ready for some dinner?"

Balint shook his head. For all he knew, at that moment Amanda was rifling through his belongings—running her tiny fingers over the incriminating ribbon. He wondered if she'd phone the police, but he doubted that she would—at least not until she first confronted him directly. But even if she *never* went to the authorities, even if he could come up with a plausible justification for owning the ribbon that did not involve homicide, the discovery would still rule out strangling Sugarman. His only hope was that Amanda hadn't bothered to look inside his wallet at all. That she couldn't be bothered. If he were lucky, she'd taken advantage of his injuries to spend the night with her lover. What he longed to do was to call her at home—to ask her to bring his wallet to the hospital immediately—but he feared that such a request might prompt her to sort through his things. Far wiser to wait. So he passed the most stressful night of his adult life, anticipating the worst. When Salt dropped by again the next morning, with a team of residents in tow, Balint hadn't slept a wink.

"You cured yet?" asked the neurologist.

"I will be when I get out of here. You haven't seen my wife, have you?"

"Nope. But I have seen the inside of your skull. Take it easy for the next few days, okay? And try not to use your face as a punching bag." Salt turned to his house officers and added, "Dr. Balint is a fine cardiologist, but he's not the world's best boxer."

"It was a sucker punch," insisted Balint.

"That's what they all say."

The house officers took turns listening to Balint's chest and palpating his cranium. Another two hours elapsed before Amanda arrived. She wore her tennis sweats under her open coat and carried a racket under one arm—her outfit announcing to the world that she wasn't particularly concerned for her husband's health. Balint scoured her face for signs that she'd searched his wallet. "I didn't realize you'd be lucid already," she said. "The emergency doctors said they might keep you sedated for a day or two." He detected a twinge of disappointment in her voice.

"Did you bring my clothes?" he asked.

"They're in the car."

"Can you get them? I'm ready to go home."

"You sure the doctors are okay with that?"

Balint sat up—too rapidly. As the blood drained from his brain, he felt dizzy, yet his head throbbed much less than it had the previous night. "I don't give a damn what the doctors think. I *am* a doctor. Now bring me my pants and let's get the hell out of here."

Amanda rolled her eyes, but agreed to retrieve his clothing. She returned ten minutes later toting a brown paper bag. "Here you go," she said—reaching into the bag—and, for an instant, Balint was certain she was going to pull out a strand of green ribbon, like a magician performing a particularly cruel trick. Instead, she handed him his slacks and shirt. "Satisfied?"

Never in his entire life had the presence of any physical object brought Balint such relief—such joy—as the feel of his cotton trousers. He stepped into the bathroom and locked the door. His wallet remained in the back pocket, precisely as he'd left it. The ribbon appeared untouched. If Amanda had discovered his secret, she'd concealed the evidence of her discovery impeccably. He dressed quickly and then slid the door slightly ajar—just far enough so that he could spy on his wife. Amanda sat cross-legged on the bed, examining her nails, looking jaded with life. Nothing in her expression suggested a woman who'd just discovered that her husband was murdering strangers for a hobby. But nothing in her earlier demeanor had ever suggested she was sleeping with his colleague—so Balint couldn't be certain. He opened the door fully and cleared his throat.

"Did they arrest that lunatic?" he asked.

"They didn't tell you?"

"Tell me what?"

"About Tim Goldhammer . . ."

"*What* about Tim Goldhammer?" demanded Balint, growing impatient.

"The police felt bad about Abby, so they apparently wrote him a ticket for disorderly conduct and let him go home. But he *didn't* go home. He drove up to Asbury Park and jumped off an overpass."

"Dead?"

Amanda paused and gazed out the window. "Not dead. But in pretty lousy shape."

"Serves him right."

Amanda didn't respond.

"Well, it *does* serve him right," said Balint. "He could have broken my jaw."

"His daughter died. Imagine how we'd feel if something happened to Jessie or Phoebe—if someone *let* something happen to Jessie or Phoebe."

"I'd give that someone more than a punch in the face."

Balint buckled his belt and tossed the rumpled hospital gown onto the bed. He examined himself in the mirror, running his fingers along his swollen chin. Secretly he was relieved that Goldhammer had been severely injured—that the banker no longer posed a threat to his own daughters. "Bet there's going to be hell to pay for the cop who let him go home. Shows there's no upside to being a patsy."

"I feel terrible for Sally," said Amanda. "I genuinely do."

Of course, you do, thought Balint—but I don't. That's the difference between us. But all he said was, "I'm sure she'll be okay in the long run."

WHEN BALINT arrived at work the next day—around one o'clock, after taking the morning off to sleep late and recover—he was greeted by another unexpected visitor: Etan Steinhoff. The rabbi stood in Balint's waiting area, pacing and speaking on his cellular phone. From the snippets of dialogue that Balint overheard, he picked up that Steinhoff was trying to set up another Project Cain clinic, this one in Camden. "I was here visiting a congregant," the rabbi explained, "and I figured I'd take advantage of the opportunity to chat with you. I promise I'll only take a moment. I know how busy you must be"—he glanced at his watch—"and I have a meeting across town at three."

Balint scanned the suite; a handful of patients appeared to be waiting for one of his junior colleagues, but he didn't recognize any of his own. "No sign of my one thirty?" he asked his receptionist.

"She's running late. Traffic. Called to say she'd be here by one forty-five."

"There you go," replied Balint—none too pleased. "We have forty-five minutes."

"I won't take nearly that long."

Steinhoff followed him into his office. He thought he knew what was coming: in light of the ongoing negative publicity surrounding Abby Goldhammer's death, he expected the rabbi to relieve him of his duties as medical director of the free clinic. Little did Steinhoff realize how welcome this dismissal would be.

"So I wanted to touch base about Project Cain," said the rabbi. "As you may know, at the beginning of the coming year, we're hoping to open three more clinics—in Camden, Atlantic City, and South Philadelphia."

"And I imagine you'll want new medical leadership," offered Balint, trying to make his discharge easier on the rabbi.

"Maybe at some point, I suppose," said Steinhoff. "We've discussed bringing on board a full-time clinician to oversee our four regional medical directors. But that's a long way off—and, I might add, you'd be the leading candidate for the job. A shoo-in, quite frankly, if we could lure you away from the hospital."

Balint sensed that the conversation was not headed where he'd hoped. "I'll bear that in mind. If I'm ever up for luring . . ."

"What I wanted to speak to you about is something much more pressing," continued Steinhoff, glancing at his watch again. "My data people have been crunching numbers, and it seems we're not giving away enough free care."

"Maybe people aren't sick enough."

"I don't think that's it," said Steinhoff. "What I think—"

"Because we could make them sicker," interjected Balint. "And then we could make them better again. That would vastly improve your numbers, I'm sure."

"What I think," repeated Steinhoff, "is that we have a visibility problem. To put it bluntly, not enough people in the community know about our services. And if you don't know about them, you can't possibly access them."

"You have a point there," agreed Balint.

"I'm glad we see eye to eye. Because what I'd like to do, God willing, is to start advertising directly to the population we're trying to serve. I'm thinking a series of sixty-second radio spots. Maybe television too—during the local news—if we can raise the funds. What do you think?"

"I guess it can't hurt trying."

"Great. So when would be a good time to set up the taping? Ideally I'd like to have you record the first handful of segments sometime within the next week."

"You want *me* to tape the ads?"

"Who else? I already took the liberty of jotting down a few loose ideas for the text." He reached into his canvas bag and handed Balint a manila folder. "But nothing is carved in stone, so feel free to add ideas of your own . . ."

Balint opened the folder. Steinhoff's "loose ideas" were, in reality, polished scripts. The first of these began: "I'm Dr. Jeremy Balint and saving lives is my job. It's also my passion . . ."

The rabbi stood up. "I can't thank you enough for your involvement in this effort," he said. "Volunteers like you make Project Cain possible. But I don't want to take up any more of your time. Why don't I call you tomorrow and we can hammer out the scheduling details?"

He didn't give Balint an opportunity to disagree.

"And send my love to that charming wife of yours, Dr. Balint," said Steinhoff. "You'll forgive me for saying that you're a very lucky man."

Balint slid the folder onto his desk. "If I had any more luck," he griped, "I wouldn't have enough time in the day to thank God for my good fortune."

"I couldn't have said the words better myself," agreed the clueless rabbi, clasping Balint's hand and then retreating to the door. "If you ever give up medicine, you'd make a fine rabbi, Dr. Balint. And I don't say that to many people."

THE IMAGE of the security camera had been emblazoned indelibly upon Balint's consciousness. In hindsight he realized that trawling the streets for a suitable target had been the height of madness. He'd gotten lucky *three times*—first in Cobb's Crossing, then with Kenny McCord, and finally outside the church—but only a fool would rely on luck with the stakes so high. Now he determined to be far more prudent. Rather than choosing his victims on the spot, he decided to scout for them in advance—to identify promising individuals long before he actually approached them. His initial idea had been to use the hospital's brand new electronic medical record system to look up promising patients at Laurendale-Methodist's affiliates in Nassau County. He'd intended to check the records from somebody else's account—accessing a public computer after a nurse or social worker forgot to log out of the network— in order to identify vulnerable candidates who lived alone. Then he realized the flaw in his scheme: once he'd killed these people, their bodies would likely be transported to the same affiliate hospitals, where internal security might later screen for unauthorized access to their charts. The IT probe would be looking for inappropriate access by curiosity seekers, bored technicians, and medical students seeking the inside scoop on an Emerald Choker victim, not for suspects. Yet the computer folks might inadvertently notice his own hospital's electronic fingerprints and launch an inquiry. The odds of that happening were exceedingly low—but exceedingly low was not the same as zero.

Balint ultimately decided to cull his victims from the obituaries. He'd once caught the tail end of a radio call-in show where a female participant "of a certain age" explained that she found her boyfriends by combing the death notices for recent widowers. So why not use the same info to help select murder victims? The process entailed a small risk: he had to look up the various Nassau County newspapers online at the Pontefract Library, so it was theoretically possible that his trail might be traced. But in this case, the danger truly did approach zero. The only real risk was being seen by Bonnie Kluger once again—but what could she possibly do? Lots of people visited libraries every day, and few of them were cold-blooded killers.

He proceeded with caution. His optimal target, he decided, was a widow over sixty whose husband's obit didn't list any other survivors. It was also essential that she live in a free-standing dwelling, either a private home or a duplex, because apartment buildings contained meddlesome neighbors and superintendents and hidden security monitors. To his surprise, and frustration, very few notices met these criteria. Eventually, he recognized why: an actual human being had to place a death notice—and to pay for it. If you died with survivors, particularly adult children, this increased the pool of persons who might arrange for such an announcement. Solitary widows apparently preferred to save the money and the effort.

So days elapsed with no optimal candidate, while life in Laurendale continued all around him.

Amanda attended her "bridge tournament" in Philadelphia—and had the audacity to telephone him to announce that she'd be staying over an extra day because she'd qualified for the final round. On New Year's Day, he took the girls ice-skating at the rink in Musselburgh, affording his wife yet another afternoon alone with Sugarman. But he refused to let her philandering get under his skin. He kept his eyes focused on his prize. Finally, during the first week of January, he spotted a notice in the *Queensferry Sentinel* that passed muster.

The death announcement was for Stavros Constantinou, eighty-one, a retired sanitation worker and Korean War veteran who'd died of lung cancer. He left behind a wife of fifty-eight years, Sofia—and nobody else. Balint looked up their home address on the Internet, then used an online mapping program to find a visual of Mrs. Constantinou's house. He'd hit the jackpot: the elderly woman lived in a stand-alone bungalow situated near the end of a winding backstreet. On paper, Balint could not have asked for a more perfect target: it was as though Sofia Constantinou had been born for the sole purpose of helping him revenge himself upon Warren Sugarman.

———

WHILE BALINT was scouting for Nassau County widows, the police announced that they'd identified a "person of interest" in the previous slayings. For weeks, pressure had been mounting on the authorities to crack the case. At a personal level, Chief Putnam was extremely popular. His plainspoken candor and seemingly perpetual five-o'clock shadow instilled confidence that his officers were leaving no stone unturned. The pundits even predicted that after the chief made an arrest, he'd become a leading candidate for the open congressional seat in his district—although nobody even knew for certain to which political party he belonged. But as much as the public liked Chief Putnam, popular frustration had been growing with the lack of progress on the case. So as soon as it appeared that the authorities had identified a suspect, the killings once again became national headlines.

The police themselves revealed no additional information about their investigation. At first Balint feared *he* might be their "person of interest." But then word leaked to the media that this "person of interest" had been interrogated by police in New York City. Two days later, the *New York Post* identified him as a twenty-five-year-old handyman from Brooklyn who'd been detained at a routine DUI checkpoint. The cops had reportedly found a spool of green ribbon in his glove compartment. When they searched his apartment, they also uncovered newspaper clippings describing both the Rockingham and McCord killings, as well as a collection of fake military outfits, a counterfeit NYPD badge, and an arsenal of semiautomatic firearms. In addition, someone had recently used the suspect's computer to search for information on the victims and on strangulation methods. The handyman, whose name the *Post* did not release, was the sort of angry white loner who matched perfectly the predictions of the pundits. Two days after his interrogation, the district attorney filed felony weapons-possession charges against the suspect and officially detained him as a "material witness" in the Rockingham killings.

For Balint, the news could not have come at a worse time. If the police had apprehended this suspect *after* he'd killed Sugarman, that would have provided an excuse to halt his murder spree and permanently retire his strangling gloves with little worry. But being in custody afforded the suspect an unshakeable alibi for when Balint killed the surgeon. Of course Balint still hadn't thought through what he'd do if the state charged the wrong man after Sugarman was dead. Would he really let an innocent stranger serve life in prison—or face possible execution—in order to secure his own peace of mind? The answer, he realized, was probably yes. That might be crueler, in some ways, than merely killing strangers, but it was another necessary evil. The alternative would be to contact the authorities anonymously in order to exonerate the accused—maybe supplying a detail that only the legitimate killer might know. But at the end of the day, it would be difficult to justify such an unnecessary—and even arrogant—risk.

This time around, Balint didn't have to confront such ethical dilemmas: the case against the Brooklyn handyman soon fell apart. It turned out that he'd been hospitalized on the psychiatric unit at Bellevue for the entire month of December, providing an airtight alibi for the time of the Kenny McCord slaying. At first, the pundits predicted that he'd been plotting a copycat offense—but even that proved to be so much hot air. According to the *Post*, the suspect had informed police that he'd actually been planning to reenact the Emerald Choker killings in an effort to solve them. Further evidence for this claim emerged when the authorities discovered a list of potential "suspects" among his belongings. The list reportedly included the "real Zodiac killer" and "Satan."

———

BALINT BIDED his time before paying a visit to Sofia Constantinou. He figured that the woman might have friends or neighbors who'd look after her during the first days of her widowhood, before returning to their own busy lives, so he allowed a window for these well-intentioned folks to offer their compassion. Fortunately, Amanda—obviously emboldened by his indifference—revealed plans to attend yet another "bridge tournament" in the middle of January.

"Maybe I'll come with you to an event one of these days," he suggested, seeking to rankle her a bit.

"That would be great," Amanda replied as smooth as ever. "Not this time, of course—because we'd have to make arrangements for the girls. But maybe over the summer, when they're at camp."

"If you're still into bridge by the summer," said Balint.

A glint of hostility flickered across his wife's face. "Do you really think I'd give up bridge that easily?"

It crossed Balint's mind that his wife understood exactly what he was talking about—that they were both speaking in the same code—but that as long as neither acknowledged it, their marriage remained on safe ground. "I have no idea," he replied. "I gave up figuring out what games you're into a long time ago."

That concluded their discussion. Two weeks later, Balint deposited his daughters with their grandparents, kissed them each on the head, promised to make them hot chocolate before bedtime, and drove the two hours and twenty minutes to the working-class hamlet of Queensferry, New York. He paused on the outskirts of the town and wrapped burlap over the license plates of the Mercedes.

The nineteenth-century coastal village had once been a whaling port, the final stop for harpoon vessels bound from Nantucket and New Bedford to their hunting grounds in the southern Pacific. Following the Second World War, the hamlet had remade itself as a bedroom community for teachers and firefighters from New York City. Low-slung, one-story dwellings sprung up on the farmland that ringed the original town, including the tidy bungalow on Crescent Court where Sofia Constantinou lived under the shade of two towering Norway spruces. When Balint pulled up at the curbside, shortly after one o'clock, the trees already cast long shadows over the shingled roof.

Balint glanced up and down the block. Not another human being in sight. In fact, the nearest house was hardly visible around the bend. He pulled on his leather gloves—which would have to suffice, as latex was bound to draw the widow's attention. Then he strode rapidly up the brick path and rang the front bell.

Half a minute elapsed. Then a minute. Balint thought he saw movement at the drapes in the bay windows. Finally, the door opened a crack and a throaty voice addressed him from behind the chain. "Yes?"

"I'm looking for Mrs. Sofia Constantinou, the wife of the late Stavros Constantinou," said Balint—striving to sound calm. "I'm Dr. Balint with the New York City Municipal Workers' Benefits Fund."

"Do you have identification?"

Balint removed his hospital ID card from his wallet and slipped it between the door and the frame. That appeared to satisfy her. A moment later, the door shut and he heard her slide open the latch.

Mrs. Constantinou was a tall, big-boned woman with distinctly masculine features, whose face appeared to be frozen in an expression of mild displeasure. She wore a threadbare terrycloth robe.

"What can I do for you, Dr. Balint?" she asked.

The widow stood in the doorway, arms akimbo. She did not invite Balint inside.

"As I said, I'm from the New York City Municipal Workers' Benefits Fund. Your husband had an insurance plan with us—and I've come to settle the policy. Would it be all right if I stepped inside for a moment?"

Mrs. Constantinou raked her eyes up and down his body, then seemed to decide that he posed no immediate threat, and beckoned him into the house. He followed her through a dimly lit foyer into an equally dim parlor. Balint felt his heartbeat accelerating, but at the same time, he enjoyed the thrill of pretending to be something that he was not.

As he trailed the widow along the narrow passageway, he might easily have wrapped his hands around her throat. That's what a novice would have done—at his own peril. But Balint held back because he wasn't yet certain that the woman was alone in the house.

At his host's urging, he seated himself on a sofa shrouded in a plastic cover. The widow sunk into the armchair opposite him. The room was too warm and smelled oppressively of lavender and potpourri.

"You'll have to forgive me," said Mrs. Constantinou, "I don't have anything to offer you. I've been meaning to go shopping all week . . . but I just haven't . . ."

"I fully understand. You don't have anybody to help you?"

The widow stiffened. "I'm well looked after," she said defensively. "Now what's this about an insurance policy?"

Balint removed his handheld computer from his jacket pocket and punched in a few random numbers as though pulling up Constantinou's account.

"New York City salaried employees have an option to buy into a life insurance program," he explained, spinning his carefully premeditated tale. "I am delighted to say that your husband bought into our plan when it was first offered . . . and that you're the beneficiary. The amount should come out to $88,471.15."

"What's the catch?" demanded Mrs. Constantinou.

"No catch. All I need is to verify the death certificate and I'll have them send you a check within thirty days."

His host's expression softened. "Sammy was a wonderful man, Dr. Balint. He promised to take care of me forever and he did—even now . . ."

Balint assured himself that Sofia Constantinou's death, if not as unequivocally a public service as Kenny McCord's, was nonetheless a net positive. The widow had apparently led a good life. By promising her the insurance payout, he was enabling her to die happy—rather than alone and demented someday in a nursing home.

"If you could just show me the death certificate," prompted Balint.

The widow stood up. "It should be with the other papers."

Mrs. Constantinou crossed the room to the television and removed a shoe box from the shelf below. She began to sort through the contents. "I've got Sammy's naturalization papers, his Medicare card, his hospital bills . . ." Balint now felt confident that they were alone in the house. He eased himself off the couch and took three rapid steps across the carpet. "I know they gave it to me. It's just that I was so overwhelmed and—"

He had his gloves around her throat. She reached her hands up, and at first he thought she was going to grab his fingers, but then he noticed a medallion hanging just above her sternum. It was one of those medical panic buttons. He managed to block her hands at the last second, but that meant releasing half of his grasp on her neck.

She screamed and dug her nails into his cheek. Instinctively he used the full force of his body to ram her head face-first into the front of the mantelpiece. The blow proved strong enough to knock the fight from her.

Blood trickled down Balint's right cheek—warm and unpleasant. He finished the job quickly, squeezing until his victim yielded her carotid pulse. Then he dragged her cadaver into the kitchen and scrubbed her right hand for twenty minutes, hoping that the scalding water would wash any traces of his DNA from under her fingernails.

As a final touch, he retrieved the ribbon from his pocket and cut off *five* identical strands, wrapping each one around her neck. Only his fourth killing, but five ribbons. That, he mused, should keep the authorities scratching their heads.

———

THE CLAW marks on his cheek were too severe to pass off as a shaving injury. He'd managed to stanch the blood flow on the drive home, but the bandages that covered the wound also hid half of his face. At first he considered blaming the marks on one of Bonnie Kluger's numerous outdoor cats—of actually scooping one of these noxious beasts off her lawn and knocking on the peculiar woman's door to complain. Yet that required interacting with his wife's former friend, an owl-like creature whose piercing gray eyes and lack of an appropriate filter always gave him the willies. Instead he attributed the scratches to a feral raccoon that had assaulted him as he carried trash bags to the curbside. When he picked up the girls that evening and his mother grilled him on his injury, he described in vivid detail how he'd surprised the animal during its midday meal and how it had escaped down a sewer grate. Later, in narrating the episode for Amanda, he added that he'd received a full round of prophylactic rabies shots in the Laurendale emergency room.

Nobody questioned his story. This confirmed what he'd already suspected: small lies usually unravel quickly, but big lies often survive without scrutiny. He repeated the tale of the rabies shots again at the hospital: Who could second-guess him? If anyone dared look in his medical chart, their snooping would trigger the instant investigation that occurred when an employee accessed the health records of a colleague.

The one person who raised any doubts was Delilah. He'd taken her out for dinner that Sunday night, foisting the girls on Amanda. Since his wife had been away all weekend at her tournament, she couldn't reasonably object when he claimed that he needed to check up on a few patients at the hospital. But the closest he got to Laurendale-Methodist was a Turkish kabob house in Pontefract Beach.

"Did you really get scratched by a raccoon?" asked his mistress. "I'll understand if it was something else . . ."

Balint wondered if his story truly seemed that transparent. "Of course it was a raccoon. What else could it have been?"

Delilah reached her hand across the table and wrapped her fingers around his. "I thought you might have gotten into a fight with *a person* . . . maybe another woman . . ."

Balint wondered how much his mistress already knew—if she knew anything at all. He suspected that she was merely fishing. "What would I want with another woman when I'm in love with the most beautiful woman in the world?"

"Some men like variety."

"You're the only variety I need," pledged Balint.

He paid the bill and they strolled along the moonlit avenue toward his car. The evening was warm for January, yet the air carried a hint of impending snow. He savored the feeling of Delilah's hands in the pocket of his overcoat.

"Can we discuss something serious?" she asked.

Balint let his breath out slowly. "Sure."

"I don't mean to pressure you, but you haven't said anything about my father in weeks. Is he going to get a heart? I want the truth."

So that was all.

"Of course, he's going to get a heart," Balint reassured her. "There were a number of obstacles to overcome before we could list him—but now that he's on the list, all we need is a heart . . . and a suitable organ could come along any day now." He had just boxed himself in, time-wise, he realized—but he was glad that he had. "I promised you that I was going to get your father a heart and I am going to get your father a heart. It's not a matter of if, only of when . . ."

"You sound so certain," said Delilah.

"Because I *am* certain. As far as I'm concerned, your father might live another thirty years."

CHAPTER NINE

Norman Navare would die two days later. The call from Delilah came during Balint's monthly meeting with the chairman—and he excused himself early by telling Dr. Sanditz that he'd suffered a death in the family. Then he raced down to the emergency room, anticipating the worst. He even feared that his mistress might cause a scene, although he sensed that the nursing student wasn't the disturbance-provoking type. But it turned out that the "medical emergency" Delilah had described proved far less alarming than he'd expected. At least, for him. Navare was indeed critically ill—but his condition had nothing to do with his heart. The housepainter had fallen off a stepladder.

"I found him when I came home from my shift," explained Delilah. She'd managed to remain surprisingly calm. "He'd been trying to change one of the light bulbs in the foyer, and he must have lost his footing."

They stood on either side of her father's stretcher in the "resuscitation" unit of the emergency department, waiting for a bed in the ICU. Assorted tubes and wires protruded from every corner of the housepainter's body. Balint had skimmed the electronic chart. Navare's CT scan showed considerable cerebral hemorrhage, but his lab values looked stable. It was one of those cases that might go either way. However, from Balint's vantage point, the best possible outcome was death. That would spare the debilitated old man months of recovery and possible brain damage. At a personal level, it would also relieve him of any responsibility for securing the man a heart.

Delilah appeared to be thinking along the same lines—or at least along parallel lines. "Will this keep Papa from staying listed for a heart?" she asked.

"Let's focus on one thing at a time. Once he recovers, we'll have to see where we stand . . ."

Delilah placed her hand on her father's forehead. "I warned him not to climb up on that stepladder. I must have warned him a thousand times . . . The college kid next door was always willing to change the bulbs for us, but Papa was too ashamed to ask."

Balint remembered how it had felt when his own father had died—the torment of being yanked out of his high school chemistry class by the assistant principal, then driven to the hospital by his Aunt Clara. He remembered seeing his father spread out on a gurney with a ghostly sheet tucked up around his neck. Breathless. Like a wax display in a museum. Before that day, he'd believed—without ever thinking about it too deeply—that life was inherently fair. If you worked hard and took care of yourself and looked after your family, then God smiled upon you and let you win the cosmic chess game. And Balint had believed in God back then—a benevolent, hands-off God who periodically tipped the scales of justice in favor of the universal good. After that day, he'd accepted that God only helped those who helped themselves. In college, he'd even worn a T-shirt that read: "Praise the Lord and pass the ammunition." And at some point, the Lord dropped out of the equation entirely, and it was all about ammunition. He'd never shared these thoughts with anybody—not with Delilah, certainly not with Amanda, not even with the know-it-all therapist they'd sent him to see when his father died. This was the sort of secret that, if divulged, could unravel a person forever.

"You're crying," said Delilah. "Oh, Jeremy."

His lover stepped around her father's body and wrapped her arms around him.

"I'm sorry," he said. "I don't know what came over me."

How absurd that she'd thought he was crying for her father, when he was actually crying for his own loss. Absurd—but convenient.

"We'll get through this," said Delilah. "Together. One way or another."

At the recommendation of the ER attending, who predicted at least another hour before an ICU bed became available, they stepped upstairs to the cafeteria to grab a quick lunch. When it came to space in the intensive care unit, even the chief of cardiology had little pull. After all, you couldn't simply dump one of the current ICU occupants out of a bed, so you had to wait for one of them to recover—or expire.

Balint canceled all of his patient appointments for the afternoon. He was aware that his colleagues might witness him strolling through the hospital with Delilah, but what was so wrong about comforting a patient's daughter? As it turned out, the few familiar faces he encountered in the cafeteria—Myron Salt, Sid Crandall from rheumatology—greeted him at a distance, but chose to stay clear.

Over lunch, Delilah talked about her father's boyhood in Venezuela and her paternal grandfather's involvement in the coup d'état of 1945. When they returned to the emergency room, the same ER attending informed them that Navare's

EEG had flatlined and asked if they'd like for him to summon a priest.

"He's brain dead," Balint explained to Delilah. "I'm sorry."

"But his heart's still beating . . ."

"On the machine. When the machine stops, his heart and lungs will also stop."

Delilah nodded and sat mute for ten minutes. Then she rose suddenly and had a brief, pointed conversation with the ER physician.

At 2:14 P.M., the nurses turned off all the machines.

———

THE FUNERAL was scheduled for Thursday afternoon. On his way out of the office, Balint ran into Warren Sugarman opposite the hemodialysis suite. Although he had no way of proving it, gut instinct told him that this encounter hadn't been a coincidence, that his rival had been lying in wait. Sugarman lacked his usual entourage of obsequious surgical residents sporting immaculate scrubs.

"I can't talk right now," said Balint as he hurried toward the elevators. "I'm on my way to a funeral."

Sugarman followed him. "I'm headed downstairs."

"It was that patient you wouldn't give the heart to."

Balint felt no need to inform him that Navare had fallen on his head.

"I'm sorry. Truly, I am."

They boarded the bustling elevator. When they reached the lobby, Sugarman resumed the conversation. "I didn't realize you were going to patients' funerals these days," he said. "That's mighty generous of you."

Balint couldn't discern whether he was being mocked. Then it struck him that Sugarman had no memory of refusing to list Delilah's father for an organ—that the surgeon didn't even recall their conversation about Navare being a family friend. He obviously hadn't connected the patient with Balint's mistress.

"I need to be at the cemetery in twenty minutes," lied Balint, picking up his pace as he crossed the plaza en route to the parking garage. A light snow was falling, coating the statues of medical luminaries in glistening flakes. "Is there something specific you wanted to talk about?"

"I ran into your wife," said Sugarman.

Balint kept walking. He shielded his eyes from the snow with his hand.

"Gloria's father had back surgery, so I was picking up Davey from school."

They'd arrived at Balint's car. He didn't give a damn for Sugarman's explanations—as long as he didn't have to hear them. "So you ran into Amanda . . ."

"Your wife tells me that your daughters are into ice-skating. It planted the idea in my head that we could all go skating together—give my boy, Davey, an opportunity to spend some time with your kids." Sugarman lowered his voice. "He's hit a rough patch since Gloria and I split up. Frankly it would do him some good."

The last thing on earth that Balint wanted was to spend a day ice-skating with Warren Sugarman and his idiot son. It suddenly crossed his mind that this might be the final occasion he ever saw the surgeon alive—or the final occasion, minus one. Even if he agreed to the skating date, he could always kill the prick beforehand.

"Why don't you and Amanda work something out?" suggested Balint.

"Sure. If that's okay with you."

"Why *wouldn't* it be okay?"

He faced his rival over the trunk of the Mercedes. Sugarman sported a broad, oafish grin, but looked to be at a loss for words. In the distance, someone's car alarm raged for help. Balint didn't understand how he'd once considered this ignorant slab of meat to be his friend.

"Okay, then I'll call Amanda," said Sugarman. "And I'm very sorry about your patient. We should all really make a habit of going to patients' funerals, when we can . . . You are a genuinely good soul, Balint. I've got to hand it to you."

If only you knew, thought Balint. If only you knew . . .

———

THE FUNERAL itself was a modest affair. A mass at Saint Rahab's Church in Hollowell was followed by a brief graveside service. Afterward, they'd retired to a mom-and-pop diner for a light afternoon meal.

Among the mourners were several of the dead man's cousins, his partners in the painting business, and a band of nursing students from his daughter's graduate program. Delilah held Balint's arm through both events and introduced him around as her boyfriend. Mercifully, none of the nursing students looked familiar. The only awkward moment occurred during the Mass, when his mistress nudged him forward to accept communion. Balint shook his head and let her slide past. While he had no scruples against enjoying a free cracker and a sip of wine, he realized that Delilah might at some point discover the truth—at least, about his religion—and that taking communion was the sort of offense for which she might struggle to pardon him. He prided himself on his foresight in this regard.

Balint paid no attention to the service. His thoughts were consumed with the fate of Mrs. Constantinou, whose body apparently still had not been discovered. That was the downside of selecting a victim with limited social connections. In theory, weeks might elapse before anybody noticed the woman missing. The impulse even entered his head that he might try to speed up the process—for instance, by calling 911 from a pay phone and summoning the police to her address—but that, Balint realized, was sheer insanity. His only realistic option was to wait.

To his consternation, the news finally broke while he was driving Delilah home from the restaurant. They'd gotten delayed in traffic on the turnpike, and since Amanda was expecting him for supper, he'd flipped on the traffic report. Instead, a newsflash announced that the Emerald Choker had choked once again. This time, of course, Balint already knew the identity of the victim before the media reported it. Her decomposing body had been discovered, it turned out, by a concerned letter carrier.

Balint shut off the radio—even though he longed to listen for more. "You can always count on the post office."

"I thought you wanted to hear the traffic," said Delilah.

"I'll turn it back on in a few minutes. I don't like listening to that serial killer business. It makes me sick to my stomach . . ."

Delilah nodded. "Why do you think a person does something like that?"

"Kills people? Probably because he's mad as a hatter."

"But *why*? Do you think it's because he had an unhappy childhood or do you believe some people are just born that way . . . ?"

Balint didn't have a good answer. "Probably some combination of both. You need to be born with the capacity for evil—and then something has to go terribly awry."

"I don't know," replied Delilah. "Sometimes I think we're all capable of that. I realize that sounds crazy, but what I mean is, if any of us found ourselves desperate enough, or suffered the right trauma, we could end up going haywire. I'm not saying that's an excuse—don't get me wrong. It's still wicked. But just like the church teaches we're all capable of great good, I can't help thinking that we're all capable of great wrongdoing."

"You might be correct," said Balint. "But I hope not."

The traffic cleared a few minutes later and he was able to get Delilah home with time to spare for his commute back to Laurendale. Balint walked her to her front door and embraced her. He wished he could stay over—but, unfortunately, he explained to her, he had night duty at the hospital. Delilah understood. She always did. She didn't even say a word about communion.

———

AMANDA HAD dinner waiting for him when he arrived home. Macaroni for Phoebe, hot dogs for Jessie, and swordfish steak for the adults. Whatever Balint might say about Amanda's inadequate fidelity, she remained as efficient a household manager as ever—on top of her thirty-six-hour workweek at the library. Over the past several days, he'd watched with some surprise as Delilah struggled to manage the responsibilities related to her father's death: locating his will, paying for the casket, arranging the hearse. Balint couldn't imagine his mistress raising children, let alone caring for children in addition to working a full-time job as a nurse. But, unlike Amanda, the girl was totally devoted to him.

He had wanted to discuss Warren Sugarman's proposal over dinner, but he didn't dare mention the subject of ice-skating in front of his daughters. They'd have reacted to the mention of the "I-word" with the same intensity that other children did to words like "kitten" or "pony." But after the meal, he received a genuine emergency phone call from the hospital—one of his cardiology fellows had shown up for his shift drunk—and it was nearly eleven o'clock when Balint was finally able to arrange for emergency coverage. By then, his wife was sleeping soundly.

Balint finally had a moment alone with Amanda the following night. It had been a momentous day: Chief Putnam had taken the bait of the five ribbons, and was reporting that the authorities now had reason to suspect an as yet undiscovered crime in addition to the four known killings. The chief held a joint press conference with Detective Mazzotta, the imposing brunette who headed the Queensberry homicide squad. Mazzotta appeared about forty, good-looking, but with a sharp edge that contrasted with Putnam's easygoing manner. Together they'd formed something called the "Ad-hoc Task Force on Serial Killings"—or simply "The Task Force"—with the goal of coordinating resources across jurisdictions. During the press conference, Mazzotta even quoted a poem:

> *Though the mills of God grind slowly,*
> *Yet they grind exceeding small;*
> *Though with patience he stands waiting,*
> *With exactness grinds he all.*

"It's by the poet Henry Longfellow. We memorized it in high school," explained the detective. "At the time, I didn't really understand what it meant or why it mattered—but today, I finally know. It means that it may take us more time than we'd like to solve these brutal murders. But mark my words, *we will solve them.* So I ask for the public's patience and understanding during these difficult days." All it required was one stanza and Detective Mazzotta became a media darling overnight.

Balint had listened to the radio between patients all after-noon. Now that they'd found Sofia Constantinou's corpse, no obstacle remained that would prevent him from killing his nemesis. By the time he discussed Sugarman with his wife, Norman Navare's funeral felt like a distant memory.

Balint entered the bathroom while Amanda was brushing her teeth and sat down on the lid of the toilet. She'd had the room painted bright yellow—and he despised the color scheme. Half-rolled tubes of her assorted creams and oint-ments covered the countertops.

"I ran into Warren Sugarman a few days ago," he said.

Amanda spit into the sink and rinsed. Her eyes widened.

"What's this about us going on an ice-skating trip with his kid?"

His wife gargled again and shut off the faucet. "It was my idea. His son, Davey, is having a hard time. The boy doesn't make friends easily . . . He's not the most inspiring child, to tell you the truth. You've seen him. Other children just don't seem to like him."

"And what makes you think Jessie and Phoebe are going to like him?"

"They probably won't. But they *do* like skating. I thought maybe it would do the poor child some good if the girls spent an afternoon with him."

"And what good will that do Jessie and Phoebe?"

His wife began lacquering her face with a pale green lotion called Cucumber Rejuvenator. "I remember what it was like to be an unpopular kid, Jer. And, to be honest, it's absolutely goddamn miserable. Anyway, I don't see how it will kill Jessie to spend an afternoon with one of her classmates."

Balint had been an extremely popular child from as far back as he could remember. That had been his one comfort—even after his father passed away. It genuinely irked him to think that his own wife had once been a friendless creature like Davey Sugarman. "I'm sorry that you had a hard time of it," he said, "but that's no reason to turn our daughters into guinea pigs. It's not my fault that Davey Sugarman is a tubby little dolt—any more than it was my fault that Abby Goldhammer couldn't swim. I'm raising children, Amanda, not running a charity for wayward delinquents."

Amanda spun around. "I can't believe you just said that."

"Said *what?*"

"Something's wrong with your brain, Jeremy Balint. He's an eight-year-old boy, for Christ's sake. Can't you show some compassion?"

"Not when it comes at my daughters' expense. Do you think they're going to gain any popularity hanging out with that boy?"

"They'll learn empathy," snapped Amanda. "That's just as important."

"Are you going to phrase it that way to them?" pressed Balint. "They're not stupid. Are you going to tell them that they have to play with Davey Sugarman because he's an ugly, awkward loser, but it's important to show compassion for ugly losers?"

Amanda swung shut the door of the medicine cabinet. The mirror rattled—and for a second, Balint feared that it might shatter.

"I'm going skating with Warren and his son," she said firmly. "And I'm taking along your daughters. You can decide whether you'd like to join us . . . Or whether associating with an unpopular eight-year-old might compromise your sterling reputation."

His wife stormed out of the bathroom and slammed the door. Then she slammed it a second time for effect. Balint waited until he was confident that she'd settled under the covers—and then crossed silently through the dark bedroom. He stayed up until the early hours of the morning, listening to radio callers discuss the Emerald Choker case with two "experts" on serial killings. That night—for the first time since a bout of poison oak six years earlier—he slept on the couch in the living room.

———

AMANDA DIDN'T mention their spat over breakfast the next morning. She acted as though nothing had happened, so he did the same. Her principal concern appeared to be that she'd managed to double-book them for the following Saturday evening—both for dinner with the Sucrams and for a gathering at the van Houtens'. "I don't know *what* I was thinking," she said. "Maria van Houten is having a farewell party for Alyssa Pickering—now that Herb's dead, Alyssa can't afford the property taxes—and I didn't think twice about agreeing to come. But we've been pledged to Betsy and Vince Sucram for months . . ." If Amanda truly cared about Herb Pickering's widow, she'd pay the property taxes herself, he noted—but Balint didn't dare suggest as much. She'd either take him up on his offer, as nutty as it sounded, or she'd complain that he was ridiculing her.

"I'm sure you'll work something out," said Balint.

"I'm sure I will too. Still, it's frustrating." His wife cleared away his plate and called the girls downstairs for their oatmeal. "But remember. We're doing *something* on Saturday night. So don't get yourself called into the hospital . . ."

"I'll ask my patients to hold off on having their heart attacks until Monday," responded Balint. He considered kissing Amanda on the forehead—but didn't. Only when he was already headed into town did he second-guess himself.

This was to be the morning that he was taping four sixty-second radio spots for Etan Steinhoff. He'd anticipated that four minutes worth of tape would require about twenty minutes of studio time, or half an hour, at most. The rabbi stunned him when he demanded a block of five hours. "It's a complicated process," explained Steinhoff. "We'll try to get through things quickly, but it's always better to err on the safe side." So Balint was committed to the pointless project until one o'clock.

The recording studio occupied a loft over Laurendale Lanes, the local bowling alley, but the chamber was fully sound-proofed. "If the building caught fire," said the audio engineer, Eve, who hooked up his microphone, "they couldn't hear your screams."

"Then let's hope there's not a fire."

The technician laughed. "That's a good one. 'Let's hope there's not a fire.'" She was cute enough—although she wore blue liner around brown eyes. Balint even considered inviting her out for coffee. He ultimately decided against it, but not because of any ethical scruples against betraying Delilah. Unlike cheating on one's wife, cheating on one's mistress seemed a minor transgression. The logistics of another intrigue, on the other hand, struck him as daunting.

Eve retreated behind a glass shield and settled into a chair beside the rabbi. "I need to test the mic," she said into Balint's headphones. "Say something."

He thought for a moment. "Though the mills of God grind slowly," he quoted. "Yet they grind exceeding small."

She flashed him a thumbs-up. "And thanks for not saying 'Testing 1-2-3,' by the way," she added. Of course, that had been his second choice.

Balint smiled at Steinhoff through the glass. The rabbi, who was speaking into his cell phone, gave him a vigorous nod.

"When you see the green light go on," said the girl, "start reading."

Balint glanced at the wall clock. He couldn't imagine how this business could possibly take five hours. When the green light flashed, he started reading from the script that the rabbi had provided: "I'm Dr. Jeremy Balint and saving lives is my job. It's also my passion. Every year in this state, thousands of adult men and women go without routine medical care. Many of these men and women die. The tragedy is that these people are entitled to free comprehensive care—often only minutes from their own homes . . ." He watched the second hand on the clock as he read. At fifty-nine seconds, he hit the final word. Perfect.

He shut the script and turned to Steinhoff. "How'd I do?"

The rabbi held his hand over his cell phone. "Good—but not good enough. There's a long and complex history here, Dr. Balint. The Tuskegee experiments, Henrietta Lacks. These people have every reason to distrust doctors. So if we're going to convince them to come to our clinics—clinics that are, quite frankly, run by rich white Jews from places like Laurendale and Hager Park—you're going to have to sound like the most honest and moral man they've ever heard in their entire lives. I want to hear Martin Luther King meets Marcus Welby, okay? And keep in mind that we're not deceiving anybody. As far as we're concerned, you *are* the most honest and moral man around. Got it?"

"I think so," said Balint. "Would you like me to imitate Dr. King's voice?"

"That won't be necessary," answered Steinhoff. "Just channel his spirit."

Balint read the script again. All he had in common with Martin Luther King was that they'd both cheated on their wives—at least, if the media reports about King were to be believed—but he didn't suspect Steinhoff would view that as a selling point. When he was done, the rabbi still wasn't satisfied.

"You sound like a doctor. Like a *real* doctor. These people don't know doctors from a hole in the ground. You need to sound like what they *want* a doctor to sound like. Pretend you're a twenty-five-year-old mother in Newark with an eleven-year-old kid who has already been arrested twice for criminal mischief, and you haven't been to a physician since your son was born—and that physician was some nitwit from Ghana or Pakistan who barely spoke English and operated out of a run-down basement. Pretend you're *that woman* for a moment—and try to sound like the doctor who she's wanted to take care of her for her entire life."

"It might be easier to pretend," quipped Balint, "if I did it in blackface."

The audio technician grinned. Steinhoff shook his head.

"We don't have time for costumes," he said. "Just do the best you can."

His best required exactly five hours, it turned out. The rabbi claimed that the final versions were indeed perfect—far better than the earlier takes—but the truth was that Balint couldn't tell the difference.

———

Now THAT Sofia Constantinou's death was front-page news, Balint had no excuse for putting off his final encounter with Warren Sugarman. Nevertheless, January drifted into February and he found himself delaying the necessary preparations. He still had enough green ribbon on his person for one more crime, but he'd made no effort to map out Sugarman's schedule or to find a window when he might slip away from Amanda. Securing sufficient time apart from his wife would prove more complicated in this case, because he couldn't kill the surgeon while Amanda was away at a "bridge tournament" or similar event, if she was actually meeting up with Sugarman on these occasions. Of course, now that Norman Navare had died, the immediate time pressure was off. He could act quickly or wait as long as he wished; some serial killers disappeared and resurfaced years later. As much as he hated to admit it, he actually enjoyed following the efforts of Chief Putnam and Detective Mazzotta as they tried to reassure the public that they had the situation under control—when anyone with half a brain realized that they didn't. By now the bounty on the killer of Kenny McCord exceeded $300,000.

Whatever was causing Balint to drag his feet, it certainly wasn't any sympathy for his rival. He despised Warren Sugarman more than he ever had. If he could have pressed a button and vaporized the man without any consequences for himself, he'd have done so in a heartbeat. The real obstacle, he realized, was fear. Killing strangers seemed fundamentally different from killing someone whom he knew well—a colleague he interacted with on a weekly, and often a daily, basis. Once again Balint feared he might freeze up at the last instant. Or that Sugarman, who was smart enough in his own way, might utter something during those final seconds to knock him off his guard. Maybe it was merely that he'd come so close to victory that he feared taking any steps which might jeopardize his previous successes.

This was Balint's state of mind on the Saturday night that they joined the Sucrams for dinner at the new oyster house in Pontefract. Amanda had salvaged the evening by dropping by the van Houtens' home earlier in the day and leaving a crystal salad bowl for Alyssa Pickering. Balint didn't understand what a woman who couldn't afford to pay her property taxes was supposed to do with a $200 bowl—unless she was supposed to sleep in it—but he kept his commentary to himself.

He'd been forewarned that his job was to tell Betsy and Vince Sucram how much he'd enjoyed their daughter's wedding, and then to steer clear of politics and religion and anything else that might insult them. "Just don't cause any trouble, Jer," pleaded Amanda. "If you have to ask yourself whether something will offend anybody, please don't say it. Trust me, it will."

"Give me some credit," he replied. "I'm not a Neanderthal."

"I'm not saying you are. But you do have a track record. And the Sucrams are the leading donors on Rabbi Steinhoff's new tabernacle. Etan will have my head if you manage to insult them."

"You and Etan are on a first-name basis now?"

"Yes, we are," said Amanda. "And that would be precisely the sort of remark I'd rather you didn't air in front of Vince and Betsy."

"Duly noted."

He pulled up the Mercedes in front of the restaurant and handed his keys to the valet. The Sucrams were already waiting for them at the bar. Balint found himself in the midst of a flurry of handshakes and kisses, then whisked off to a table in an oak-paneled side room. On the opposite wall hung an enormous sailfish.

"Your daughter had a fine wedding," said Balint. "We had a marvelous time."

"Thank you," said Betsy Sucram. "We were so glad you could join us."

"That fellow you sat us with—tax lawyer—the guy was hilarious."

"Must have been Vincent Hearn," interjected Vince Sucram. "My namesake."

"That's right. Hearn. He and I had a long debate over whether we should be referring to your daughter and her partner as 'bride and bride' or 'spouse and spouse.'"

Amanda kicked him in the knee. Hard.

Betsy Sucram pursed her lips. "And what, pray tell, did you decide?"

Balint shrugged. "I can't remember anymore. Five martinis and they could have been two grooms for all I knew."

This time, Amanda's shoe came inches from his groin, and he grabbed the tablecloth—nearly toppling their water glasses. "Sorry," he said.

That was about the time when he first noticed two women who'd just been seated at the far end of the nearly empty dining room. One was their peculiar neighbor, Bonnie Kluger, who wore an odd, kimono-style robe and a bright crimson hat. Her outfit looked a bit like casual wear for the Pope—if the Pope had been Japanese. The other patron was Sally Gold-hammer. Balint hadn't seen Sally since the day her daughter had drowned.

He drew Amanda's attention to the newcomers. The Sucrams also noted their arrival and maintained an awkward silence.

"You really *must* say *something*, Jeremy," Amanda said. "She's seen us. We can't just pretend she's not here."

"So why do *I* have to say something?"

"Trust me. It's better that way. She's already made it clear that she wants nothing to do with *me*—but if you went up to her and apologized, it might go a long way toward making her feel better."

"I can't apologize," said Balint. "That's practically an admission of guilt. Her lawyers will eat me alive." He turned to Sucram for support. "You're a businessman, Vince. You understand where I'm coming from."

Vince Sucram nodded politely. Later, Balint learned that he'd been mistaken and their dinner companion was actually an anthropology professor—that the money came from his wife's family enterprise. "Maybe you could express your sadness over the situation without actually taking any blame."

"Could this get any more awkward?" asked Amanda. "Please just get it over with, Jeremy. Before we all die of embarrassment."

So he dropped his napkin on his chair and strode across the dining room. A look of sheer terror suffused across Sally Goldhammer's face. Bonnie Kluger, unfazed, gnawed a crust of bread.

"I hope I'm not intruding, Sally," said Balint. "I wanted to let you know how sorry I am about all you've been through."

The woman stared at him without acknowledgment.

"She appreciates the thought," Bonnie answered for her. "But you'll forgive her if she's in no mood to talk to you at the moment."

"I understand."

He was about to return to his own table when Bonnie said, "I hear you were bitten by a raccoon."

"Scratched," he corrected her.

"Yes, scratched. Very unusual."

Balint felt threatened. "I interrupted its lunch, I'm afraid. But I learned my lesson. Next time I'm going to be much more careful."

Bonnie's eyes latched into him like fishhooks. "I know all of the raccoons on our street intimately," she said—as though claiming to know all of their human neighbors. "It would be *highly* out of character for any one of them to attack you unprovoked. Surely you must have done *something* to antagonize him."

If he could have chosen a second local victim after Sugarman, this woman would certainly have been next on his hit list.

"You're mistaken, Bonnie," he said. "I did nothing of the sort."

The strange woman stared straight through him—as though she alone could sense his inner core of iniquity. Then she waved her hand before her face, sweeping him toward inconsequence and oblivion.

"Very well. No sense in arguing," said Bonnie. "But I urge you to take care of yourself. If you do provoke raccoons, they're capable of gouging your eyes out."

Apparently Bonnie's voice had carried across the dining room, because when Balint returned to his own table, after a brief detour to the restroom, Vince Sucram was already whispering an anecdote about eye-gouging rituals among the Pau-Gha people of Indonesia.

CHAPTER TEN

Balint dithered so long that Sugarman was still alive when the weekend arrived for their family ice-skating adventure. He had only himself to blame. Yet the prospect of spending an afternoon in the company of both the surgeon and Amanda together was so repugnant to him that, on the night before the outing, he contemplated throwing caution to the wind and attempting to kill the surgeon without any advance preparation. In the end, good sense prevailed—and instead of murdering his rival, he spent the night fantasizing that an outside force might intervene. He imagined that the skating rink burned to the ground or that Davey Sugarman contracted an acute and fatal case of meningitis. But when dawn arrived the next day, the world hadn't ended in nuclear holocaust and gorillas hadn't escaped from the zoo to carry off his rival's dopey offspring. So Balint loaded his wife and daughters into the Mercedes and resigned himself to his fate.

A burst of arctic air had swept across the region overnight and the bitter chill ached in Balint's lungs. His daughters blew on the car windows and fingered patterns in the condensed moisture. "Listen to me, Jessie," said Amanda. "I want you to be nice to Davey Sugarman, okay?"

Jessie didn't respond.

"*Okay?*"

"Okay, Mommy."

Balint heard the resistance in his daughter's voice—but he wasn't in a mood to argue with Amanda. He'd been too busy before they left home to update himself regarding developments in the murder investigation and now he was burning to learn the latest details. Claiming that he wanted to check the weather, he flipped on the radio news. To his amazement, he heard his own voice: *The tragedy is that these people are entitled to free comprehensive care—often only minutes from their own homes . . .*

"Wow," said Balint. "That's my ad."

The girls recognized his voice too. "Daddy's on the radio!" exclaimed Phoebe. "Daddy's on the radio!"

Balint glanced at them through the rearview mirror. Jessie wore a doubtful expression. "Is that really you, Daddy?" she asked.

"Yes, it is," said Amanda. "Your father is fast becoming a radio celebrity."

The expression of delight on Jessie's face was worth the five hours he'd squandered at Steinhoff's studio.

"You sound good," said his wife. "Very professional."

"Steinhoff thought I sounded too much like a real doctor."

"As opposed to . . . ?"

"The idealized image that disenfranchised ghetto dwellers have of the kind of physicians who serve rich white people, or something like that. Although I'm sure your friend wouldn't describe it exactly in those terms."

Amanda folded her arms across her chest. "I'm sure he wouldn't."

After that, they drove in silence—except for the drone of the radio. As they were approaching Musselburgh Township, the station ran a short update on "The Choker." First, they played an audio clip of Detective Mazzotta urging the public to come forward with knowledge of the crimes. *"Anything* out of the ordinary," she said. "If you know of someone preoccupied with news about these killings, for instance, or someone who has been acting strangely of late. Please let law enforcement judge what's important and what's not. No suspicion is too trivial to report." Balint also learned that the Saint Nicholas Society of Long Island, to which Stavros Constantinou once belonged, had raised $15,000 for clues leading to a conviction in the Queensferry case. At the rate that these bounties kept mounting, Balint reflected, he'd soon be worth more as a felon than as a physician. It genuinely frustrated him that he couldn't share this irony with anyone. He reached forward to turn off the radio, then caught his mistake.

They arrived at the rink around ten o'clock. During the summer, the structure served as home court for the Musselburgh Mud Hens' basketball team; in the winter, the municipality lacquered the gymnasium floor in a thin veneer of ice and used the structure as a hockey arena. On weekends, when the team was on the road, the town opened the facility to the public. Despite the weather, Balint found the parking lot nearly full. Sugarman and his son had already rented their skates and waited for them near the concession stand.

"Cold enough for you, Balint?" asked Sugarman.

The surgeon wore a Columbia Lions sweatshirt. His son sported a knit cap and matching mittens, but he'd taken off one of the mittens to stick a finger up his nose. No wonder that the girls showed no interest in him.

"Is it cold?" asked Balint. "I hadn't noticed."

Sugarman and Amanda shared a polite greeting. They didn't shake hands or hug.

Balint had determined to make the most out of this encounter—to use the afternoon to pry from his nemesis any information he could glean about his schedule. Yet he feared this might appear incriminating and he realized he had to tread rather lightly. Then fate sailed his way once again. "I can't tell you how good it feels to get out of the house," said Sugarman. "I have an IRB proposal due first thing Monday morning—we're testing Pfizer's new antirejection drug—and I'm still not done with the protocol. It's looking like the minute I get home, I'm going to be working straight through until the deadline." He stretched his arms over his head. "I haven't pulled an all-nighter since residency."

The gears of Balint's mind kicked into overdrive.

"What are you going to do with Davey?" he asked.

"Gloria's taking him off my hands. Her father's back on his feet—and not a moment too soon. I love that kid—don't misunderstand me—but I didn't go to medical school to drive carpools and pack lunch boxes. You know what I mean."

Balint wondered if Sugarman would have had more time for a likable child. "I'd go crazy if anyone tried to take my girls away from me," he said.

"Each to his own, I suppose. Being a father is important to me . . . but so is getting my research proposal approved."

While they were chatting, Amanda had taken the girls to rent ice skates. His wife was now helping them tie the laces. Balint ordered his own pair and exchanged them for his sneakers with the teenage attendant. He did not enjoy skating. In hindsight he regretted having introduced the girls to the activity. Overhead the loudspeakers piped a wordless chorus of "Winter Wonderland" into the gymnasium.

Sugarman asked Balint, "Would you mind if I borrowed your wife?"

A moment passed before Balint registered that his rival meant as a skating partner. "That's between you and her," he said. His thoughts had already skipped ahead to the next day—when his rival would be alone at home.

Sugarman took Amanda by the hand and led her onto the rink. The man immediately demonstrated his skills: he was by far the most talented amateur skater that anyone present had likely ever witnessed. Balint's wife had received lessons as an adolescent, but with Sugarman leading, she performed spins that rivaled Peggy Fleming. Her partner kept her on the ice through "Frosty the Snowman" and Tchaikovsky's "Waltz of the Flowers." Other skaters cleared space for the couple and watched in awe. At the end of the routine, many of these spectators applauded. Amanda whispered into the surgeon's ear and giggled. Delight radiated from her every feature. She returned to the sidelines for hugs from Jessie and Phoebe.

"I didn't know you were a ringer," said Balint.

Sugarman beamed. "I played hockey in high school. The coach insisted we study some basic figure work in the off-season. At the time, I thought it was bullshit . . ."

"But now you can wow the ladies," offered Balint.

"Something like that."

Davey Sugarman tugged at his father's elbow. The kid apparently had to use the restroom, but didn't feel comfortable going alone. "We'll be back," said Sugarman.

After the pair departed, Amanda sat down on a nearby bench and adjusted her skates. Perspiration beaded her forehead.

"Can we go on the ice now?" asked Jessie.

"I'll take them," offered Balint.

Amanda shook her head. "Wait until Warren's son gets back." She turned to Jessie and added, "Please show Davey how to ice-skate."

"I don't want to," said Jessie. "He's dis*gu*sting."

Amanda's expression sharpened. "I'm not asking you, Jessica. I'm *telling* you. He's our guest and we have to be kind to him."

"I wish he hadn't come," said Jessie. "He's not *my* guest."

"Yes," replied Amanda. "He is." She clasped her daughter's coat by both forearms and looked firmly into her eyes. "If you want us to bring you skating again this winter, you're going to have to include Davey. Am I making myself clear?"

Balint had heard enough. "Don't pressure her. She's capable of choosing her own friends," he warned. He smiled at his daughter and added, "It's okay, honey . . ."

His wife glowered at him.

"Your father is mistaken. It is *not* okay."

Jessie appeared frightened. She glanced over her shoulder, looking for reassurance from her sister, but Phoebe was occupied performing spins on dry land. For a moment, Balint feared his daughter might start to cry. Ultimately, Amanda relented.

"It's all right, darling," she said. "Never mind."

Immediately the girls cavorted off toward the ice, where they'd spend the afternoon ignoring Sugarman's nose-picking dolt of a child. Balint stood up to follow, holding onto the railing to maintain his balance. Behind him, he heard Amanda's voice fire like a frozen bullet: "I truly hate you sometimes."

Those were the final words she spoke to him all day.

———

His wife's silent treatment lasted through the evening. The only reason Balint didn't sleep on the sofa again was that he didn't want to cede territory to her—either moral or physical. As far as he was concerned, she'd been way out of line to bully Jessie into socializing with that unpopular misfit. How could she possibly value the interests of her lover's child over the welfare of her own daughter? It raised serious questions about Amanda's judgment.

That night, Balint experienced one of the most intense and vivid dreams of his adult life. In the dream, he found himself seated in a courtroom—on trial for the murders of the Rockinghams, Kenny McCord, and Sofia Constantinou. Among the jurors, he recognized several colleagues from the hospital: Myron Salt, Andy Price, Sid Crandall. Also Ellen Arcaya and Matilda Rothschild. The forewoman, to his delight, was none other than Delilah. His mistress wore the same floral-print skirt and ruffled yellow blouse that he'd enjoyed removing from her body on their first date. As the prosecutor rose for his closing argument, the nursing student winked at him— and he felt confident he had the case in the bag. Even when the lawyer decried his villainy in the starkest terms, describing each death in dramatic and highly embellished detail, Balint remained confident that his fate was secure. But then he looked up—and the judge, wearing his Columbia Lions sweatshirt, was Warren Sugarman. His rival wielded a scalpel in place of a gavel. "The service of the jury will no longer be necessary," declared the surgeon. "I will decide this matter myself." In his dream, Balint felt himself seized with panic.

Somehow, in the landscape of his unconscious, Sugarman transmuted into Etan Steinhoff. The rabbi sported a white lab coat. At first, Balint feared that the rabbi was also going to condemn him—yet, to his amazement, Steinhoff lavished praise upon his actions. "God plays a mean game of chess," said the Israeli. "But sometimes, He needs help moving around the pieces. That takes courage. So I've come here to honor a genuine hero, a man who devotes as much passion to snuffing out life as to saving it . . ." Balint experienced a surge of relief—and then he was awake.

It was already seven o'clock and sunlight peeked around the blinds. Out in the neighboring yard, he heard the Robustellis' beagle howling at the dew. If he'd believed in the meaning of dreams, he'd have devoted the next hour to exploring his psyche. But Balint had no more patience for dream interpretation than for faith healing or the laying on of hands. To him, all were varieties of quackery. So instead of inventorying his soul, he spent the next hour mapping out his assassination plan.

The pretext Balint had determined upon to escape his family was another trip to his parents'—but to keep Amanda from sending the girls with him, he'd explain that the purpose of the visit was to discuss "living wills" and end-of-life planning. This conversation was a morbid affair, but one he'd been meaning to have with them for some time—and, for reasons he couldn't articulate well, even to himself, the matter had taken on an added urgency since his killing spree began. Obviously such a discussion couldn't take place in the company of small children.

Balint brewed himself a cup of coffee and read the *New York Times*. The Metropolitan Section contained a brief update on the Choker investigation, but the article revealed no new details. About twenty minutes later, Amanda appeared in the kitchen—her expression a blanket of exhaustion. His wife poured herself a glass of orange juice without acknowledging him. Balint informed her that he planned to meet his parents for lunch to review "advance directives." In response, his wife glared at him and walked out of the room.

On any other morning, Balint would have pursued her and sought to reconcile. Instead he phoned his mother to make certain that his parents would be at home when he arrived. Then he looked in on his sleeping daughters, but refrained from kissing their foreheads, as he usually did, for fear that they'd wake up and delay him. By nine A.M., he was on the road—*on his mission.*

The day was dreary and windswept, punctuated by bursts of cold rain. On the golf course, an abandoned cart rested near the center of the green—the only evidence of any human presence. Balint was reminded of the August morning half a year earlier when he'd collided with the brindled dachshund. How strange that only six months had elapsed. He could no longer remember who he'd been before he'd started plotting his revenge against Warren Sugarman.

Balint's parents were, as always, thrilled to see him. Even though it wasn't yet ten in the morning, his stepdad wore a sport jacket and bow tie. He deflected their questions about Amanda and reassured them that he'd return the following Saturday with their granddaughters. Then the three of them settled down around the table in the living room. His mother passed him a cup of coffee.

"If you'd given me more notice," she said, "I'd have prepared a hot breakfast. I'm afraid all we have are bagels and cream cheese."

"I come for the company, not the food," answered Balint—as he'd emphasized thousands of times before. "Anything new on the home front?"

"Well, the ignoramuses on the board of managers rejected my idea for distributing Iron Necks," said Henry Serspinsky, shaking his head. "I'd be lying if I didn't say I was mightily disappointed."

"They didn't see the risk?"

"Oh, no. They agreed with us about the danger. One of the numbskulls even acknowledged that my invention could save lives. The problem—Get this, Jeremy—is that they're afraid of patent infringement. According to the legal department, some guy in Arizona markets protective equipment for circus performers with a similar design."

"They call it the 'Juggler's Pal,'" interjected Balint's mother.

Serspinsky scowled. "Can you believe that? Lives are at stake and they're worried about intellectual property codes."

Balint suspected the board was relying on the other invention as an excuse, rather than as a reason, but there was no point in pulling the wool from his stepfather's eyes. "I wouldn't worry too much about the Emerald Choker," he counseled them. "If nothing else, it looks like you're beyond the southern tier of his range."

"I forgot you were the expert," said his mother. "All I can say is, if you show up one day and we have green cords wrapped around our throats, don't say we didn't warn you."

"I'm sure I'll be kicking myself," answered Balint with a smile.

His mother offered him a second bagel. "Very well. Joke about it. See if I care."

Balint wondered if his parents were genuinely concerned about the Choker, or whether they'd merely latched onto the serial killings as a way of filling their ample expanses of free time. In either case, fear of strangulation offered an excellent segue into the end-of-life conversation he'd been wanting to have for months. "On the subject of dying," he said, "I've been meaning to talk to the two of you about living wills."

"Our wills are already with the lawyer," said his mother. "Everything goes to you—except a few pieces of jewelry I'd like to leave to my cousins on the Kimball side."

"Not regular wills. *Living* wills," said Balint. He described the concept of advance directives, highlighting his concerns. Henry listened closely; his mother appeared bored. "Now I hope we don't have to deal with this for another fifty years," said Balint. "But in case something happens—let's say you get injured fighting off the Emerald Choker—it's important for me to know your wishes."

Lilly Serspinsky refilled his coffee cup. "We'll leave it to you to decide whatever you think is best. Won't we, Henry?"

"As long as I'm not in pain," said Balint's stepfather.

Balint had feared this response. "But I'd like to know what *you* want, Mom. It should be about what *you* think is best."

"Nonsense. We've raised a wonderful son—the most ethical human being on the planet, as far as Henry and I are concerned—and we have every right to trust you to make the best decisions for us. Capisce? Now we've had enough morbid conversation for one morning. Let's talk about something uplifting . . ."

Balint winced internally when his mother called him "the most ethical human being on the planet." Had his life always been filled with so many routine references to morality and justice? And was he only noticing now, for the first time, because of the circumstances? Or was this focus something new? These were purely academic questions, of course. The bottom line—and this was what mattered—was that he'd be the last person anybody might suspect of homicide.

Balint gave up his efforts to engage his parents in a discussion of advance directives, and instead they chatted about Jessie's struggles with fractions and Henry's conflict with a neighbor whom the retired veterinarian believed to be overfeeding her cat. At noon, he permitted his mother to kiss him on the cheek and then he set off for Meadow Court. His intention was to finish off his rival and still return home before two o'clock.

The dreary morning had degenerated into a dismal afternoon. Visibility dropped nearly to zero as he exited from Hager Parkway onto Chestnut Street. The weather played perfectly into his hands: if he were delayed excessively, he could always use the downpour as an excuse. At the Meadow Drive intersection, while waiting for the traffic light to change, he slipped on a never-before-worn pair of leather gloves. He'd already precut identical strands of green ribbon and transferred them from his wallet to the pocket of his jeans.

Balint circled the side streets around Meadow Drive for ten minutes, waiting for the worst of the downpour to subside. When the rain abated to a steady shower, he drew up in front of Sugarman's address. To his surprise, an unfamiliar vehicle was stationed under the basketball hoop.

He didn't dare ring the front doorbell, as he'd originally planned. Instead he once again stole into Sugarman's backyard and mounted the wooden deck. The cedar boards squeaked beneath his feet. Raindrops pattered the lid of the kettle grill. Under the eaves, he paused a moment to dry his face.

Neither the first nor the second windows revealed anything of interest. Peering inside the third window, he saw Sugarman—stark naked—holding a cocktail glass in one hand. A woman knelt in front of him—also naked, at least from the waist up. So this was what his rival had really meant when he said that he'd be pulling an all-nighter.

Balint instinctively wanted to look away, but the woman's thicket of stringy auburn hair struck him as strangely familiar. When she turned to wipe her mouth on her elbow, he was shocked to recognize the ravaged face of Gloria Sugarman/ Picardo.

———◆———

BALINT ARRIVED home weighed down with failure. Although he recognized rationally that he'd have ample other opportunities to kill Sugarman, he nonetheless felt as though a crucial moment had passed him by. His limbs hung from his body like lead. It didn't help matters any that his pants had soaked through to his underwear.

While he was changing his clothing, Amanda stormed into the bedroom.

"So you decided to come home," she said.

"I told you I'd be at my parents'."

His wife sat down at the foot of the bed. "Whatever. We really can't go on like this, Jeremy."

"What's that supposed to mean?"

Phoebe chose that unfortunate moment to run into the room. "Mommy! Can you show me how to braid Jessie's hair?"

"Not now," said Amanda. "Go to your room. Mommy and Daddy are about to have a fight."

His daughter looked toward him for a second opinion. He had no choice but to support Amanda. "We'll show you how later, princess," he said. "I promise."

Phoebe hurried away and again Balint found himself alone with his wife. He could sense that Amanda was seething.

"If we're going to have a fight," he said, "let's get it over with."

Amanda didn't answer immediately. Instead she removed her shoe and threw it against the closet door. Its heel left a black scar on the paint.

"I don't think you realize how angry I am right now," she said. "I take care of everything around here. I get the girls ready for school and I pay the bills and I make sure there's food in the refrigerator and that the laundry is done and that nobody misses their dentist appointments—and that's on top of a full-time job. Do you realize that?"

"I *do* realize that. And I really appreciate it."

"No, I don't think you do," retorted Amanda. "Because I almost never ask you for anything. At least, nothing taxing. I don't even ask where you're going or what you're doing with your time. Do you understand what I'm saying?"

"You're always welcome to ask," offered Balint.

"To what end? I'd prefer not to be lied to." So that was it: Sugarman had told her about his affair with Delilah. Now, at least, his wife's rage made more sense. "But the one time I do ask you for something—something important to me—you make a total goddamn mockery of it."

"You mean Davey Sugarman?"

"What the fuck is wrong with you?" demanded his wife. "What else could I possibly mean?"

"Look, I'm sorry—"

"Not only did you hurt that poor boy's feelings, but you undermined my authority in front of Jessie. I don't need to be humiliated in front of my own daughter. I swear to you, Jeremy, I won't put up with that."

He'd been an idiot not to foresee this happening. Of course, Sugarman had told her. What better way to distract her from his own double-dealing?

"I'm sorry," he said. "It won't happen again."

"You bet your ass it won't," cried Amanda. "I'm going to invite that child over for a play date with Jessica next week and you're going to welcome the poor boy with open arms— like he's the fucking King of Siam. Got it? Because if you don't, I swear to God, I'll castrate you in your sleep."

———

BALINT WAS still reeling from his fight with Amanda when—at precisely eight o'clock the following morning—he received a call summoning him to the office of chairman of the medicine department. Nothing good ever came out of such an urgent meeting, he knew, although he couldn't figure out specifically what he'd done wrong. Surely they couldn't blame him for the intoxicated cardiology fellow, especially since he'd removed the offending trainee from duty immediately. The only transgression he'd committed of late—unless one included his killing spree—was his affair with Delilah, and he didn't imagine that was the sort of offense that the chairman gave a rat's ass about. But when he stepped into Dr. Sanditz's office, one glance at the eminent nephrologist's flinty face told him that he'd screwed up royally.

Bruce Sanditz has once been a leading researcher on glomerular diseases at Johns Hopkins, but in his fifties, after several Nobel-prize-caliber discoveries, he'd given up the laboratory for a cushy administrative appointment at Laurendale. On the whole, he was widely regarded as a benevolent and easygoing chairman. As long as you brought in grants and your division ran in the black, he rarely gave you a hard time. Sanditz also had a dark sense of humor, and a penchant for practical jokes: for instance, he'd once distributed a memo asking for suggestions on setting up a program for live-donor heart transplants—obviously in jest—and then he'd posted the earnest protests he'd received from indignant colleagues on a bulletin board in the faculty lounge. Yet Balint had seen his boss display genuine anger on several prior occasions, most memorably when a junior attending complained about the cost of tickets to the department's annual banquet. That junior attending—otherwise very talented—had been shocked to discover that his employment contract wasn't renewed the following year. In short, Bruce Sanditz was not a man to cross.

The chairman beckoned for Balint to take a seat. "Jeremy," he said, "I hope I didn't drag you away from anything important."

"Not at all," lied Balint.

He actually had three catheterizations lined up for that morning.

"Let me ask you something. Something personal," said Sanditz in a voice that gave away nothing. "What's the hardest decision you've ever made?"

"Do you mean in medicine?"

"In anything," said Sanditz. "*In life.*"

Balint saw where this was going. He could already envision the chairman saying, *Well, the hardest decision I ever have to make is when I relieve a division chief of his duties. Unfortunately, in your case, I can see no other way . . .*

His situation, he recognized, was desperate. A day earlier, he'd been on the brink of pulling off the murder of the century, but now he was just a peon about to be sent packing. That was the cruel reality that lurked beneath life's surface: *everyone* was expendable. The president resigns and they swear in a new president. The queen dies and they find another queen. But in this case, he refused to go down without a fight.

Balint actually contemplated answering the chairman's question truthfully. How could he possibly forget the most difficult decision of his life? He had been seven years old and they were on a family trip to visit his mother's cousins, the Kimballs. The Kimballs had a daughter, Beatrice, six months older than he was, who had been born missing most of her facial bones; even with multiple surgeries, she still looked hideous—and Balint had been terrified of her. That day, pressured by his parents to "be nice" to his deformed cousin, he'd played a game of hide-and-seek with her—and Beatrice had made the mistake of concealing herself inside the refrigerator in the Kimballs' basement. Balint had heard her pounding inside, listened to her screaming that she couldn't get out, but he hadn't told anyone. He'd simply gone back upstairs to play with his own toys. He couldn't even explain why. When they found Beatrice Kimball eight hours later, after a frantic search, she'd already asphyxiated. Nobody had ever suspected him of any wrongdoing—and, looking back, he wasn't convinced he'd done anything *that* wrong. It wasn't as though he'd locked his cousin in the refrigerator. The girl had done it to herself. And then a crazy notion popped into his head: if he revealed this remote incident to Sanditz, the confession might unsettle the chairman enough to derail his boss's plan to fire him.

"My hardest decision," replied Balint—returning to his senses. "When I was seventeen, I rescued a drowning woman at the beach. It seems like an obvious choice in hindsight, but I might easily have been carried out to sea by the riptide. I still remember the split second before I jumped into the ocean—the moment of reckoning when I decided to risk my own life to save someone else."

"Good. Very good," said Sanditz. "Do you know what the most difficult decision I've had to make is?"

Here it comes, thought Balint. "Sometimes a decision is difficult for a reason," he ventured. "Sometimes it even requires reconsideration . . ."

"Nonsense," replied Sanditz. "I make a decision and I stick with it. That's the medical man's creed, isn't it? Sometimes right but always certain."

"I guess so."

"So the hardest decision I've ever had to make," said Sanditz, "relates to this award from the American College of Physicians." Suddenly, the chairman's eyes twinkled, and then a grin spread across his face. "I was going to nominate Andy Price, the leukemia guy, for that mission hospital he set up in Haiti. I also hear that Price saved *your* life, by the way—that you narrowly missed getting yourself decapitated by a crazy person. But then I learned about the great work you've been doing at that free clinic in Newark, and I decided you're the better man for the part. Price will have his chances. Only not this time."

Balint struggled to wrap his mind around his reprieve. "What award?" he stammered.

"It's called the Wenger Award for Ethics in Medicine. Two hundred grand—no strings attached. To be given to a clinician who has mastered the art of ethical decision-making. Every institution can nominate one candidate." Sanditz leaned forward and his balding crown reflected the overhead light. "There are no guarantees, mind you, but the head of the selection committee did his post-doc under me—and that certainly won't hurt."

Balint started to regain his composure. "Thank you. I'm really honored."

"Send me your updated CV and I'll write you a letter," said Sanditz. The chairman chuckled. "Confess, Jeremy. You thought you were in the doghouse, didn't you?"

"You did catch me off guard."

Sanditz leaned back in his swivel chair. "You've got nothing to worry about, Dr. Balint. I like you. You remind me *of me* when I was an up-and-coming division chief at Hopkins. There's not much you could do to get on my bad side . . . I suppose you might start embezzling funds or killing off your patients, but short of that, you're golden. At least, as long as I'm chairman around here, and I'm planning on being carried out of this office in a pine box, so you're a very lucky man." The smile vanished from Sanditz's face as rapidly as it had appeared. "Of course, don't go testing me . . ."

"Thanks for the vote of confidence," said Balint. "I really appreciate it."

"Nonsense. No need to thank me." Sanditz glanced at his watch. "If you want to thank anyone, it's Sugarman in surgery who deserves the credit."

"Warren Sugarman?"

"That's the only Sugarman we've got, as far as I know," said Sanditz. "First-rate young fellow. Between you and me, he's been taking my Jeanine out for the last couple of months and he's made quite an impression on Angela and myself."

"Sugarman's dating your daughter?"

"Off the record. No need to jinx things. But we had him over for dinner last Friday night and he spent the entire meal talking you up. He says you and your wife have taken his son under your wings. Quite frankly, that's what ultimately sold me on you for the award."

"It's mostly my wife's doing," said Balint. "Amanda is good with children."

"Sugarman made it sound as though you were *both* equally responsible," replied Sanditz. "And I see no reason to doubt him."

"That was very kind of him," said Balint, clenching his fist in his pocket. "I know just the way to thank him."

Somehow, Sugarman's kindness—assuming he lacked an ulterior motive—was even more infuriating than his betrayal. Never, not even when he first discovered the affair, had he despised another human being so much.

———

BALINT's MEETING with Sanditz swept away his despair. He again found himself as determined as ever to murder Sugarman at the first opportunity. Unfortunately, he had no reason to expect another easy opening to arise.

Most of the week passed in a whirlwind of clinical duties: Balint filled in for the scheduled service attending on Monday and Tuesday after the assigned cardiologist came down with the flu, and on Wednesday afternoon, he delivered the first of his annual lectures to the medical students. At night he churned out draft after draft of his "statement of purpose" for the Wenger Award. Even Amanda was delighted to learn about the nomination—and she managed to share the news with half of Laurendale. Yet through all of this, the itch to murder was never far from Balint's thoughts.

And then fate twisted in his direction one final time. On Friday, after dinner, Amanda came down with a stomach bug. Hardly an hour passed that night without his wife racing to the bathroom to vomit. In her condition, it seemed highly improbable that she'd be meeting up with Warren Sugarman the next day for a romantic interlude.

"You'd better leave the girls at your mother's overnight. Better than letting me get everybody sick," she instructed him as he prepared for their biweekly drive out to Hager Heights. "Tell her I'll pick them up tomorrow evening when I feel better." It was theoretically possible, of course, that his wife was faking—that her illness was part of a scheme to get the girls out of the house. But that made little sense. After all, she'd have had an opportunity to meet up with Sugarman either way. And since Balint was returning home that afternoon, she wouldn't have gained any extra time alone.

To Balint, Amanda's illness offered the second chance he'd been hoping for. Even Sugarman was unlikely to arrange a substitute tryst at the last minute, so he felt relatively confident that he'd find his victim home alone. His parents proved so excited to see their granddaughters that they didn't notice his early departure from lunch.

Balint stopped at the Meadow Drive intersection and pulled on his gloves. Outside, the air was mild for early March. Crocus heads poked from the dead earth alongside Sugarman's front path. Today the driveway stood vacant. All that lay beneath the basketball hoop was a puddle streaked with oil. Balint drew in a deep breath and rang the bell.

Sugarman answered the door almost instantly, looking dapper in a silk smoking jacket. He carried a Champagne flute in one hand. "Balint! What a surprise!"

"I was in the neighborhood. I hope you don't mind . . ."

"Not at all. Not at all."

Sugarman invited him inside and steered them into the den. The room hadn't changed since their dinner the previous September, except for a goldfish bowl at the end of the bar. A stack of journal abstracts lay on one of the love seats.

The surgeon noticed him looking at the goldfish. "Davey won him last week at the Purim carnival," he said. "I figured it was better to leave him here than to take him back to Gloria's. I mean: it's only a matter of time before he goes down the toilet."

"Not just him," said Balint. "All of us."

Sugarman laughed. "You have a point there. If you choose to look at it that way . . ."

Balint related the tale of Phoebe's gourami. While he talked, he scanned his surroundings for weapons. One option was a fireplace poker, but these stood at the far end of the room—and he didn't see how he could slide one from its iron holder rapidly enough. On the table nearest him rested a kaleidoscope and a wooden African statuette, but both looked rather flimsy. And then he caught sight of a marble ashtray on the opposite table. At present, the ashtray brimmed with hard candies.

"So? To what do I owe the pleasure?" asked Sugarman.

"You must have some idea why I'm here," taunted Balint. "Take a guess."

"I honestly haven't an inkling . . . But hold that thought, Balint, while I top off my glass. Incidentally, can I offer you a drink? I'm out of whiskey glasses—but the bourbon itself is first-rate . . ."

Sugarman walked toward the bar, exposing the back of his skull to Balint. This was his opportunity. "Scotch and soda," he said. As soon as the words had safely crossed his lips, he scooped the ashtray from the table and carried it toward his enemy. At the last moment, Sugarman caught sight of his attacker's reflection in the mirror behind the bar—but too late. He turned his head and raised his arm just as Balint brought the hunk of marble down upon him. The blow caught him in the temple and he staggered backward, toppling into the row of bar stools.

Sugarman tried to rise from the carpet, but Balint slugged him with the ashtray once again. This time, the thud of stone against flesh resounded across the den. The wide-eyed, unconscious face of Balint's rival stared up at him. He clasped Sugarman by the throat and squeezed the life from his body until the man's tongue dangled from his lips. He looked just as Balint had envisioned he would: face mottled and bloated, ears bloodshot at the tips. As he eased the surgeon's lifeless body to the floor, Balint sensed the heavy burden of death in the weight of the corpse. It all felt surreal.

He spread out his rival's corpse alongside the sofa and tied each of the six green ribbons around the dead man's neck. Never again, he realized, would he hear the oafish welcome of "Balint!" rising from his rival's throat; never again would he have to endure imagining those coarse hands fondling Amanda's breasts. This was checkmate. He had challenged God to a game of chess—and he had trounced Him.

Balint felt only one emotion: relief. Less than a minute later, he was cruising along Hamilton Boulevard with hardly a care in the world.

ACT III

CHAPTER ELEVEN

Balint arrived early for the monthly heart-transplant summit the following Monday. He'd spent the previous afternoon glued to the radio in his study, but if the police had found Warren Sugarman's corpse, they weren't yet publicizing the discovery. Amanda hadn't intruded upon him—but she'd clearly suspected something amiss, because each time he'd visited the kitchen to replenish his coffee, she'd had her cell phone pressed to her ear. Presumably she'd been dialing her lover—now her *former* lover—and, needless to say, Sugarman hadn't answered her calls. By breakfast that morning, Balint's wife had appeared blatantly anxious, but he pretended not to notice. Similarly he feigned surprise when Sugarman didn't appear to chair the transplant meeting.

The summit would serve no purpose without a surgeon present who could agree to list the prospective organ recipients under his name. Balint nibbled on his croissant and skimmed his *New York Times*, waiting for a man he knew would never arrive. In fact, this would be the last early morning conference he'd have to attend for quite some time, he expected, because he'd recently learned that Chester Pastarnack—Sugarman's only potential short-term replacement—had accepted a position as a paid consultant to a venture capital firm and relocated to Arizona.

"I got a ride home from Warren on Friday," reported one of the anesthesiologists. "I even said to him, see you bright and early on Monday. He didn't mention a word about not being here."

The senior nursing coordinator gathered together her files. It was already 7:20. "Let's hope he's all right." When she stood up, that somehow granted permission for the other attendees to disperse.

Balint accompanied the German consult-liaison psychiatrist into the corridor. "I have served on this committee twenty-six years," said the headshrinker. "Under Chester Pastarnack and before that under Allan Drevitz and before Drevitz under Rachel Glendening. *Not once* did any of them stand us up."

"Something must have happened," said Balint—trying to sound just as he might have on any other occasion. "This is so unlike Warren."

The psychiatrist snorted. "Dr. Glendening chaired this meeting once when she was nine months pregnant. The woman was practically in labor. You don't surmise Dr. Sugarman is giving birth to a child, do you?"

Balint wasn't sure whether the question was rhetorical.

"I doubt it," he said.

"In that case," answered the shrink, "I am highly disappointed."

The word 'disappointed' from her lips suggested something closer to outrage.

———

LAURENDALE COUNTY's Sheriff Ralph Spitford, announced the murder in a hastily arranged press conference shortly after noon. The sheriff was a broad-shouldered African American officer who wore his sunglasses perched on his forehead. His cousin was Reverend Spotty Spitford, the perennial left-wing presidential candidate. Unlike Chief Putnam or Detective Mazzotta, Spitford *looked* like a cop. He answered reporters' questions in short, declarative sentences, as though pained to part with each syllable. Balint caught the tail end of the announcement during a quick foray into the cafeteria for a sandwich. In pairs and small groups, physicians and nurses stood transfixed around the television screens. Intermittently Balint heard Sugarman's name and that of the Emerald Choker rising above the murmurs of alarm. A female surgery resident hurried past him toward the women's restroom, tears streaming down her cheeks.

Balint strolled back to his office suite, his hands in his pockets. He resisted the overwhelming urge to whistle a cheerful tune.

News of Sugarman's murder ricocheted swiftly through the hospital. Shortly before four o'clock, the vice president for external affairs sent out an e-mail message confirming the death and recapping the victim's "illustrious" career. Balint wrote back on a whim, suggesting the creation of a memorial fund for Sugarman's son. By the end of the workday, to his considerable amusement, he found himself in charge of a drive to raise college tuition for Davey Sugarman. Waiting at the elevator bay, Balint kept thinking to himself: *I'm not going to run into Warren Sugarman. Never again.* Although he'd been looking forward to this moment for many months, even he found himself genuinely surprised at how much pleasure he derived from knowing that he'd never again share another elevator car or endure another promenade across the parking garage in the company of his wife's lover. On his way out of the building, Balint noticed that the hospital's national and state flags had been lowered to half-mast.

Myron Salt caught up with him at the snack stand in the lobby, where Balint was buying a chocolate cruller for the drive home.

"You heard about Sugarman?" asked Salt.

"It's awful. I'm practically shaking."

He paid for his donut and waited while the neurologist ordered a latte.

"The Emerald Choker," said Salt. "You *read* about these things. You don't really believe they could happen to someone you know."

"It's uncanny."

"I played squash with him on Saturday morning," said Salt. "Or rather, I played squash *against* him. You know how Warren was about winning . . ."

"Losing certainly wasn't his style."

He registered that Salt was speaking of Sugarman in the past tense—and he dug his teeth into his lower lip to fight off an involuntary smile.

"And now I'm thinking, we were playing squash and he had only hours to live. And then I'm thinking, what if that lunatic had followed *me* home instead of Warren? What if *I'd* been the one who got wrapped up in ribbon?"

"You think you were followed?"

"I don't have a clue. I'm just saying . . ."

The squash game came as a surprise to Balint. It meant Sugarman must have returned from his racquet club only a short time before Balint rang his doorbell—that he had lucked out to find his rival at home. For all he knew, the entire Institutional Review Board proposal of the previous weekend might have been an outright lie to conceal plans with Amanda, plans foiled when Balint insisted upon leaving the girls in her care.

Gloria might merely have been a last-minute stand-in. What a relief, he reflected, that this weekend Sugarman had substituted a sporting match for a stymied tryst rather than another romance.

"It still hasn't sunk in," said Balint—striving to strike the right chord. "Warren—of all people! It goes to show that no good deed goes unpunished."

"How so?" asked Salt.

Balint hadn't anticipated having to explain himself. "All I'm saying is that Warren was one of the kindest, most generous, upstanding human beings I've ever met—and it's hard to see how, in a fair world, he'd be the one to get murdered."

Myron Salt laughed, but with a glance around them, as though Balint had told an off-color joke. "Warren? *Upstanding*? Now that's some radical historical revisionism if ever I heard it. Warren was a philandering prick and a selfish bastard. And he was also my best friend since second grade, so I should know."

"You certainly don't mince words," said Balint.

"I cared about him too much when he was alive to lie about him now that he's dead."

Their conversation paused while they passed through the revolving doors into a wintry mix of snow and slush. Myron Salt opened his umbrella.

"How are *you* doing?" he asked Balint. "I figured if there were any residual effects from your boxing match, I'd have heard from you by now."

"I'm back to baseline—at least as far as I can tell. I suppose I could have major deficits without realizing it."

"*You* might not realize it," answered Salt. "But your wife would. Half the calls I get these days are from concerned spouses. Only last week, a woman whose husband I'd treated phoned me and said, 'He's more or less back to normal—except he's been going to work wearing only one shoe and sock.'" The neurologist laughed again. "Isn't that classic? *Only one shoe and sock.* I guess it's all a matter of your perspective on normal.

"Anyway," said Salt, "I'm glad to see you're wearing shoes on both feet."

He wished Balint a safe trip home and set out into the darkness.

BALINT HAD expected to find Amanda on the verge of a breakdown. To his surprise, his wife greeted him as though nothing were amiss. She was camped out at the kitchen table, surrounded by balls of crumpled paper, navigating Jessie through her math homework. "Dinner's running late," she apologized. "Phoebe left her backpack at school and I had to drive her there to pick it up." How well she's taking this, thought Balint—or, more accurately, what a great show she's putting on. But then it struck him that she didn't know. Why should she? What was devastating news bound to spread rapidly through the hospital might not seem nearly as significant at the public library, where most likely nobody other than Amanda had ever heard of Warren Sugarman. Before today, at least. As he listened to his wife explain how to convert fractions into decimals, he grew increasingly convinced that she wasn't faking.

After a twelve-hour workday, Balint's stomach gnawed with hunger. He realized that his wife wasn't to blame for their late dinner, but the delay irritated him nonetheless. When he failed to find a satisfactory snack in the refrigerator that might tide him over until the meal, a cruel impulse got the best of him. "What a crazy day at the hospital," he said. "I imagine you heard the news about Sugarman."

Amanda looked up, concerned. "What news?"

Balint sorted though the day's mail—forcing himself to appear indifferent.

"*What news?*" she demanded again. "Did something happen to Warren?"

"You really don't know?"

"Oh my God. Is he hurt?"

He looked up from the mail—wearing an expression of polite concern.

"Not hurt . . . Dead," he said. "Murdered."

A subtle change swept across Amanda's face: her eyebrows slanted closer together and the muscles around her mouth tightened. To Balint, attuned to these subtle nuances, it was as though he were watching as the final vestiges of youthful beauty drained from his wife's features. She set down her calculator. Jessie recognized her mother's distress and dropped her pencil.

"I don't believe you," said Amanda.

Balint continued to sort through the mail. "Why would I make that up?"

"You know exactly why . . . To torment me. To throw things in my face. If this is your idea of a joke, Jeremy, it's not the slightest bit amusing. It's sick."

"Do I sound like I'm joking?"

Amanda's eyes were fixed on him. "Jessie, please go watch TV."

"Are you mad, Mommy?"

"No, darling, I'm not mad. But Daddy and I need to talk. About adult things."

Their daughter didn't protest further. A moment later, they were alone. Amanda held her arms to chest as though to protect herself from attack.

"Did you do something to Warren?" she demanded.

"*Me?* Nothing. It was the Emerald Choker."

A puzzled look sparked in his wife's eyes, and color surged into her cheeks. "You *are* fucking with me. You bastard!"

Balint feared she might throw something at him—something more lethal than a high-heeled shoe. "If you don't believe me, turn on the news . . ."

Amanda rose in silence and crossed the room to the vintage black-and-white television that perched on the countertop. They'd inherited it from her father when he passed away—rabbit ears and all. She turned on the device and flipped through the channels to the six o'clock news. On the screen, a grizzled crime reporter in a trench coat broadcast from Meadow Court; while he spoke, the camera cut to footage of a body bag being removed from Sugarman's home.

"It can't be . . ." gasped Amanda.

"Satisfied?" asked Balint. "I don't blame you for not believing me. When you get right down to it, what are the odds that someone we know would be murdered by a serial killer? It's going to be a challenge for the transplant program . . ."

Amanda switched off the television.

"Are you okay?" he asked.

His wife shook her head. Her face had turned a ghastly shade of ash. She didn't cry. She didn't move. She merely stood with her back leaning against the counter, paralyzed with grief, staring blankly out at the room. If she'd exploded with rage or collapsed into tears, Balint might have savored his payback. But his mind didn't know how to process Amanda's catatonic agony, an emotion utterly alien to him, and the longer she remained mute and motionless, the less pleasure he could find in his success. That brief interval—before his wife regained control of her senses and inquired after Sugarman's funeral—was the only time when Balint entertained the notion that he'd actually done something wrong.

THE NEXT few days were the most critical for Balint's scheme. Up until now, he'd had no connection to his victims; as long as he wasn't spotted entering or exiting their homes, and didn't leave incriminating evidence at the crime scenes, the authorities had no way of tracing their deaths to his doorstep. In contrast, he'd been deeply enmeshed in Sugarman's life. Even a superficial investigation of his rival's personal affairs would have uncovered multiple motives for Balint to kill him. Yet for all of his apprehension, the police and the public never considered the slaying as anything other than a random act of violence perpetrated by a lunatic. The media reported every minute detail of the crime, and hailed the glories of Sugarman's medical career, but no mention was made of his pending divorce or his multiple mistresses or the dead dog he'd discovered seven months earlier in his rose bushes.

In the immediate aftermath of the killing, Sheriff Spitford established a command center inside a mobile trailer opposite Sugarman's house. His deputies knocked on every door within a square-mile radius in search of witnesses. Meanwhile across the New York City Metropolitan Area, what had previously been a matter of passing concern increasingly gave way to general panic. The networks ran stories about extended families that had temporarily moved in together so elderly parents or unmarried siblings wouldn't find themselves alone with the Choker. The authorities compounded this anxiety with mass e-mail messages and text alerts offering "safety tips" to protect oneself from attack. Neighborhood patrols, like the one proposed by Henry Serspinsky, sprang up in housing projects and sleepy exurbs. All of these efforts occurred against a background of wild speculation by various self-proclaimed experts on unsolved crimes. Using various algorithms, these experts predicted the precise locations of the next murders—which they claimed would occur in sites as varied as suburban

Albany and on the steps of the Chrysler Building. Nobody ever seemed to question that another slaying would ultimately occur, that the culprit might not simply rest on his laurels and retire. One British website even offered pari-mutuel betting on the location of the next killing and the demographics of future victims.

In the absence of clear progress in apprehending the killer, the media focused on supposed tensions among the various investigators. Days passed before Sheriff Spitford was invited to join Chief Putnam's task force, fueling further rumors of disagreement over strategy. Putnam and Mazzotta apparently wanted to devote resources to finding the "missing" body of the hypothetical victim who'd been tagged with four ribbons. Spitford doubted the existence of a fifth fatality. He'd been quoted as saying, during a closed-door meeting, "I won't be dragged on a wild goose chase, when there probably isn't any goose. That extra ribbon was a twisted joke. You can bet your Sherlock Holmes hats that the perpetrator is laughing his ass off at us right now." But Putnam and Mazzotta weren't convinced; they didn't believe sociopaths were capable of pranks. Isabel Crosby from *Trenton Today* claimed that Spitford and the founders of the task force were no longer on speaking terms, although all parties vehemently denied this charge. Crosby also broke the news that State Senate Majority Leader Veronica Sanchez-McCord was receiving electroshock therapy for depression at an out-of-state clinic.

In keeping with Jewish tradition, Warren Sugarman's burial occurred on the first day following the discovery of his body. The previous evening, Balint's home telephone had rung shortly after eleven o'clock, while Amanda was in the girls' bedroom, comforting Phoebe over a nightmare. He let the answering machine pick up. Only when he heard Bruce Sanditz's stentorian voice on the tape did he race into the kitchen for the receiver. Never before, as far as he could recall, had his boss called him at home—certainly not in the middle of the night. "Sorry," he apologized. "I'm here."

"Glad I caught you awake," replied Dr. Sanditz. "You have a minute?"

"For you, an hour," agreed Balint. "What's going on?"

Through the plaster, he heard Amanda reading another bedtime story to Phoebe.

"My sense is that you and Warren Sugarman were good friends, right?"

Balint felt his stomach roiling. "You could say that," he conceded.

"Good. Because I need another eulogy for tomorrow's memorial," said the chairman. "I agreed to coordinate this damn thing for Jeanine's sake—they were practically engaged, just so you know—but I'm having a doozy of a time lining up speakers. So far, all I have is Myron Salt from neurology. Can I count on you for a brief speech? It doesn't have to run more than five to ten minutes."

"Are you sure?" asked Balint. "What about a surgeon?"

"I tried. They all said no. I'd never say this in front of Jeanine, but that fellow had more enemies than I ever would have guessed. So can you help me out?"

Balint agreed. What choice did he have? Unfortunately public speaking had never been one of his strong suits, and he stayed up another four hours churning out a draft of his remarks. Yet as he jotted down platitudes of praise, he cursed Sugarman's memory. The bastard was having one last laugh, even from beyond the grave. When Balint arrived at Sewell Auditorium for the ten o'clock tribute, accompanied by Amanda, his eyes were bloodshot from exhaustion. According to the photocopied program, a graveside service in Elizabeth Lakes would follow the memorial.

The turnout amazed Balint. For a man who'd so recently run short on eulogists, Sugarman attracted more than his fair share of mourners—or, at least, of the idly curious. Balint recognized many of his colleagues in the crowd, including Andy Price from hematology, Sid Crandall from endocrinology, and even Dr. Liao, the visiting Taiwanese pulmonologist who'd subbed for him at the free clinic. There were also faces he hadn't seen in years: Allan Drevitz, the retired surgeon who'd directed the transplant program before Pastarnack; a social work coordinator with an artificial voice box who'd retired when Balint was still an intern. And there were countless mourners he didn't recognize at all—including a disproportionate number of attractive young females. At the urging of Dr. Sanditz, Balint and Amanda settled into the second row. Myron Salt and his most recent wife—his much younger wife—sat to their right. In the front row, on the opposite aisle, Rabbi Steinhoff conferred with Gloria Sugarman/Picardo. The late surgeon's son squirmed in his nearby seat and tugged at his necktie. Immediately in front of Balint, the chairman's daughter wept softly into her mother's shoulder.

"I had no idea Sugarman had so many friends," he said to Amanda.

His wife looked at him as though she hardly recognized him. "There are lots of things you don't know. As hard as that is for you to imagine." Amanda didn't sound angry, merely depleted. She'd hardly spoken to him since she'd learned of her lover's death. Balint considered reaching for her hand—but he feared that she might pull away. He didn't want to risk forcing their reconciliation prematurely.

At precisely five minutes after ten, Steinhoff stepped to the lectern and welcomed the mourners. On this occasion, the young rabbi did not appear to be in any hurry; his cellular phone was nowhere to be seen. He offered a prayer—in both English and Hebrew—and then yielded the floor to Bruce Sanditz. As though the microphone were a hot potato, the chairman quickly handed it over to Myron Salt. Only then did Balint examine the program more carefully. He had not merely been billed as the final speaker, it turned out; he was described as Sugarman's "lifelong friend." Listening to Myron Salt tell stories of his boyhood antics with the dead man growing up in Bergen County—how they'd trapped a songbird and placed it inside their third grade teacher's desk drawer, and how Salt had slept on Sugarman's couch after each of his divorces—Balint's own prepared remarks about the deceased man's "collegial spirit" and surgical skills felt woefully inadequate. He wished he'd had Delilah beside him for moral support, rather than Amanda's cool civility.

"And our final tribute of the morning," announced Dr. Sanditz after Salt returned to his seat, "is Warren's closest friend both from college and from medical school, the chief of our own division of cardiology, Dr. Jeremy Balint."

Balint stepped up to the podium. The stage lights nearly blinded him for an instant, but soon his eyes adjusted. In front of him, only inches from his feet, Jeanine Sanditz sniffled into a tissue. A few yards to his left, Gloria bore a stoic grimace. Amanda's face remained an inscrutable blank. All at once, the cardiologist was struck by how much human suffering Warren Sugarman had caused. If he'd had any doubts about wiping out his rival, as his eyes panned across each of these betrayed, grieving women, Balint felt himself thoroughly and unequivocally vindicated. That was what he truly wanted to talk about: Vindication. Justice. With each passing second, the silence in the auditorium grew heavier. He removed his prepared remarks from his breast pocket and glanced over them; then he set them aside.

"It is only fitting that our beloved friend and colleague, Warren Sugarman, was murdered by the Emerald Choker," he declared, "because it reminds us that it requires an enormous evil to eradicate as powerful a force for good as was Warren." His voice rose as his confidence grew. "I used to joke with Warren that if he had been born Catholic, they'd have made him a saint. His response was always the same: he warned me not to let his secret out of the bag. Because Warren's modesty and deep humility kept him from publicizing his most generous deeds. For instance, many of you remember Warren's 'vacation' in Peru last year. But how many of you know that Warren secretly donated all of the proceeds from his industry-sponsored lectures to free clinics in Lima . . . ?"

None of them knew about donations to the free clinics, of course, because they'd never taken place. Nor had the nights in medical school when Sugarman allowed homeless former patients to crash on the couch in his dormitory room. For nearly half an hour, Balint rattled off his rival's unheralded good deeds—his life-saving bone-marrow donations, the hours he volunteered recording medical journals for blind physicians, the many occasions when together they skipped their Columbia classes and served meals at a South Bronx soup kitchen. "The world's indigent and downtrodden had had no greater ally," avowed Balint, "than the late Warren Sugarman." His portrait of the murder victim was complete nonsense, but nobody was in any position to object.

"At the time of his death," Balint concluded, "Warren had just told me that he planned on donating one of his kidneys to a complete stranger. *What do I need with an extra kidney?* he asked. And while, as we all know, Warren never had an opportunity to give that kidney away while here with us on earth, I'd like to believe he's already had himself listed as an organ donor in heaven." By the end of his eulogy, Balint had been so moved by his own words that he found himself wiping tears from his eyes.

Gloria thanked him for his kind remarks. Jeanine Sanditz assured him that he'd captured perfectly "the essence" of the Warren she'd known and loved. Etan Steinhoff patted him on the back and reminded him that he'd make a fine rabbi. Balint also received handshakes and hugs from dozens of strangers.

The interment itself was a far more intimate affair. Only a handful of friends followed the hearse to the cemetery. A bitter chill had dropped the temperature below freezing. Steinhoff said the mourners' *kaddish* and the *shema*, then read the twenty-third Psalm. Balint took his turn shoveling soil onto the casket. By two o'clock, the body rested underground and they were headed back to Laurendale.

Amanda didn't utter one word on their drive home. He feared that she alone might have seen through his lavish praise of Sugarman—that his wife might even have interpreted his remarks as mockery. But time, Balint knew, was on his side. His rival no longer had a dog in the fight. Now that he'd eliminated the competition, Balint was ready to start rebuilding his marriage.

———

AMANDA HAD taken a bereavement day at the library, but Balint was still planning to see patients in the late afternoon. He pulled up in front of their home and waited for his wife to exit the car. "What are you doing?" she asked.

"Dropping you off. I have a four o'clock patient."

She didn't respond at first. After a pause, she said, "Would you please come inside? I'd like to have a conversation with you."

"Can it wait until tonight?"

"No," replied Amanda. "It *cannot* wait until tonight."

So Balint shut off the engine and followed her into the house. He sensed she was displeased with his eulogy, but he didn't see why their discussion couldn't be postponed until after supper. Amanda keyed off the burglar alarm and hung her coat in the closet; then she climbed the stairs to their bedroom and slumped down on the bedspread. He stood opposite her, leaning against his exercise bike. Neither of them had turned on the overhead fixture, so a cloak of pale winter sunlight draped over the room.

He decided to preempt her. "If you're upset about something I said at the memorial, I want you to know that I did the best I could on short notice."

Amanda shrugged. "I'd like you to do something for me. Something important."

"Sure. Anything—if it's *that* important."

"It *is* important." Her eyes focused on her hands; Balint could hardly hear her voice. "I'd like you to move out."

That hadn't been what he'd anticipated. He willed himself to remain calm—as he did on the rare occasions when a patient suffered a cardiac arrest in his office. "You're upset. And maybe you have a right to be upset. But is this really what you want? Jesus, Amanda. Nine years is a long time. Once you've had a chance to think things over, you may see them differently."

"I'm not upset, Jeremy. I have every right to be upset, but I'm not. And I *have* thought things through. Now if you care about me the slightest bit—or even if you don't—I'm asking you to pack your things and move out."

A shiver ran up Balint's spine. His eyes darted around the bedroom—the room they'd shared for nearly a decade. On the carpet in front of the bookcase lay his wife's valise, still half-packed from their trip to Disney World. An unfinished latch-hook rug rested on her nightstand. It seemed impossible that at the very moment he'd finally removed the chief obstacle to their happiness, his wife suddenly wanted out.

"May I ask why?" he asked.

Amanda nodded. "If what you said today at Warren's service wasn't true—and I doubt it was—then you're a total asshole and I'm ashamed to be married to you. But if for some reason it were true—if Warren really did lead this double life as a saint and a bone-marrow donor, then that reminded me that I'm married to the wrong person. I don't love you, Jeremy. It's that simple."

"You mean you're not *in love* with me. That happens. After seven, eight, nine years, marriages change."

"You're not listening to me, Jeremy. I'm not *in love* with you. That's true. But it's not what I'm saying. I don't *love* you. Period. The sad part is that I haven't loved you for a very long time . . . If not for Warren, I'd have left you ages ago."

"Warren?"

"Don't pretend, okay? I'm tired of pretending. You know I was having an affair with Warren and I know you're screwing some nursing student—and the only reason I didn't say something sooner was that Warren preferred it this way. On account of Gloria, before they split up, and then for his son . . ." Amanda rose from the bed. "So now you see why I think that it's best for you to move out."

"Why should *I* move out?" demanded Balint. He felt his anger mounting; he cupped his fist in his palm. "*You* were fucking Warren Sugarman so *I* should move out. That doesn't make a hell of a lot of sense."

"Okay, I'll move out," Amanda replied without emotion. "I'll move out and you drive Phoebe to her violin lessons and buy Jessie's favorite brand of ice pops and call the water company next month to turn the sprinklers back on for the summer. Do you have any fucking idea what it's like to run a house, Jeremy? Do you know how to prepare the estimated taxes for the accountant? Or how often the flue should be swept out so the fireplace doesn't explode? My God, I bet you don't even know the names of your daughters' teachers!"

"Mrs. Duncrest and Miss Grossman."

"That was last year," Amanda corrected him. "I don't think you have the slightest clue how to do what I do every day. Not a fucking clue. But if you want to try, goddammit, be my guest."

Balint realized that his entire future depended on what he said next, but he could no longer conceive of a path forward—at least, not one in which he persuaded Amanda to change her mind. Her offer hung in the air like poison. Balint's body felt as frigid as ice.

"I don't want to try," he murmured.

"What?"

"I said, *I don't want to try.*"

Amanda retrieved her purse from the bed. "I'm going to pick your daughters up from school and I'm going to take them to Animal Palace for dinner. Please don't be here when I get back."

Again she'd caught him off guard. "You can't really expect me to move out right now?" he asked. "Where am I supposed to go?"

His wife walked to the door. "Where do you go when you're claiming you're at dinner talks and continuing education conferences?" she asked. "You're a smart guy, Jeremy—and you have a gift for deception. I'm sure you'll figure something out."

Amanda disappeared into the corridor, leaving him alone in the shadow-filled room. "What about the girls?" he called after her. "What are you going to tell them?" But she was already gone.

For the longest minute of his life, Balint stared at the spot where she'd been standing. Then he adjusted to his new situation and started packing clothes and toiletries into his suitcases. What other option remained? He'd have to rent a room at the Hager Heights Motor Inn until he could find an apartment. And once he was settled into his new lodgings, he'd have to murder again. Two more times. What a waste, he thought. What a nuisance. But it was far too late to alter his course, so he would still have to sacrifice two more lives for the sake of a marriage that could no longer be salvaged.

CHAPTER TWELVE

From the outset, Balint had understood that he'd have to kill six times—now seven, counting each of the Rockingham slayings separately. He'd planned on three killings before Sugarman's murder and two more after. Otherwise—even should the authorities never figure out that Sugarman had been his intended target all along—they'd likely focus a disproportionate amount of time and effort on the final crime. Yet the prospect of two more murders weighed heavily on him: if murdering strangers had been mildly distasteful before his rival's death, now the prospect of stalking additional victims felt like an unreasonable burden to bear. But Balint steeled himself to the task. Even as he registered at the Hager Heights Motor Inn—surprising the night clerk when he requested a room for seven days, rather than merely three hours—his mind was already focused on putting the final two killings behind him. What mattered most, of course, was not cutting corners. He couldn't afford to let Amanda's poor judgment drive him toward negligence. That was why he'd seen his four o'clock and four-thirty patients that afternoon, despite his intense desire to drink himself into oblivion.

Once he'd settled into the stark motel room—which, on arrival, he registered was Room 101—Balint telephoned Delilah and asked if she could meet him that evening. *Urgently.* His mistress had been scheduled for an overnight shift at her hospital, but when he emphasized the importance of meeting him, she agreed to request a sub. Ninety minutes later, she pushed open the unlocked motel room door. Balint felt overjoyed to see her. He'd already polished off half the bottle of Scotch that he'd brought with him from home—or what had once been home—and the furniture was beginning to sway around him.

Delilah's flushed face blazed beneath her jet-black bangs. Her knee-length cloth coat only accentuated her curves.

"You look ravishing," declared Balint.

"Oh goodness, Jeremy. You're intoxicated."

He felt ashamed and set down his drink. "Just tipsy."

Delilah tossed her coat and scarf on the bedspread. She approached him with professional alacrity—first appropriating both the glass and whiskey bottle, then insisting that he remove his shoes and socks. "What you need is a cup of hot coffee and a cold shower," she announced.

"Can we talk first?" he asked. "Please. Something's happened."

Delilah looked indecisively from Balint to the motel's coffeemaker and back. To his relief, she settled down alongside him on the bed. For a moment, she even nuzzled her face against his neck. "I'm worried about you, darling," she said. "But please do *me* a favor: Next time, if something happens, call me *before* you get tipsy, okay?"

"Okay," he agreed. "But it happened so fast."

Delilah squeezed his hand sympathetically. "Tell me all about it."

"I'm afraid you'll be mad," he said. "You *will* be mad. And you'll have every reason to be mad. I suppose what I'm really afraid of is that you'll leave me."

The nursing student scoffed. "Don't count on it, buster," she said. "You're stuck with me—whether you like it or not."

"How can you be so certain? What if I told you I was a war criminal? Or the Emerald Choker?"

"Then we'd deal with it. I may seem sweet and innocent to you, but I can be a stubborn bitch when I want to be." She kissed him on each wrist. "I love you. And even if I didn't love you, I'd still owe you for everything you did for me and Papa. I'm not only a stubborn bitch, but I'm a stubborn, loyal bitch. Now what is this awful, dark secret that you're going to reveal that's supposedly going to have me running for the hills?"

The girl's eyes never left his; her grip on his hands never loosened. How different this odd creature was from Amanda, he realized—how much better a human being. Not more competent or more presentable. But better in the moral sense. For all of the pain he'd suffered over Amanda's rejection—and worse than pain, *humiliation*—he recognized that he'd have been far happier all along with Delilah Navare. It now seemed so obvious that if he hadn't let Amanda wear down his resistance in medical school, he'd never have found himself murdering strangers. The last laugh, in other words, would still belong to him. If Delilah was willing to forgive him, that was. But he had to try.

"I'm married," he said.

Delilah nodded and waited for him to say more.

"I should have told you that first day I met you. But you were so beautiful and my relationship with Amanda was such a goddamn mess—and I don't know how you'll ever forgive me, but I hope you will. I left her tonight, by the way. I couldn't take leading two lives anymore . . ."

To his relief, Delilah wrapped her arms around his chest and hugged him.

"Is that all?"

"That's a lot," said Balint. "Isn't it?"

"It *is* a lot," she replied. "But I already knew."

Once again, he found himself reeling. The furniture had come back into focus, but now he realized that it was still rocking slightly.

"How?"

"I wasn't sure if you knew that I knew," replied Delilah. "But I was afraid to say anything. To be candid, I had a hunch all along. You never invited me to your house or to meet your parents . . ."

"So it was that obvious?"

"Kind of. And on top of all that, it just didn't make any sense that an attractive, charming doctor would be single at your age. So, at some level, I already suspected. And then I read about that accident in the newspaper—the little girl who drowned—and I understood immediately that you were the same Jeremy Balint. The difficult part was keeping the knowledge to myself. You must have been under so much pressure, and I was powerless to help you deal with it."

"You *did* help. More than you know."

He let her revelation sink in. "So you also know I have two daughters?"

Delilah nodded. "There's not much I don't know about you. You're a wonderful man, but you're pretty transparent."

Balint kissed her on the lips. "I am transparent. Aren't I?"

"Most men are. At least the good ones."

Delilah clasped his hands between hers again. "Can I ask you one thing?"

"I'm out of secrets," said Balint.

"Did you really leave your wife? Or did she throw you out?" she asked. "I'll love you as much either way—but I just want to know the truth."

She wasn't lying, he realized. She would love him as much either way.

"I really did leave her," he said. "Not that she's particularly distraught. The man she was having an affair with died this week. Was killed, actually. I know it sounds like a lousy thing to leave her at a moment like this—but I gave the eulogy at the man's funeral, and I realized I couldn't go on leading a double life. You don't think any less of me, do you?"

"Of course not. I'm sure whatever you did was the right choice." Delilah stood up and started fiddling with the coffee machine. "Now that we've had our heart-to-heart, it's time we get you sobered up."

"I am sober," he said—but he heard his speech slurring.

"Nonsense. Now get undressed."

He struggled to unbutton his shirt. Eventually she saw what a difficult time he was having and she came over to help him.

"So what does this mean?" he asked. "For us?"

"What do you want it to mean?" she responded. "I'd like us to find a place for you to live and then I'd like to move into it. Both of us. And then, since we're putting all of our cards on the table, I'd like us to get married. In a church *or* a synagogue . . . It's not that important to me."

"You know *that* too?"

"I'm sweet, darling. I'm not an idiot."

She continued to unbutton his shirt.

"I've heard your radio ads for that Jewish organization," she said. "And I remembered when you first told me your name was Jeremiah in Hebrew. Between that and when you refused communion, I put together the pieces . . ."

She hung his shirt over the chair. Then she unbuckled his belt.

"Anyway, like I was saying, that's what *I* want. Of course, I only get one vote. It takes two to tango."

Balint realized that this wasn't the sort of decision he ought to make while he was drunk—or even tipsy. "Two votes," he said. "I want to tango."

"Tell me that again when you're sober and then we'll have a deal. I only wish Papa had lived to see this moment. He liked you, by the way. *A lot.* He'd never have said anything like that in front of you—he always held his cards close to his vest—but after that first time he met you, he told me he thought you were an honest man, which was his highest compliment. And my father was an excellent judge of character, if I do say so myself."

"I don't doubt it."

Balint was finally naked. He braced himself against the wall, fearful that he might topple over backward. Now that he'd revealed his marriage to Delilah, he felt like an utter ass for getting drunk. The nursing student tugged him into the bathroom and turned on the shower. Soon the room filled with steam. To his surprise, she began to undress herself—and his face must have betrayed his astonishment. "You don't think I'm going to trust you to shower on your own," she said with a smile. "Not on the first day of our new life together."

They kissed again.

"All I ask of you is one thing, Jeremy. No secrets. If you can promise me that, I'll support you in absolutely anything."

He almost did trust her. But *almost* carried only so far when murder was at stake.

"No secrets," he agreed. "I promise."

A SURPRISE visitor greeted Balint in his office the next morning. He had arrived at the hospital with a pounding headache that was part hangover and part tension. Ahead of him lay a series of unwelcome tasks: revealing his split with Amanda to his parents, hiring a divorce attorney, renting a home. And on top of all these stresses, he still had to murder two more strangers. He was contemplating an early evening drive to Lake Shearwater to acquire more ribbon when he nearly collided with Etan Steinhoff. The rabbi was speaking on his telephone in Hebrew—in a tone more suited for a drill sergeant than a clergyman—and pacing a hole in the carpet of the cardiology suite. When Balint appeared, Steinhoff ended his conversation abruptly.

"I was in the neighborhood," said the rabbi. "Visiting the sick. I thought I'd drop by for a moment. Is that all right?"

"Even if it's not all right," replied Balint, "you're already here . . ."

Balint motioned for Steinhoff to follow him into his office. As soon as Balint shut the door behind them, the rabbi said, "Amanda phoned me this morning. She told me what happened."

"Did she? *Everything?*"

"She told me that you two had decided to separate—at least for the time being," said Steinhoff. "Obviously nothing is carved in stone."

"Almost nothing," replied Balint. "*Headstones* are carved in stone."

He hung his overcoat on a hook inside the closet door.

"*Cornerstones* are also carved in stone," mused Balint.

Steinhoff smiled. "I suppose that wasn't the best choice of words," he said. "In any case, I thought you might want some moral support. I'm here as a rabbi, of course, but I'm also here as a friend."

"That's very kind of you. But I'm fine."

He stepped away from the door, hoping the rabbi might take his leave.

"Sometimes these things don't hit you all at once," observed Steinhoff. "If you do want to talk . . . my door is always open." The rabbi offered him a kind-yet-somber nod that Balint suspected was designed to reassure him. "I know how busy you must be, Jeremy. But even busy professionals can struggle."

"I suppose they can. But I'm *not* struggling." Balint settled down behind his mahogany desk. "In fact, I haven't felt better in years." He booted up his computer and added, "I had no idea how liberating divorce could feel. You really ought to try it sometime." He couldn't resist adding, "Or if you'd like to have an affair, I can fix you up with one of my patients . . ."

Steinhoff raised his hand to his lips, clearly straining for a suitable response. "You've had a shock," he finally said. "I won't pressure you. If you *do* want to talk, you know where to find me." He paused. His eyes darted around the office, avoiding direct contact with Balint's gaze. "While I'm here, I also wanted to make sure that you're still committed to the Project Cain health center—that your separation hasn't put you under too much stress to continue."

So *that* was it, thought Balint. The rabbi was afraid he'd jump ship, that he might divorce himself from the clinic as well as from Amanda.

"I hadn't actually thought of that," said Balint. "Now that you mention it, I might find myself under a lot of additional stress."

A shroud of disappointment fell over the rabbi's face.

"On the other hand, I might not. How is the project coming along, by the way? How many crimes have you prevented?"

"It's not that kind of project," replied Steinhoff—apparently relieved to be discussing a subject about which he felt more comfortable. "Our goal is to prevent crimes *in the future.* Years from now. When these kids are teenagers."

Balint frowned. "But surely, you must have prevented a few crimes already . . ."

"Maybe. You can never know for certain."

"You don't know? You mean you're not keeping records."

Steinhoff's neck was turning crimson. "Our project is coming along splendidly. We've generated enthusiasm in the community. That's our most important objective right now."

Balint's spirits had soared since he'd started poking fun at the rabbi. He hardly felt his hangover anymore. "I'm glad people are enthusiastic. But you're going to have a hard time sustaining that enthusiasm, if you ask me, unless you're able to show some results."

The rabbi's cell phone rang to the tune of "Hatikvah." "I should be going," said Steinhoff.

"One quick question," said Balint.

"Yes?"

"I'm just wondering. Do you think a program like yours could have made a difference in a case like the Emerald Choker?"

"I'd like to believe so. With the right intervention, I'd like to believe that *any* child can be rescued from a life of violence."

"And Project Cain is the right intervention?"

"I'm sure of it," said the rabbi. "If we'd gotten the Emerald Choker into one of our programs early enough, he'd probably be an upstanding citizen right now."

"Maybe a doctor or a rabbi?"

"Why not?"

"Indeed. Why not?" echoed Balint. "I'll tell you what. If I run into him on the street, I'll invite him on a free tour of the clinic."

The rabbi shook his hand to end the conversation.

As soon as Steinhoff departed, Balint telephoned Delilah. "I'm calling you now that I'm sober. I *still* want to get married," he announced. "And I'll be happy to get married in a church. I know how important that is to you."

———

BALINT'S FINAL patient of the afternoon was the same blind, demented woman whose poor medication compliance had delayed him on the night of his first date with Delilah. Fortunately this time Mrs. April arrived in the company of her adult son. At first, the appointment progressed like any other ordinary checkup. He listened to the old woman's heart and lungs, palpated her abdomen, and checked her ankles for swelling; then he reviewed the results of her recent EKG and echocardiogram. "The good news is that your ejection fraction has stabilized," he noted. "Unfortunately your blood pressure is still running high."

"It's probably all the stress we've been under," interjected the son. "I might as well tell you, doc. My boy has had a rough year—he was arrested for killing animals—and Mother's had a difficult time handling it. Jared has always been her favorite."

"Killing animals?"

"It's not how it sounds. We had this crazy woman living on our block, real vicious lady, and she owned a pair of German shepherds who used to terrorize the neighborhood. Scaring children. Attacking the postman. Straight out of a concentration camp. And then one day last summer, one of the dogs bit my little girl. So Jared did what any protective older brother might do: he stabbed the animal with a carving knife. I'm not saying it was the right response, but the beast had it coming."

"It certainly sounds that way," agreed Balint.

"To you and me. But not to the police. They get my kid to admit that he also shot a couple of squirrels with a BB gun once—what eleven-year-old hasn't?—and all of a sudden they're blaming him for murdering cats and dogs across the whole damn state. They even accused him of blinding a horse in the Catskills. I mean: How could my son possibly get to the Catskills? But it has practically ruined our lives."

Balint had nearly forgotten about the boy who'd been charged with killing Sugarman's neighbor's dog. How strange, he reflected, that the wheels of destiny turned even when he wasn't paying attention.

"I'm truly sorry you've had such a hard time of it," said Balint. "All I can say is that life is full of surprises. Everything may look grim right now, but the future is long. Your boy sounds like the kind of well-grounded young man who'll get himself back on his feet—one way or another."

"Amen to that," declared Mrs. April.

"And in the interim, Mrs. April," he continued, "I'm going to recommend we increase the doses of your blood-pressure medications."

Balint wrote the demented woman a handful of new prescriptions. By six o'clock, he was out the door and on the road to Hager Heights. Several times he found himself thinking that he could visit both his parents and Lake Shearwater, and still make it back to Laurendale for his daughters' bedtime, before he caught himself. He'd already spoken to Amanda that morning, and they'd agreed that his calling every evening was likely to upset the girls, at least for now. Instead they'd agreed that he'd take them out on Saturday and Sunday afternoons. Once he had a permanent address of his own, then they'd consider other arrangements. While he'd been on the phone with Amanda, Balint had been impressed with how easily they'd come to an agreement. For all of his shortcomings, Sugarman had been right when he'd said that Balint and Amanda had a knack for teamwork. And now that his rival was dead and his marriage had collapsed, Balint couldn't even muster much anger toward his soon-to-be ex-wife.

He pulled into Hager Estates shortly after nightfall. The street lamps cast a pink glow over the rows of identical duplexes. Even the yard signs campaigned for the same handful of candidates in the upcoming legislative primaries. Balint parked opposite his parents' house and rang the bell. Nobody answered. Then he knocked. After a long wait, he let himself in with his key.

"Mom!" he called. "Henry!"

An irrational sensation of unease took hold of him. His parents never went out after dark. His mother drove only short distances in clear weather; his stepdad didn't drive at all. Balint hadn't bothered to call in advance, because he'd never considered the possibility that he wouldn't find them both at home. Yet walking from room to room, it became increasingly clear that he was alone in the house. Suddenly he was seized with the ridiculous—paranoid—fear that they'd been murdered. That, of course, would have been the ultimate irony: if another serial killer, maybe an Emerald Choker copycat, randomly chose his parents to slaughter.

He found no indications of foul play. His impulse was to call Amanda for instructions on what to do next; the phone was already out of his pocket when he again recalled that he was now on his own.

Balint sat down on the living room sofa to think. A few moments later, he heard the front door rattling. He was in the process of scanning the room for a suitable object with which to defend himself when his parents appeared in the entryway.

The couple wore matching orange outfits bright enough to blind passing motorists.

"Jeremy! What a surprise!" exclaimed his mother.

She hugged him and kissed his cheek and hugged him again.

"Stop futzing over the boy, Lilly, and get him some food," insisted Henry. "He's probably starving."

"Hold your horses. Since when can't I hug my own son?" demanded Balint's mother. "If you're so afraid he might starve, you know where the refrigerator is."

Yet the protest was hardly out of Lilly Serspinsky's mouth when she disappeared into the kitchen. Less than a minute later, she reemerged with three cups of instant coffee. A platter of bagels, lox, and whitefish followed. "We'll get a head start on tomorrow's breakfast," she said. "Unless you'd like me to heat up some chicken for you."

"Breakfast is fine."

Balint scooped up a slice of whitefish. "You had me worried. I figured it was late for you to be out."

"I'm sorry we weren't home. You haven't been waiting long, have you?"

Balint shook his head; his mouth was already full of fish.

"You didn't think the Emerald Choker got us, did you?" asked Henry.

Balint couldn't tell whether his stepfather was joking.

"Your father's captain of our neighborhood watch," added his mother. "We're doing exactly what the police suggested. We're making Hager Estates an inhospitable environment for serial killers."

"If it makes you happy."

"It makes us *safe*," countered Henry. "Now what brings the hardworking man out here on a weekday night? Is anything wrong?"

"Nothing's the matter with the girls, is it?" asked Lilly.

"If it's a money problem," added Henry, "you know we'll help any way we can."

"The girls are fine. And this has nothing to do with money," he said quickly. "I guess I just better lay it out on the table: Amanda's leaving me."

His mother flashed her husband a telling look—one that suggested she'd predicted the demise of his marriage all along.

"Can you change her mind?" asked Henry.

"Why should he try to change her mind?" demanded his mother. "I knew from day one that girl wasn't good enough for you. How many times did I say that girl was a bad apple and Jeremy was simply too good-hearted to see it?"

"Please, Lilly," his stepdad cut in. "I don't understand. Can't you go to counseling or something? We had neighbors—the Lustgartens—who swore by their marriage counselor. And they always seemed happy as clams."

Balint sipped his coffee. As much as he'd dreaded telling his parents, now that he'd made his announcement, he felt surprisingly relaxed. "It's too late for counseling. Amanda has been having an affair."

"How dare she!" exclaimed Balint's mother.

"For *years*. With one of my colleagues."

"Better to find out now," said Henry, "than twenty years from now."

Balint wondered how long his stepfather's reasoning applied. Would he have said the same thing if Balint had been married thirty years? Forty?

"I'll never understand," said Henry. "How can a mother do that to her daughters?"

"I hope the Choker gets her," said Balint's mother. "I swear I do."

"Lilly! Don't say such things," cried her husband.

"Well, it's the truth. Pure evil, that's what it is. Pure evil."

Balint interjected to explain the logistics of his arrangement with Amanda. In explaining why *he'd* moved out, he didn't mention any of the practical issues. "By all rights, I should have made her leave," he said. "But what kind of man throws his wife out of the house? I just didn't have it in me. It's better this way."

"Such a *mensch* isn't born once a century," said his mother. "You'll forgive me for saying this in front of you, Henry, but he takes after his father. The man, rest his soul, had only one flaw: he was always putting other people ahead of himself."

———

DESPITE THE late hour and intermittent flurries, Balint drove directly from Hager Estates into the Onaswego Hills. He'd been riding a streak of luck—first with Delilah, then with his parents—and he was determined to get the final two killings over with. During the hour-long trip, his radio station played the Project Cain ad twice. *I'm Dr. Jeremy Balint and saving lives is my job . . .*

At first, the cabin appeared as he'd left it. He once again bound cloth around his shoes to avoid leaving footprints. Only as he approached the entrance did he notice a second set of prints in the ice; they appeared to have been partially eroded by successive freezes and thaws. When he turned the knob, the cabin door opened easily. Someone had unlocked the latch from inside. He glanced at the window: sure enough, this same someone had bashed in enough panes to create a makeshift entrance.

Balint flipped on the overhead light, but the bulb had burned out. Luckily the lamps in the kitchen and bedroom remained functional.

A brief investigation revealed that a squatter had been living in the cabin. Mud stains scarred the throw rugs in the vestibule. The remains of a small animal, possibly a weasel or badger, decomposed on a plate beside the kitchen sink. In the bedroom, Balint discovered that the squatter had dragged the mattress off its frame. He prided himself on his foresight: a lesser criminal would have concealed the spare ribbons among the box springs—and would now be awaiting trial in the county lockup. Once again, Balint reflected, he'd handily out-smarted fate.

Although the squatter had rummaged through the boxes in the closet—and Balint suspected some of the fishing tackle was missing—he'd shown little interest in the steamer trunk of women's undergarments. He'd broken the lock, but left the contents largely unscathed. Balint retrieved the remaining green ribbon from the bottom of the trunk and pared it into twenty-four-inch strands. A total of thirteen. He coiled up the first eleven strands and secured them inside his wallet. Then he carried the final two strands outside, tied them to the broken metal handle of a wagon, and threw the handle as far as he could into the water.

One step closer to victory, he assured himself. He was almost there.

The next time he visited Lake Shearwater, it would be to go fishing.

CHAPTER THIRTEEN

He spent the weekend with Delilah touring houses. They had decided to rent—at least until the divorce was settled and his financial situation became clearer—and this substantially narrowed their options. The Hager Heights-Laurendale-Pontefract triangle simply wasn't the sort of place where starter couples leased first homes. By the time you had enough capital and children to reside in these communities, you were ready to commit for life, or to a thirty-year mortgage, which often felt like the same thing.

They explored a split-level in Hager Park owned by the Ecuadorian consulate, but Balint was reluctant to have a landlord with diplomatic immunity. They also considered a luxury apartment complex in Rolleston; the thirty-minute commute to the hospital proved the major sticking point. All other matters being equal, he would have preferred a house to a condo, so the girls might have a yard in which to play, but he reminded himself that these were minor concerns, because whatever property they ultimately settled upon would only be temporary. Delilah, for her part, proved as flexible in residential tastes as in everything else. "I got to choose the husband," she said. "I'll leave the rest of the decisions to you." Yet unlike with Amanda, he felt confident that his second wife wouldn't later hold his preferences against him.

On Sunday morning, he found the house he wanted. One glimpse at the listing on a real estate website had him sold—he didn't even need to tour the place. Of course, he already knew the building well from the outside. It stood only two doors away from his former home, on the corner with Bonaventure Lane. That meant he'd be living close to his daughters, so close they could come over after school at a moment's notice. But the real reason he wanted this house was to revenge himself on Amanda for abandoning their marriage. He recognized that she'd find his decision humiliating, although he could think of no *rational* reasons for avoiding the property. Only sentimental ones. The modest colonial with the brick façade and black shutters belonged to Sally Goldhammer. (Her husband, he'd learned, remained in a vegetative state.) Balint imagined that the woman's decision to rent, rather than to sell, reflected some complex process of denial. That wasn't his problem. All that mattered was that he required a house and she had one to let.

Although Balint didn't harbor the slightest modicum of guilt, either over Abby's drowning or his decision to rent the property, he was nevertheless glad that Sally had chosen to lease the house through an agency. Seeing the grieving mother in person offered no upside. How much easier it was to sign a handful of forms in a real estate office. By noon on Sunday, they'd put down a security deposit and two months' rent. Three hours later, he'd checked out of the motor inn. When a truck with Delilah's furniture arrived at the address midweek, the reality of their new life together finally sank in. Less than nine days had elapsed since his break with Amanda, only twelve since he'd strangled Warren Sugarman. Maybe he didn't deserve an award in medical ethics, Balint thought, but he'd certainly earned himself a prize for resilience.

Delilah proved far more effective at running a household than Balint had anticipated. She lacked Amanda's sophistication, but she set lower goals and generally made do with less. Why broil a chicken, she asked, when the Gourmet Factory sold ready-to-eat poultry dinners for $7.99 each? Yet the most striking difference between living with Amanda and with Delilah was the freedom. No longer did he have to attend anniversary parties and benefit gatherings to satisfy people whom he hardly knew. Not once did Delilah command his presence at a wedding or a funeral.

On the following Saturday, he strolled up the street to retrieve his daughters. That was when he revealed to Amanda that he'd rented the Goldhammers' property. In order to avoid a fight, he'd asked Delilah to join him on the visit. Amanda was too concerned with appearances to lose her temper in front of the nursing student.

"We've actually rented down the block," he announced. "I figured that would be easiest on the girls."

"You don't mean . . . ?"

"Why does it matter?" asked Balint. "If anything, I'm doing that woman a favor. She'd have a hell of a time finding anyone else to rent the house at that price."

Amanda looked from Balint to his mistress. "You're something else, Jeremy. You really don't see how insensitive this is, do you?"

"It will be convenient," he replied—refusing to take her bait. "This way, the girls can drop by whenever they wish. Besides, it's only short term."

His wife glowered at him. "I shudder to think what your long-term plans are. If you're thinking of buying Warren's house—and I wouldn't put it past you—I'd advise you against it. I swear I'd burn the place out from beneath your feet."

Balint smiled. "I'll take that under advisement."

Delilah hardly spoke during the encounter. To Balint's delight, she proved a sensation with his daughters. He'd feared the girls might resent her or shut her out: instead they peppered her with questions about being a nurse. She asked them to call her by her first name, a novelty that caused them considerable joy. "They're absolutely adorable," she told him that evening. "Just like you."

As splendidly as his daughters had hit it off with Delilah, Balint refused to leave anything to chance. One morning he ducked out of the hospital and strolled over to the pet shop opposite the discount pharmacy. An aroma of fecundity and bodily fluids assailed his nostrils. He strode quickly toward the feline cages, intending to buy his girls a kitten. In his experience, female human beings of a certain age were highly susceptible to the charms of baby cats. Personally, Balint had never desired a house pet—they struck him as far more effort than reward, and he hated the stench—but he was willing to sacrifice fresh air if that meant impressing his children. He'd almost settled upon a calico tabby, and was returning to the counter to negotiate the price, when he suddenly caught sight of a brindled dachshund puppy. The hound yapped at him cheerily, a spitting image of the creature he'd run over on Meadow Drive. In an instant, he realized he *had* to have it—extra work be damned. So much to Delilah's surprise, and his own, he returned home from the hospital that evening with a three-month-old canine. In one final swipe at Amanda, he named the animal "Sugardog."

The girls fell in love with the puppy immediately. Balint was slower to adjust to the duty of walking the animal at six each morning. It didn't help that several of his neighbors, whom he often encountered during these walks, had grown less than friendly—likely under Amanda's influence. Matilda Rothschild and Ellen Arcaya offered him only terse good mornings. Vicki Robustelli felt compelled to make small talk while her beagle sniffed the dachshund's behind, but the woman kept glancing up the street uncomfortably. The truth of the matter was that Balint didn't give a rat's ass if these women took his soon-to-be ex-wife's side. He hardly remembered their names.

Only one encounter left a mark on him.

About a week after he'd purchased Sugardog, he ran into Bonnie Kluger in front of her garage. The peculiar woman was calling after one of her cats; she held a saucer of milk in one hand and a hypodermic needle in the other. Bonnie sported a bizarre outfit of solid-colored patchwork that might have belonged to a medieval jester.

Balint hurried past rapidly without even acknowledging the woman—and he thought he'd escaped safely, when she called after him. "You can run, Balint, but you can't hide!"

He ought to have continued on his way without acknowledging her. Instead, he made the mistake of turning around.

"What's that?" he asked.

"I said that you can scurry about like a common thief," said Bonnie. "But you can't hide from the sight of God."

"I don't know what you're talking about."

"Everyone else on this street does. You murdered that little girl—let her drown as though her life was worth less than nothing—and now you've had the gall to move into her home. For shame, Jeremy Balint. For shame!"

"Good morning to you too, Bonnie," replied Balint. "Have a pleasant day."

As much as he felt he'd gotten the better of her during this exchange, Balint found himself replaying the conversation in his head for weeks. Somehow that woman always managed to make him feel worthless. On several occasions, he dreamed about strangling her. He must have talked during his sleep, because when he woke up one morning, Delilah asked him who Bonnie Kluger was.

———

DURING HIS first month living with Delilah, Balint conjured up ample excuses to put off his final two killings. Many of these excuses were highly implausible, such as the worry that Amanda had hired a private detective to trail him in the hope of acquiring evidence that might improve her divorce settlement. The underlying cause of his reluctance to act was far simpler: he wanted to savor his triumph. Deep down, he recognized that his victory wouldn't be truly complete until he'd exhausted his remaining strands of ribbon—but with Sugarman gone forever, the entire enterprise seemed far less pressing. Only when he heard Chief Putnam, in his daily news briefing, describe the Emerald Choker as "mystifyingly inactive of late," did he recognize that he couldn't delay the last pair of murders forever. Killing again involved risk, but in the long run, *not* killing again entailed far more risk.

The diversity among his first five victims—both in terms of geography and demographics—afforded him far more latitude in selecting his final targets. He could drive north of New York City, even into Connecticut, and pick off another middle-class suburbanite, but he might just as easily trek into downtown Newark or Camden and strangle a homeless junkie. At the end of the day, Balint decided that—all other factors being equal—he'd try to cause as little collateral damage as possible. If he'd needed to murder a police officer or the CEO of a *Fortune* 500 company, he'd have done so, but in the absence of a compelling reason, he saw no point in not choosing a target of far less social worth. That was how the following Wednesday night, while Delilah was working a double shift at the Rolleston Maternity Clinic, he ended up on a deserted backstreet in Jersey City, trawling for prostitutes. Once again, he'd cloaked the license plates of the Mercedes in burlap.

Balint had very limited experience with sex workers—largely confined to one raucous bachelor party he'd attended in New Orleans as a first-year medical student. He was genuinely stunned at how openly the hookers along Garfield Avenue flaunted their wares. Scantily clad women and statuesque transvestites knocked on his car windows at nearly every intersection. Unfortunately, despite the subfreezing temperatures, the streets swarmed with assorted agents of vice and their clientele. Moreover, many of these women appeared to be working in teams of two or three, so even if he lured one away, others would remain behind to identify him to the authorities. As Balint cruised the Red Light District, his foremost thought was that, as a taxpayer and a father, he couldn't understand why the police didn't clear these derelicts from the streets.

Around midnight, on the verge of quitting for the evening, Balint passed a blue arrow directing drivers toward the public bus station—and a novel idea suddenly dawned upon him. Ten minutes later, he was circling the streets several blocks away from the terminal; he dared not approach any closer, because he feared that cameras might record the entrances. On television, he'd once watched a news magazine that exposed how pimps congregated outside transportation centers, recruiting stray teenagers who'd run away from homes in the heartland. So why not him? After all, given the choice between his companionship and the protection of local hoodlums, what middle-class adolescent wouldn't feel more comfortable with a clean-cut, thirty-something white guy driving a Mercedes sedan? Once the plan dawned on him, Balint felt like a fool for not having thought of it earlier.

The night was overcast and damp. Only a block away from the bus station, the neighborhood consisted largely of warehouses and storage facilities, with an occasional residential building tucked into the mix. That minimized the risk of running into late-night partygoers or dog walkers. Balint drove past three men sporting hooded sweatshirts who appeared as though they might be casing parked cars. He also spotted a homeless person sleeping in an alcove, but he dismissed this potential target: he couldn't get a good sense of the person's size or strength from the road—and, more important, he couldn't be certain that the man or woman would actually be missed. The last thing Balint wanted was to murder a stranger in cold blood and then have the victim's body go undiscovered for weeks or months. That made as little sense as hunting ducks for sport. Yet, at the same time, he dared not transport a corpse into a more visible location. So he kept driving . . .

A solitary streetlamp illuminated the corner of Fox Place and Bontea Slip. Beneath it stood the most promising target Balint had seen all night: a scrawny teenage white girl carrying a knapsack. The girl looked to be sixteen or seventeen—and lost. He pulled the Mercedes to the curbside.

"Can I help you?" he asked.

The girl shook her head. "I'm okay."

"I'll be glad to give you a lift. There's a youth hostel downtown, if you're looking for a place to stay," he said. "I'm Dr. Balint with Laurendale Hospital's Adolescence Outreach Program. I can show you my ID card . . ."

The girl eyed him warily. He held his ID badge out the window.

A siren rose and fell several blocks in the distance. All of the buildings around the intersection remained dark.

Balint's target approached the vehicle slowly, took the ID badge from his hand, and examined it. Then she handed it back. "How do I get to that hostel?"

"Stay on Fox until you reach Garfield Avenue," he lied. "You'll go about three miles down Garfield and then turn left on Arthur. You shouldn't be able to miss it."

The girl shivered. "Three miles?"

"You can walk or I can drive you," said Balint—striving to sound indifferent. "The decision is entirely up to you."

She stepped away from the car, and for a moment, he feared she might choose to walk. But then she crossed in front of the vehicle, and seconds later she was settled into the passenger seat with the knapsack braced between her legs. He smiled at her and eased the car gently on its way.

"You have a name?" he asked.

"Jane," she said.

He'd have wagered his entire salary that the girl had given him an alias. No matter. It probably served him right.

"Good to meet you, Jane," he said. "I'm Jeremy."

They coasted along the deserted backstreets of Jersey City. Balint navigated the potholes while searching for a suitable spot to deposit a body. About a half mile down Fox Place, the commercial district gave way to rows of dingy wood-frame homes.

"Where you from?" asked Balint.

"Someplace," said the girl. "You sure you know where you're going?"

"Almost there," said Balint.

And then he slammed on the brakes.

"Dammit," he shouted. "I think I hit something."

He climbed out of the vehicle quickly. As he'd hoped, the girl followed. To their right stood a rather inhospitable playground, its jungle gym and monkey bars towering over the iron gate that surrounded the perimeter. During the day, Balint suspected the site crawled with schoolchildren. On the opposite side of the street stood a vacant parking lot advertising low monthly rates.

He popped open the trunk and slid out his snow shovel.

"Can you check the front tires?" he asked the girl.

Jane did as instructed. As she conducted her inspection, leaning slightly forward, he brought the head of the shovel down upon her skull. He had taken a risk, he knew—another vehicle might have come along at that moment. In that case, he'd have denied offering her a lift and instead claimed that he'd merely hit her with his car, an accident; it would have been her word against his. Thankfully, no other cars appeared.

Balint quickly carried the girl's limp body to the playground entrance. Then he squeezed his hands around her neck. What amazed him most was how calm he felt as he wrung the life from her. Gone were the tingling nerves and the adrenaline rush. Now, killing was merely a routine task. As he tied each of the seven green ribbons around her neck, all he experienced was a numbing sense of indifference.

———

THE NEXT day drew another summons to Bruce Sanditz's office. Balint found the department chairman at his desk, gorging himself on a pastrami sandwich. Specks of lettuce clung to the nephrologist's bicuspids. Even wearing a cashmere sweater, instead of a jacket, Balint's boss did not appear casual. "Take a seat, Jeremy," he urged. "I know what you're thinking—that I'm killing myself with these cold cuts. Well, what would you say if I told you that my father is 102 years old and has been eating two pastrami sandwiches a day for nearly a century?"

"I'd say he has excellent genes," said Balint. "And very good luck."

"So would I," agreed Sanditz, grinning. "Unfortunately, my father died from malignant melanoma at age sixty-three. But if he hadn't, mind you, he'd still be devouring red meat like there's no tomorrow."

"I don't doubt it."

"Anyway, I didn't drag you in here to gab about my hardening arteries. Now do you want the good news first or the bad news first?"

Balint wondered if this were a trick question—if he were somehow stumbling headlong into a trap that might cost him his job.

"The bad news," he said.

"Exactly. A man after my own heart," replied Sanditz. "Always take care of the storm before you enjoy the calm." The chairman paused, likely for effect. "So the bad news, Dr. Balint, is that I intend to live forever. Or, at least, until I reach 102 . . . And I don't intend to retire. *Ever.*"

"That's the *bad* news?"

"For you, it is. Because the good news is that if I had to recommend someone to Dr. Kimball to serve as the next department chairman, it would be you."

"Thank you. That means a lot."

"And do you want to know why?"

Balint searched the chairman's features, but they yielded nothing. "I'm not sure. *Do* I want to know why?"

"You do, Dr. Balint. You most certainly do." Sanditz removed his handkerchief from his slacks pocket and patted down his forehead. "The reason I would unequivocally recommend you as my successor is because Laurendale-Methodist's reputation is based only partially on our state-of-the-art medicine. Equally important to our success—if not more so—is our good name. And our good name stems from our commitment to ethics. Now do you see what I'm driving at?"

"I confess I'm not sure."

"Well, I *am* sure. I have an inside tip from my former graduate student that you are going to be named the first recipient of the Wenger Award for Ethics in Medicine by the American College of Physicians."

Balint hadn't expected to win. "Jesus Christ," he exclaimed.

"I doubt Jesus Christ had anything to do with it. It's all your doing, Jeremy. They were very impressed by that health project you're running with the rabbi."

"It's nothing, really . . ."

"The only other person who deserves any credit is poor Sugarman, for bringing your brilliant work to my attention. Too bad about Sugarman, isn't it?"

"Not a day goes by," replied Balint, "when I don't think of Warren."

"Same here. Jeanine is still a wreck. Between you and me, she's seeing someone now—a therapist, I mean. Not that I expect it will do her much good. What she needs is time and more time. But insurance pays for therapy, not time . . ."

"I am truly sorry."

The funny thing was that Balint actually *did* feel sorrow for a brief moment—not regret that he'd killed his rival, but rather the detached sadness he might experience if someone else had murdered the supposed fiancé of the chairman's daughter.

"I do hope they catch that bastard," said Balint. "Although honestly, I'm not too optimistic."

"They'll catch him all right," countered Sanditz. "Trust me on this one, Jeremy. I have more experience in these matters than you do—I've been hearing the media report on unsolved crimes for nearly sixty years. And do you know what I've learned?"

"What?"

"These men *always* get caught. They talk too much—they brag to a girlfriend, they confide in a neighbor . . . or they get arrested for something else entirely and spill the beans to the guy in the adjoining cell. Half the time, that other inmate turns state's evidence—and the other half of the time he's an undercover cop. So mark my words, Jeremy: by this time next year, we'll be sitting in this office, watching them try that Choker fellow on live television . . ."

"I hope you're right."

"I *know* I'm right. Anyway I'm confident you have better things to do than gab about serial killers. So get back to work. Make some money for the hospital. And congratulations once again—only remember, the award's not public yet. You'll be named a finalist next week and they'll invite you to their annual banquet in New York City—but the actual winner won't be revealed until the event. So when they call out your name, make sure you look surprised."

"I won't breathe a word. Now take good care of those arteries."

"Strongest arteries on the planet," answered Sanditz, already browsing the next folder on his desk. "Practically lined with Teflon."

———

As soon as he arrived home, Balint shared his success with Delilah. If he'd still been living with Amanda, he'd have had to keep the secret to himself; otherwise, half of New Jersey would have been in on the news within hours. But Delilah was as discreet as she was devoted—so discreet that when he added that he'd promised Sanditz not to share the information with anyone until the award ceremony, she wondered aloud if he hadn't done wrong by taking her into his confidence. "I'll try to look surprised," she said. "But I'd hate to make a mistake that gives anything away." She added that she'd read a novel about a breeder who fixed horse races—and how he'd been discovered because his wife always wore fancy outfits on days that his animals were slated to win.

"I promised you no secrets," said Balint. "Not even small ones."

She responded by hugging him to her chest. "I don't know how I duped you into falling for me. But even if you left me tomorrow, I'd still be grateful for the time we had together. Truly."

Balint savored the warmth of her slender body.

"Nobody's leaving anyone," he pledged.

They made love in three different rooms that evening, and the next day he arrived at work in one of the best moods of his adult life. He'd nearly blocked out the knowledge that he still had yet another murder to perpetrate. Even when Chief Putnam announced the discovery of his most recent victim, whose name actually did turn out to be Jane—Jane Johnson of Belfast, Maine—Balint found himself surprisingly unconcerned with the news. His own life and the killings somehow seemed increasingly disconnected.

Balint didn't notice the stack of pink phone messages on his desk until the receptionist reminded him that he'd received three phone calls from the same extension. Only then did he recognize the name: Dr. Kimball! That was Dr. Marion Robbins Kimball IV, the president of the hospital. Balint knew the man by sight and had strolled past the oak-paneled doors of his second-story office on countless occasions—but his knowledge of the institution's patriarch came largely secondhand.

For Dr. Kimball kept an extremely low profile at Laurendale-Methodist, leaving most public matters to his army of executive vice presidents and department chairpersons. At the same time, Kimball was rumored to be both savvy and ruthless. His great-grandfather, Francis Marion Kimball, had founded the hospital as a community dispensary in the late nineteenth century. His uncle, Marion Robbins Kimball III, later transformed the facility from a small-time clinic into a nationally renowned tertiary care center. If a leading research scientist like Bruce Sanditz was willing to relocate from Johns Hopkins to central New Jersey, that alone served as a testament to Kimball's skill as a recruiter.

Balint's hand trembled while he dialed the number. He feared the worst: that Kimball was cleaning house—firing both Sanditz and all of the chairman's division chiefs. Why else contact him directly?

"This is Dr. Balint," he said, "returning a call."

"Jeremy Balint? Kimball speaking," replied the gravel-voiced president. "Would you mind popping downstairs for a minute? If now is a convenient time, that is . . ."

"I'm on my way."

Five minutes later, Balint found himself seated face-to-face with the hospital's chief executive. He was surprised to find Kimball's office as cozy as Bruce Sanditz's was spacious. Other than the computer, the chamber looked as exactly it might have appeared in the days of the administrator's great-grandfather. Velvet curtains flanked the windows. Portraits of prominent Kimballs lined the walls. On a shelf behind the intricately latticed walnut desk stood pictures of Marion shaking hands with five different United States presidents.

Marion Kimball was a slight, beak-nosed man in his fifties. He wore a pair of thin-rimmed spectacles, but he could just as easily have sported a monocle. Another man sat in the chair beside Balint: a burly, younger executive with a crew cut.

"Jeremy Balint," Kimball introduced him. "Roger Slade. External affairs."

Balint recognized the name instantly. Slade was the unseen figure behind the e-mail messages surrounding Sugarman's death.

"Good to meet you, Dr. Balint," said the vice president.

Slade wasn't an MD, he remembered. He shook the man's hand.

Kimball offered Balint a cigar; he declined. The hospital president then lit one for himself and let the blue smoke curl toward the ceiling.

"I'm sorry I haven't had an opportunity to get to know you better before today. Somehow I'm always putting these things off—and then I'm forced to introduce myself to people under tragic circumstances." Kimball puffed vigorously on his cigar. "I suppose I have nobody to blame except yours truly."

The words "tragic circumstances" welled in the pit of Balint's stomach. He instantly feared something had happened to the girls—but that made no sense. Why would he learn of a personal calamity from the president of the hospital? More likely, he realized, the institution had discovered something suspicious in his professional conduct. For all he knew, maybe they'd figured out that he was the Emerald Choker, but they wanted to paper over the matter. That would certainly explain the presence of the public relations man. His exposure would look awful for the hospital, after all—and high-ranking people had certainly tried to cover up worse offenses. Watergate, for example.

"I imagine you're wondering why I summoned you," said Kimball.

A long silence ensued until Balint realized that the administrator was actually awaiting a reply. "I am curious," he finally stammered.

"Understandably." Kimball removed his spectacles, cleaned the lenses with a tissue, and then returned them to the bridge of his nose. "I regret that I must be the bearer of misfortune, but there's no alternative. Your colleague, Bruce Sanditz, passed away this morning."

"Sanditz? Dead?"

"I'm afraid so. Rather suddenly. He was sitting in that very chair less than two hours ago—and now he lies on a cold slab in the basement. A stroke, it seems. As soon as we're through, I'm going to have Roger call his family to let them know."

Balint struggled to digest the news. "You haven't told his wife."

"Not yet," said Kimball. "We will. But there are certain priorities, you understand. The welfare of the hospital is at stake . . ."

"Of course," said Balint—for the sake of agreement.

"Bruce Sanditz was a fine fellow. A first-rate chairman. At the same time, I've been of the opinion for a while now that the medicine department was in need of new leadership—*younger* leadership. So it delights me to inform you that you are now the new chairman of the department of medicine. Effective immediately."

The president didn't appear to be *offering* him the post, because an offer implied a choice of whether or not to accept. If he turned Kimball down—and he couldn't imagine why he would—he half-feared the man might have his kneecaps shattered.

"Acting head?" inquired Balint.

"*Permanent* head," retorted Kimball. "A smooth transition is our foremost priority. Besides, I can't tell you how fed up I

am with all of these temporary appointments and search com-
mittees and whatnot. I saw a sign once that read, 'If Moses
had been a committee, the Israelites would still be wandering
in the desert.' At a time like this, what we need is leadership
and stability." The administrator stubbed out his cigar. "Now
clear your schedule for the day. We'll have a press conference
at noon. Roger will introduce you."

"I don't know what to say," said Balint. "I'm honored."

"They tell me you're an ethics guy," said Kimball. "Only
last week, Bruce sat right in that chair and called you 'The
Conscience of the Medicine Department.' Told me you're
winning some big-time award."

"The Wenger Award," interjected Balint.

"Wenger. That's right. Anyway, I just wanted to reassure you that the chairmanship shouldn't interfere with your
clinical duties." Kimball pointed directly at the vice president
and added, "You keep doing what you've been doing all
along. Only in a bigger office. Roger here will take care of
everything else."

CHAPTER FOURTEEN

Bruce Sanditz's wife had accompanied her daughter to visit Warren Sugarman's gravesite that morning, forgetting her cell phone on her kitchen table. On the way home, mother and child stopped for lunch at a diner in Marston Moor. The proprietors, a trio of Greek brothers, kept the television running above the counter at all times. As a result, after watching Detective Mazzotta brief the media on developments—or rather, the lack of developments—in the Constantinou slaying, Mrs. Sanditz was treated to an emergency twelve o'clock press conference on the local public access channel during which Roger Slade announced the death of her husband. Balint spent the next three days apologizing—to anyone who would listen—for this "gross oversight in judgment." When he finally managed to reach the chairman's widow directly, she told him to "take his new job and choke on it" before hanging up. So began his tenure as head of the Laurendale-Methodist department of medicine.

Kimball hadn't been lying: the only significant difference between his former position and his new one appeared to be the increase in office space. Sanditz's desk was large enough to practice putting golf balls along the blotter, and his corner window offered a panoramic view of the posh coastal hamlets below, but the chairmanship didn't appear to entail any tangible responsibilities. All of the hiring and firing decisions that Balint had long attributed to Sanditz apparently took place at higher levels of management. Even the nonrenewal of the junior attending who'd complained about the cost of banquet tickets appeared to be a coincidence; Balint used the perks of his new post to order the discharged physician's personnel file from storage, and learned that the man had been caught fabricating research data. Fortunately, if Balint remained as powerless as ever, his colleagues remained blissfully ignorant of his lack of authority. Oncologists and pulmonologists he hardly knew clambered over each other to offer him their congratulations. Only Myron Salt swam against the current. Balint encountered the neurologist in the parking lot after work one evening, and Salt warned, "Those who can, do; those who can't, teach; and those who can't even do that, administrate. You're too smart to spend the prime of your career ordering paper clips, Balint. Aren't you?"

Salt had a point. On the other hand, Kimball had tripled his salary overnight. At least until his divorce was settled, Balint assured himself, he'd been wise to accept the promotion. He didn't have to serve as chairman forever—or even to remain at Laurendale Hospital. In fact, over the long haul, once the slayings were well behind him, the safest move might be to depart from the region entirely.

Balint was in the process of planning the final murder, which he'd decided should take place in Connecticut, when he received an unexpected office visit from Etan Steinhoff. The rabbi, as always, had a pretext for appearing without warning. "They're opening a new gift shop in your atrium," he explained. "The public relations folks thought it might look good to have a rabbi on hand for a blessing."

Rabbi Felder, Balint was certain, had never prayed over a gift shop.

"Sometimes I think this hospital has become a giant public relations firm that happens to provide medical care on the side," observed Balint. "May I ask: Is there a proper blessing for a gift shop?"

"There is a proper blessing for *everything*," said the rabbi. "Gift shops, camels, wallpaper, even non-Kosher meat."

"How about serial killers?" asked Balint.

Steinhoff looked him over as though he had just walked off the moon—and then he flashed a broad smile. "That was a joke, wasn't it?"

"You're catching on," answered Balint. He glanced pointedly at his wristwatch. "Now what can I do for you today?"

"May I sit down?"

Balint said nothing. Steinhoff took his silence as an invitation to seat himself.

"I fear I come bearing bad news," he said. "About Project Cain."

"Let me guess. The parents aren't sick enough—so you want me to start poisoning them on the sly."

The rabbi mulled over his offer for a moment. "Not at all," he said. "The parents *are* sick. But they're getting their medical care elsewhere. Emergency rooms, church-run programs. So we've decided to pull the plug on the free clinics. I'm sorry to have to be the one to tell you . . ."

"Not the end of the world," said Balint—although, to his surprise, he found himself mildly disappointed. "I guess Cain wasn't able, you might say." He paused a moment and added, "That, just so you know, was also a joke."

The rabbi forced a smile that evaporated instantly.

"We're not giving up on Project Cain. Far from it. We're only shutting down the clinics," explained Steinhoff. "We've found a much more effective way to lure the children into our 'supplemental mothering' sessions. Free sneakers. Between Nike and Reebok, I now have enough donated footwear to shoe every indigent child in New Jersey."

Balint laughed—the first time he'd laughed in many months. Possibly the first time he'd had a genuine good laugh since his car had collided with the dachshund.

"Is something funny?" inquired Steinhoff.

Balint shook his head as he regained his composure. "It was how you used 'shoe' as a verb. Like you were shoeing horses. Struck my funny bone for some reason . . ."

"I see," said Steinhoff. He clearly didn't. The rabbi scanned his cell phone for a moment and stood up. "Are you all right, Jeremy? If you'd like to talk about your marriage—or about anything at all—I want to renew my offer."

"No, thanks. But there is something you can do for me, rabbi."

Steinhoff's dark eyes glowed eagerly. "Anything."

"How about a new pair of sneakers?"

A look of deep disappointment suffused across the rabbi's face, as though Balint had denied the omnipotence of the almighty God or had taken to worshipping idols.

"I'll see what I can do," he said. "If we have enough."

Steinhoff was already out the door when Balint called after him: "You didn't even ask me for my shoe size!"

———

As Bruce Sanditz had promised, the executive director of the American College of Physicians did phone Balint the following week to invite him to their upcoming banquet in Manhattan. "I do apologize for the short notice," she explained, "but some members of the board of directors wanted to postpone—on account of the Choker." The organization had apparently conducted an informal survey of its district committee leaders and discovered that nearly half refused to attend any event in New York City while the serial killer remained on the loose. "If you can't come," added the executive director, "we fully understand. I assure you that your decision will have no effect on whether you win the Wenger Award."

Balint surged with pride at the knowledge that his petty spree had the power to impact the lives of so many of his colleagues.

"I wouldn't miss it for the world," he said. "If you think I'm afraid of some nutcase with a spool of green ribbon, you don't know me . . ."

"That's wonderful. I wish more of our members shared your outlook."

She e-mailed him a formal invitation that afternoon, and two weeks later, he checked his coat at the Waldorf Astoria Hotel and accompanied Delilah into the mezzanine ball-room. His parents had arrived earlier in the day by commuter rail, taking his daughters to see the dinosaur exhibit at the Museum of Natural History. Now the six of them sat together at one of the head tables, along with the two other finalists and their respective spouses. By any impartial assessment, the other candidates' accomplishments dwarfed his own. Dr. Feig, an infectious disease specialist, was the whistle-blower at the Centers for Disease Control and Prevention who'd leaked to the press the details of Operation Cobalt, a Cold War-era pro-tocol during which the military tested biological weapons on unsuspecting African American peanut farmers in Mississippi. Dr. Sestito, another cardiologist, had personally rescued six-teen children from a hospital in California when its pediatric ICU caught fire during an earthquake. The woman was gor-geous, in addition to brave, despite the striking burn scars on her hands and forearms. Even after his late boss's tip-off, Balint didn't see how he could eclipse these two for the prize.

Balint relished having Delilah at his side. Unlike Amanda, she didn't dominate the conversation; in fact, she spent most of the event entertaining his daughters, allowing him an opportunity to chat with his fellow honorees. The salad course had already been served when talk shifted to the Emerald Choker.

"We almost didn't come," said Dr. Sestito's husband. "As it is, we're flying out first thing in the morning. There's no reason, as I see it, to take unnecessary chances."

"See, Jeremy," Balint's mother chimed in from across the table. "Henry and I aren't the only ones who are worried."

"We've agreed not to go anywhere alone while we're here," added the husband. "Not even the bathroom. And we left our twins back in San Diego."

"They're twelve," said the wife. "They were *so* disappointed."

Balint's mother commented that leaving the children behind in California was the correct choice. Delilah, meanwhile, showed Jessie how to fold the wax paper from the breadbasket into origami swans and cranes.

"I hate to stick my neck out," said Warner Feig, the whistle-blowing ID specialist. "But I'm going to have to disagree with you about risk. Flying here from California was far more dangerous than actually being here—and the danger of crashing in a commercial jet is still only several million to one. If you've made any high-risk decisions this week, the most hazardous was probably driving to the airport."

Balint had been thinking precisely the same thing, but he was glad he hadn't been the one to derail the conversation. An awkward silence followed. Fortunately they cleared the salad plates a few moments later, and the master of ceremonies, a Nobel Prize winner in physiology, stepped to the front of the room.

"It is now my privilege," he declared, "to introduce the first winner of the Donald S. Wenger Award for Ethics in Medicine . . ."

The academy had staged the event to mimic the Oscars, even placing the winner's name inside a glistening silver envelope. Until the final moment, Balint expected that Sanditz had been misinformed—that either Feig or Sestito had won. And then he found himself the center of attention, walking toward the head of the ballroom on a cascade of applause.

The Nobel laureate shook his hand, whispered a few inaudible words, and made room for Balint at the microphone. As he repeated the phrase *thank you*, a hush fell over the crowd. And then, out of the silence, arose the question of a small child:

"Did Daddy win?" asked Phoebe.

Her high-pitched voice carried across the silent banquet hall. All eyes shifted from the cardiologist to his daughter. Balint could not have scripted the moment better had he planned it long in advance.

"Yes, princess," he answered from the podium. "Daddy won."

The exchange drew enthusiastic cheers and laughter from the audience.

RIDING HIGH on his successive triumphs—first the chairmanship, then the ethics award—Balint determined to conclude his killing spree as soon as was feasibly possible. In fact, he even considered quitting while he was ahead—leaving the death toll at six and hoping the discovery of Jane Johnson's body proved enough to distract the authorities from the death of Warren Sugarman. If only Putnam and Mazzotta had been investigating the crimes alone, he might actually have done so, although he recognized that scaling back on his plan was precisely the sort of corner cutting that had landed his bloodthirsty predecessors in the slammer. If anything kept him on track, it was fear of Ralph Spitford. Balint sensed that the sheriff was far too shrewd an opponent to underestimate. He'd seen through the extra ribbon, hadn't he? And during a recent television interview, he'd already noted that the Johnson murder didn't fit the same profile as the earlier slayings. "One possibility is that we're dealing with a second perpetrator," said the no-nonsense lawman, noting the killer's shift from middle-class suburbanites to a runaway teen. "The other possibility is that the Choker has decided to play it safe. Why he would do that, we cannot speculate. But I assure you we will find out." That very night, Balint resolved that he'd have to sacrifice one more middle-class suburbanite to protect his ass.

Delilah's final trimester of nursing school was nearly over—and with it Balint's window of opportunity to disappear unnoticed for many hours at a stretch. So on a Friday afternoon, he canceled all of his patients, claiming a sore back, and drove north through the Bronx and Westchester County into Southern Connecticut. Balint wore his final pair of disposable latex gloves over his trusty leathers and carried the last strands of green ribbon loose in his pocket. While he drove—windows down, Golden Oldies on the radio—he savored the carefree pleasure of a man on the final leg of a long and exhausting journey. So the journey hadn't turned out precisely as he'd anticipated. What mattered was that he'd ended up far better off than when he started. If he hadn't set out to kill Sugarman, who could say that he'd have ended up living with Delilah? Or that he'd have been appointed the youngest department chairman in the Laurendale-Methodist Hospital's 146-year history?

Balint pulled off I-95 at the Cloverdale exit. He inched his way through the local business district—past upscale boutiques and a pizza shop and a funeral parlor with a hearse parked out front. Along one of the side streets, he caught sight of two women in sweat suits power walking. He circled the block—hoping that they might separate—and when he returned, the women had stopped exercising and stood chatting in front of a Tudor-style residence with a freestanding garage. The garage door stood open, displaying only one vehicle. In an upscale community like Cloverdale, where two or even three cars was the norm, this was a strong indication that his target was returning to an empty house. In preparation for his attack, Balint pulled the Mercedes to the curbside.

Balint watched from the rearview mirror as one of the women continued her power walk, while the other, a chubby matron in her forties, advanced up the path that separated the garage from the house. He fingered the ribbons in his pocket. It was now or never, he knew.

He reached forward to shut off the radio. At that very moment, the DJ broke into "Earth Angel" with a bulletin. "We have breaking news," announced Brother Charlie. "I repeat: we have breaking news. A suspect has been positively identified in the Emerald Choker slayings." Balint dared not breathe: he waited for the world to learn the identity of the serial killer—unsure whether the name revealed would be his own.

A moment later, the audio feed cut to Sheriff Spitford. "We've had the suspect in custody on a different charge for over a week now," he said. "We possess DNA evidence linking him directly to a pair of strangulation homicides in Wisconsin in 2007. In addition, we have an eyewitness—a granddaughter of the couple killed in Cobb's Crossing, New York—who has positively picked our suspect out of a lineup as the man she saw parked near her home on the morning that her grandparents were murdered."

Spitford said the man's name. Balint had never heard of him.

A journalist asked Sheriff Spitford how certain he was that his officers had the right man in custody and whether the suspect had acted alone.

"One hundred percent certain," answered Spitford. "And yes, he acted alone."

A perverse instinct urged Balint to kill one last time anyway, in order to prove Spitford wrong. He would have given almost anything to see the officer backtracking the next day in humiliation. But the key word was *almost*. What Balint wasn't willing to sacrifice was his freedom, or the future of his daughters. So that meant his killing spree had to come to a close. Instead of murdering a stranger, he'd be driving out to Lake Shearwater and discarding the last of the ribbon underwater. He removed the gloves and slid them into his pocket; these too would have to go into the lake.

A tap at the window of the Mercedes distracted Balint from his reverie. He looked up into the eyes of a cocoa-skinned female police officer. A pin on her lapel read: AUXILIARY COMMUNITY PATROL.

"Is everything all right?" she asked.

"I'm fine," replied Balint quickly. "I thought I was lost. But I'm not. I know exactly where I'm going."

"Good," replied the officer. "Please drive safely."

He pulled away from the curb and did not look back.

———

BALINT'S DIVORCE was finalized later that week. Amanda had called and offered him a settlement so reasonable that he could see no point in hiring an attorney. She wanted to divide their assets in half and to share custody of the girls: they'd switch between houses on alternate weeks. Her only other demand was that she retain the right to live in their house until Phoebe departed for college, at which point they'd sell the property and divide the proceeds. To Balint's surprise, she didn't ask for anything in the way of alimony or child support. "To be blunt, Jeremy," she'd explained on the phone, "what I want more than anything is a clean break—to get on with my life. I'd rather die in the gutter than depend on you for anything ever again." Her tone wasn't angry or bitter, but unnervingly matter-of-fact, as though she were discussing various methods for classifying library books. Already their marriage seemed remote, almost inexplicable.

Balint dropped by his former home early on Sunday morning to deliver the divorce papers himself. He also hoped to surprise his daughters, who weren't expecting him until later in the day. Amanda opened the door in her fleece dressing gown. She did not look pleased to see him.

"Really, Jeremy. You can't just show up like this," she said—making no effort to invite him inside.

He handed her the divorce papers. "I thought you might want these."

Amanda glanced over the documents and nodded. "You should have called."

"Next time. Promise." Balint stood on the front porch, the slate porch to which he technically still owned half the title, waiting for an offer to enter. His wife kept one hand clasped on the doorknob.

"Do you want something else?" she finally asked.

"Is it okay if I say hello to the girls?"

Amanda's expression hardened. "You'll see them in four hours."

"Come on. I wanted to surprise them. Just this once."

At that moment, Balint noticed a flicker of motion behind Amanda in the foyer. Then a voice called out, "Is everything all right?" He recognized the polished baritone instantly, even out of context. It belonged to Etan Steinhoff. The rabbi appeared to have taken Balint up on his suggestion to have an extra-marital affair. What amazed Balint most of all was how little he cared: if Amanda's relationship with Warren Sugarman had driven him to murder, now her sleepover with Steinhoff didn't even get under his skin.

"It's nothing. Just my ex-husband," Amanda called into the house. To Balint, she said, "Now isn't a good time, Jeremy. I'm sorry. Please come back at one o'clock."

"Very well," said Balint. "I understand."

He turned to go, then summoned the minimal Hebrew he'd retained from his childhood Sunday school classes, and shouted into the darkness: "Good morning, rabbi! *Boker tov!*"

———

No SIGN of the philandering rabbi remained when he picked up his daughters at the appointed hour. The girls hugged him simultaneously; now that they no longer saw him every day, his very presence had become a special occasion. Phoebe showed him her drawings of African and Asian elephants for his approval. "Can you see how the ears are different?" she demanded. "That's because the African elephants are smarter."

"Obviously," agreed Balint. "Does that mean *people* with big ears are smarter too?"

Phoebe giggled. "No, silly. Only elephants."

On the spur of the moment, he decided to pay Amanda back for the way she'd treated him earlier. "I have a surprise for you girls," Balint announced—when he was certain his ex-wife remained in earshot. "It's actually your new stepmother's idea," he added—although technically he wasn't yet remarried.

"Delilah and I are going to take you to the zoo." Let Etan Steinhoff try to compete with a stepparent who could produce giraffes and sea lions in an instant.

So they all bundled into the station wagon and drove over the George Washington Bridge into New York City. The afternoon was mild for May; daffodils sprouted along the paths leading to the primate house and the aviary. Balint held hands with Delilah like a high school student on a first date. While the girls explored the children's petting zoo, they waited outside the fence and kissed.

"I love you," said Balint. "What's that famous line of Lou Gehrig's: 'Today I consider myself the luckiest man on the face of the earth.' Well, that's exactly what I feel like right now."

"I'm so glad," said Delilah.

And they kissed again.

Then she asked: "One question. Who's Lou Gehrig?"

Somehow Delilah's question added perfectly to the moment. Not only were there things he could teach her, but she genuinely wanted to learn the answers. He couldn't remember the last time Amanda had displayed any sincere curiosity about something that interested him. Balint was about to answer, when his daughters came charging out of the petting zoo, cheeks bright pink, demanding more coins with which to purchase goat feed. Behind the girls, Balint spotted another familiar—if highly unwelcome—face. Davey Sugarman. A moment later, Balint found himself being greeted by Gloria Picardo.

"What a coincidence," declared Gloria. "You're everywhere."

"I could say the same," answered Balint. "If I didn't know better, I'd think you were following me." He introduced Delilah to Sugarman's widow. "How are you doing?" he asked. "How is *your son* doing?"

Gloria glanced around. The boy still stood along the edge of the petting zoo, watching other children feed the goats and sheep.

"I won't lie to you," she said. "Lousy. Or somewhere between lousy and awful, if you want to be precise. Warren was the best thing that Davey had going for him. You cannot imagine what it's like for a boy to lose a father he idolizes at a young age—and especially without any warning."

"You might be surprised what I could imagine," said Balint.

"But I am glad I ran into you," continued Gloria, taking no notice of his remark, "because I've been meaning to thank you for weeks."

"Thank me?"

"For what you said about Warren. At the memorial. I had no idea, you realize, but now it all makes sense . . . I can't believe I thought Warren was cheating on me when those meetings were so obviously related to his charity work. He told me it wasn't what it looked like—but how was I supposed to know that it really wasn't? I don't think I'll ever be able to forgive myself for doubting him . . ."

"He was a great guy," said Balint. "He never stopped loving you, by the way. He told me that himself only the week before he died . . ."

"Thank you for sharing that." Gloria reached out and patted his arm. "Even if it's not true, it's still nice to hear."

When she departed, steering her son toward the restrooms, Balint experienced a visceral surge of relief. He squeezed Delilah's hand.

"That's the wife of the guy who . . . ?" Delilah asked. She finished the sentence by glancing meaningfully at Balint's daughters. *Their* daughters now.

"Exactly," he said.

"And did he really tell you that he loved her?"

Balint smiled. "I promised you I'd always tell you the truth," he said. "In order to help me fulfill that promise, I'll have to request that you not ask certain questions."

Delilah laughed. "Request granted."

He didn't think about Gloria Picardo again all afternoon. They let the girls lead them from exhibit to exhibit—spending twenty minutes hunting zebra in the Serengeti and another thirty spying on Malagasy lemurs. As a final triumph, after a ride on the monorail through tropical Asia, Balint bought the girls a life-sized stuffed tiger; they had to open the sunroof in the Mercedes to accommodate the animal's head. Jessie had worried that the wind might hurt the creature's eyes, so they had stopped in a bodega opposite the zoo and bought a pair of disposable sunglasses and a roll of duct tape.

As Balint drove toward his new home with his new family, he reflected on how successfully he'd carried out his mission. He'd checkmated God and left no loose ends. He'd erased the lives of six people, but all had either exceeded their usefulness, like the Rockinghams, or had been rescued from future suffering, like Kenny McCord, or were, like Warren Sugarman, actively making the world a worse place. His conscience was clear, he assured himself. He had no regrets. Besides, he'd acted to protect his daughters from a broken marriage—even if matters hadn't turned out as he'd hoped. Who could fault him for killing on behalf of Phoebe and Jessie? Who could fault a man who loved his own children as much as he did?

They turned the corner onto Bonaventure Lane and, seconds later, Balint eased the Mercedes into the driveway. Delilah went to unlock the front door while he assisted the girls in extricating the enormous tiger from the car. Tiny balls of Styrofoam stuffing leaked from under the animal's paws and through its ears. He was carrying the creature in a bear hug when he heard Delilah's surprise.

"What's that?" she cried.

He saw it a moment after she did. Around the doorknob. Someone had wrapped a length of green ribbon, a light strand of satin that danced ominously in the breeze.